THE ATONEMENT

*The Bayou Hauntings
Book Eight*

Bill Thompson

Published by
Ascendente Books
Dallas, Texas

The Atonement: The Bayou Hauntings 8
All Rights Reserved
Copyright © 2021
V.1.0

Published by Ascendente Books
ISBN 978-17355661-3-9
Printed in the United States of America

Books by Bill Thompson

<u>The Bayou Hauntings</u>
CALLIE
FORGOTTEN MEN
THE NURSERY
BILLY WHISTLER
THE EXPERIMENTS
DIE AGAIN
THE PROCTOR HALL HORROR
THE ATONEMENT

<u>Brian Sadler Archaeological Mystery Series</u>
THE BETHLEHEM SCROLL
ANCIENT: A SEARCH FOR THE LOST CITY
OF THE MAYAS
THE STRANGEST THING
THE BONES IN THE PIT
ORDER OF SUCCESSION
THE BLACK CROSS
TEMPLE

<u>Apocalyptic Fiction</u>
THE OUTCASTS

<u>The Crypt Trilogy</u>
THE RELIC OF THE KING
THE CRYPT OF THE ANCIENTS
GHOST TRAIN

<u>Middle Grade Fiction</u>
THE LEGEND OF GUNNERS COVE

THE LAST CHRISTMAS

Once again, I want to thank some wonderful people in Louisiana. This time it's the folks in St. Martin Parish who gave me information, advice and even a few ghost stories. Thanks to you all, my tales have more personality and down-home flavor.

See you along the bayou!

CHAPTER ONE

Twenty-five Years Ago—Summer 1996
Merilee Plantation
Near St. Martinville, Louisiana

Tag. You're it!

Charlotte stuffed her fingers into her ears to drown out the noise. If yelling at her brother would help, she'd have done it. He was fourteen, for God's sake, not a little toddler running around the house. Twins were supposed to be in sync somehow—in tune with each other unlike other humans—but she didn't believe a word of it. Wick Ambrose never cared what she thought. He brought new friends into the house and showed them around. They marveled at the mansion and its antique furniture, and then the damn boys would run through the house, playing that damn game.

Tag. You're it!

She knew how to stop them. She'd open her bedroom door, scream as loudly as possible, and slam it so hard anybody in the house could hear it. Then she'd smile as her mother called from downstairs.

"Wick! Stop all that running, you hear? Quieten down right now, or y'all are going out in the yard to play!"

And the running would stop. They'd go into Wick's bedroom, close the door, and be really quiet.

Sometimes she'd sneak across the hall and put her ear to his door. Once she thought she heard someone crying, but that couldn't be right. They had been playing just a minute ago. Nobody was mad or sad or anything except crazy rambunctious.

Muffled words came from inside Wick's bedroom.

Tag. You're it!

CHAPTER TWO

Summer 1996

Years ago, when the twins were young and life held promise for James and Maria Ambrose, James's family welcomed his rare attempts at spontaneity. Now Wick and Charlotte were fourteen, James hadn't seen a pay increase in four years, and Maria struggled to maintain Merilee, a seven-thousand-square-foot antebellum mansion that needed far more work than a vacuum and dust mop could handle. Life was tedious and sometimes difficult.

When James burst into the house that late June afternoon around three, Maria's first thought was that Mr. Slage had fired him at last. Why else would he be home before six? But then he made her close her eyes, and when she opened them, he fanned a stack of hundred-dollar bills in front of her face.

"James! What…what on earth have you done? Where did you get that money?"

"*That money*, as you so casually describe it, is three thousand dollars. Three thousand smackers that your husband received as a bonus today. We finished the bridge project in Loreauville three months early and under budget, and our company earned a bonus. The boss split it up and gave everybody an equal share. Do you know what we're doing with ours?" He was practically dancing around the kitchen; she hadn't seen him this animated—or this happy—in years.

There hadn't been extra money for a long time, and in seconds she knew a dozen things the house needed. Fixing plumbing and heating problems, the washer that was dying, and painting the house inside and out, just for starters. "I'd vote to fix things up around here," she began, but he shushed her.

"No, no, no. You will not rain on my parade, Maria. I planned this all the way home from the office. We're going on a trip. A road trip to Florida. We'll spend tonight at the casino in Biloxi, and I'll win us a little extra cash at the craps table. Then we'll drive to Pensacola and spend a week on the beach. How does that sound?"

Maria hesitated. She dared not cross him, but they desperately needed that money, and what he suggested was foolish. "You hardly ever mentioned that bridge project," she said. "You couldn't have had much to do with it..."

"Stop it, dammit! I may not be the engineer you thought you were marrying, but I helped put together the specs for the job, and I earned that bonus!"

You only got it because the boss gave everyone an equal share. Whether he did or not, Maria realized her husband was an unambitious man in a dead-end job. Fifteen years ago, she got pregnant and they married. Then he flunked out of engineering school at LSU and got hired on at Slage Engineering because her father and old man Slage played poker together at the Elks Lodge. He asked Slage for a favor, and James went on the payroll as an assistant something-or-other. His job title hadn't changed in all those years, and he got the occasional cost-of-living increase, but never one based on merit.

"James, we need so many things around here. That money could come in really handy."

He wouldn't hear of it. In fact, he walked to the stairs and called his children from their bedrooms into the upstairs hall. "Wick! Charlotte! Throw a few days' worth of clothes in a bag and meet me down here in five minutes. Hustle, everybody!"

"I'm busy," Wick yelled down, and Charlotte protested too, but James was adamant. He sent Maria to help them get ready. "I don't know how long we'll be gone," he said. "Just pack some clothes. We can find a laundromat if we need to."

And one of us will do the washing, she thought. *That would be me. What a vacation.* But she didn't voice her complaints aloud. It wouldn't go well if she did.

Charlotte carried a small duffel down the broad circular staircase, but Wick bounded down two at a time, his hands empty.

"I told you to pack a bag…"

"And I said I'm busy, Dad. I'm in the middle of something."

"Go sit down in the library, both of you. Maria, go upstairs and pack him some clothes. We're leaving in five minutes."

Wick's eyes widened in astonishment, and Charlotte wondered what her brother was up to that was so important.

"I can't leave right now," Wick cried. "I…uh, give me maybe fifteen minutes or so."

"Out of the question. Go to the car. We leave now!"

"Dad, don't make me…" Charlotte looked at him, astonished. He was about to cry.

"Unless the Pentagon has you working on a secret project, you're out of here. Now go!"

James drove the old Volvo station wagon out to the highway and turned right. When they passed through Breaux Bridge and got on eastbound Interstate 10, Wick said, "Where are we going? Are we coming back home tonight?"

"Your old dad got a big bonus at work today, son. I'm taking the family on a road trip. It's been years since we had fun together, and we're heading to the sunny Florida Panhandle. Tonight we'll stay in Biloxi; the casino's calling my name!" He turned on the radio and told them to settle back, relax, and leave the driving to him.

"Holy shit!" Wick muttered under his breath. "Holy shit!"

"What's wrong?" Charlotte whispered.

"I'm in deep shit, that's what's wrong. Now shut up and let me think."

Over the next six days, Wick was quiet and stayed mostly to himself. He wouldn't join the others for meals or trips to the beach, instead sitting by the motel's swimming pool for hours on end. And he refused to confide in Charlotte, his twin sister, who usually knew everything about his antics, and who supported him by keeping her mouth shut when she might have gotten him in trouble.

In her wildest imagination, she couldn't have dreamed what Wick had done this time.

CHAPTER THREE

Present Day

South of St. Martinville near the Iberia Parish line, a historical marker stood alongside Highway 31 where it intersected with a seldom-used dirt road that ran down to Bayou Teche.

MERILEE PLANTATION
In 1843, during the Golden Age of this parish,
Pierre Ambrose emigrated from France and purchased
1800 acres along Bayou Teche.
He built a Greek revival mansion, named it after his wife,
and operated a sugar cane plantation.
After Merilee's tragic death in the yellow fever epidemic of
1855, Pierre sold most of the land.
The house remains in the Ambrose family.

Two vehicles slowed at the marker and turned down the road past another sign nailed to a tree—*Private Property. No Trespassing.* Maneuvering around fallen branches and debris, the drivers crossed a wide front yard and parked near the decaying old house.

"This is insane. We shouldn't have come back,"

Charlotte muttered as she followed her brother, crawling through the brambles and up onto the rotting front veranda. It was pitch dark; only the pale crescent moon and the light from Wick's phone allowed them to find their way.

Wick grabbed her arm. "Wake up, Char. You had no choice. What's insane is to ignore what we're facing, and I'm damn sure not going to deal with this alone. This is your problem as much as it is mine, so cut the dramatics."

"*My* problem? What's *your* problem—selective amnesia? After twenty-five years, have you forgotten what happened? I haven't, not for one minute. We lost everything because of you…"

He snapped, "Give it a rest, okay? *My* problem, *our* problem. What does it matter now?"

It will always matter. This was never my problem. Say what you will, everything that happened inside these walls was your fault. How many times had she wished things had ended another way, that Wick hadn't done it, or that if he had, he handled things himself. And that no one else found out. But wishes were a waste of time. Things were what they were, and they were bad.

Last week Wick had called her for the first time since 2001. It didn't surprise her when he said he had trouble finding her number. When she left Merilee, she hadn't wanted it to be easy for her brother to get in touch. She moved to Nashville, finished school, started a modest clothing design business, and tried to enjoy life for the first time since that night in 1996.

Thanks to the damned internet, Wick had found her. He'd learned Merilee was going to be sold, and they had to go back to be sure everything was okay. She'd refused at first, reminding him the situation was his to deal with, but he'd convinced her if things went wrong and a future owner learned the house's secrets, it would be her problem as well as his. And so here she was, against her better judgment and hating her brother for coercing her back to their home.

They stood before the familiar massive double doors, the fancy etched glass panes imported from France now just jagged shards. When Wick tried the door, it wouldn't budge.

He inserted a key, unlocked it, and pushed again, but the door resisted. He stood back and kicked hard once, then again, and the doors crashed inward.

A cloud of dust rose from plaster strewn about the floor of the enormous foyer that reached two stories to a cupola on the roof. Much of the railing had collapsed onto the sweeping circular staircase that led to the second floor of the once-grand mansion.

"My God, it's a wreck," Wick said. "Worse than I expected."

"Home sweet home," she snapped. "Let's get this over with. The less time I spend in here, the better."

"You're not overcome with nostalgia?"

"Not funny, Wick, especially coming from you. There's nothing humorous about this." She walked to the nearest room, a parlor with its furnishings in the late stages of deterioration. A massive chandelier lay in pieces upon the grand piano, where it had fallen long ago. She remembered this room well—it was where they had sat when…when their lives had plummeted into an awful abyss.

Charlotte paused to listen. A tinkling sound came from somewhere.

"Did you hear that?" Wick nodded and put a finger to his lips. They listened in silence.

Mommy. Daddy. Words so quiet they might have been drifting on the wind. Mournful, singsong words.

Help me, please! It's so dark.

She clamped a hand on his arm, but he jerked it away. "Wick! Do you hear that? Let's get out of here!"

"I hear it. Come on. This won't take long, and then we'll go." He led her back into the entry hall, and they walked toward the staircase. Somewhere upstairs, a door creaked and closed.

Charlotte grabbed his hand. This time he didn't stop her. "Oh God, Wick. I'm scared. You shouldn't have come back."

His cockiness disappeared, and he seemed as worried as she. "Let's finish and get out of here," he said as they raced to the next room. An enormous portrait that once hung above a massive fireplace lay in shreds on the floor, and plaster from the ceiling blanketed everything in a fine snowlike powder.

They gave the remaining first-floor rooms a cursory glance and returned to the foyer. "Do you want to do the cellar now or at the end?" he asked, and she gripped his hand even tighter.

"Are you insane? I'll never, ever go down there again. Or into your bedroom either."

"Okay, then. I'll do the cellar at the end."

A soft sound echoed through the foyer. A long, slow breath, like someone exhaled. Then soft, tinkling words.

Please don't! I'm scared. I won't tell, I promise. Just let me go home.

She dug her nails into his wrist, and he jerked back. "Stop it! It's wind that blew through a broken window upstairs."

It's not the wind. Wick knows what it is. It's a voice. His *voice.* They began ascending the staircase, dodging the pieces of broken banister that lay here and there on the risers.

Thirteen steps above the ground floor, they reached the landing and paused. Ahead lay thirteen more and the second floor, shrouded in darkness. He directed the light upwards, but its feeble beam didn't penetrate the shadows in the hallway at the top of the stairs.

In the upstairs hall, they stepped onto once-fancy carpet that lay rotting beneath their feet. She trembled and said, "Hurry, Wick. I'm seriously scared, and I can't take much more of this." They looked up at the heavy brass light fixture hanging from the ceiling. Neither of them spoke, for there were no words to express the horror of what had happened in this spot.

He led her down the hall into their parents' bedroom and bath, the guest room, and Charlotte's bedroom and dressing area.

"Look who's here," Wick said, pointing to a large stuffed clown tossed into a corner chair. "You left poor Henry behind." The doll's porcelain face leered at her through the gloom, and she remembered that odd way his eyes followed her as she moved about. She shivered.

"I hated him. He's scary. Jesus, Wick, move it. This place gives me the creeps."

When they came to the next door, she stopped.

Wick said, "You're really not going into my bedroom? Are you chicken?"

"Chicken? I'm terrified. I'm thirty-nine years old, and I'm shaking so hard I can hardly stand. We both know what happened here. If you're not scared too, then you're a fool. I understand why we had to come back one last time. I came against my better judgment, but I wouldn't go into your bedroom for a million dollars. I wish you wouldn't go either. It's not safe."

"Go on, then. Wait for me downstairs." He turned the knob, pushed the door open, and stepped through. As he disappeared in the darkness, it creaked shut with a resounding thud.

That's the sound we heard from downstairs! That creaking sound was his bedroom door closing!

Dear God.

Charlotte raced down the stairs, dodging and stepping around the debris. Her mind twisted and tore into a million disjointed thoughts. The nighttime terrors in the old house where she grew up. The sounds from Wick's bedroom— muffled thumps and thuds. Voices too. The thought that if she left her room at night, something awful would happen, but she couldn't remember what. If she had ever known.

Eerie words echoed throughout the house, jolting Charlotte back to reality.

Please don't! Please. I'm scared.

Confused, she realized she stood in the kitchen, her hand on the knob of an open door. In the blackness before her, a set of wooden stairs led down into the cellar. She screamed and drew back.

How did I get in here? I left Wick upstairs…

Oh, God, now I remember! Wick! Oh God, Wick, I have to help you!

An overwhelming sense of dread enveloped her as she raced down the hall. She tripped and fell hard, jumped up and ran into the foyer. Moonbeams from the cupola high above cast an eerie glow on the staircase as she ascended. At the top, her foot connected with something on the floor, and she fell again, crying out in pain as she landed hard on her right hip.

Charlotte reached out and ran her hand along the thing she'd tripped over—a ladder. Bile rose in her throat, and her chest constricted so that her breaths became difficult, heaving gasps. She shivered as she realized what was unfolding now had happened before.

Her fingers ran along the old ladder beside her. Although she could scarcely see in the shadows of the moonlight, she could have described every detail. She gasped for air and prayed for this nightmare to end. She willed herself to be far away from Merilee, back in the world of today, not in this house where she grew up. But this was no dream, and there was no way to stop it.

She raised her head, knowing there was something in the shadows above.

A thing that swayed slowly back and forth.

Something filled with memories. Overwhelming, dreadful ones. Horrors no one should endure.

Just before merciful darkness shuttered her mind, she heard laughter and those childish words.

Tag. You're it.

CHAPTER FOUR

The French Quarter
New Orleans

The bar at Atomic Roadhouse in the old Jax Brewery building on Decatur was packed solid. It was this way every evening—in the two years since it opened, Atomic had become the hottest place in the Quarter. Basketball games played on sixteen screens hanging from the ceilings, and four bartenders scrambled to keep drinks in the hands of patrons seated at the bar and at tables crammed so close it was difficult for servers to move about.

Opening a new venue in the French Quarter had been a gamble, but thanks to a lot of advance hype and the fame of its owner, Atomic Roadhouse was crazy busy from the day it opened. The noise level was deafening—even people next to each other on bar stools shouted to be heard—and the energy in the place was electric.

"Four Turbodogs up!" a bartender named Sissy shouted to a server, who snatched up a tray and dodged her way through the crowd. As Sissy pulled the next order, she realized that something odd was going on. In seconds, the entire place quietened. She looked up and saw that the monitors tuned to Channel Nine were broadcasting a special announcement.

"Holy shit!" someone yelled as a familiar face appeared on the screen. "Look at that!"

"Turn it up!" cried another, and Sissy grabbed the remote.

Below the mug shot of a handsome guy with a big smile were the words *POPULAR NEW ORLEANS RESTAURATEUR FOUND DEAD IN ST. MARTIN PARISH.*

"It's Wick!" Sissy cried in disbelief. "It's Wick Ambrose! Holy shit, what could have happened?" A tear ran down her cheek.

The cheers and shouts morphed into a cacophony of confusion, shouts, and questions. Everyone quietened again as the newscaster reported that Wick Ambrose, the thirty-nine-year-old owner of three popular New Orleans venues, was found hanged at Merilee Plantation, an antebellum mansion near St. Martinville that had been his childhood home. The newsflash ended with a promise for more details as they became available. The basketball game resumed, leaving the crowd in Atomic Roadhouse stunned.

"He's the guy who owns this place, right?" someone at the bar asked Sissy, who nodded. *Owned* would be a better word, she mused as she picked up the next order and stared blankly at it, unable to process anything except the news. All she could think about was him. Wick Ambrose's infectious humor and easygoing attitude endeared him to employees and customers alike. He was a guy who seemed genuinely interested in other people's welfare, and the place brightened when the boss stopped by every afternoon.

Wick's gone. He's never coming back, Sissy thought. But why? What could have happened? Why would he hang himself? He didn't, she decided, and that was all there was to it. The last person on earth to take his own life would be Wick Ambrose.

———

Landry Drake's phone rang just seconds before he got a one-line text from Channel Nine about Wick Ambrose's death.

"Hey, Jack. What's going on?"

Jack Blair was the senior investigative reporter for WCCY-TV Channel Nine, the Voice of the Crescent City and the station where Landry had worked until recently. The two had become colleagues and good friends after Landry rescued him from a life on the streets and an addiction to alcohol. He'd given Jack a job and a chance to rebuild his life, and the man had repaid Landry by becoming a valuable assistant and then earning the title of investigative reporter.

"Have you heard the news about Wick Ambrose?"

"I just got a text from the station. What the hell's that about? He seemed like a guy who had everything going his way."

"Everyone believed he was. Listen to this, though. You've heard of Merilee Plantation, the old mansion outside St. Martinville, right? That's where they found him. He grew up there."

That surprised Landry. He'd heard tales about Merilee, although he'd never been there. People said the old mansion was haunted.

"Interesting. How did he die, and who found him?"

Landry's girlfriend, Cate Adams, tugged at his sleeve and mouthed, "Who died?"

"Jack, hang on a second. Cate, Wick Ambrose died. The restaurant guy."

The news surprised her too, and Landry put the phone on speaker.

Jack said, "The cops aren't saying much. Someone found him hanged in the house. I'm heading up there now, and I wondered if you'd like to come along."

He glanced at his watch; it was after ten. "How did you get permission?"

"Permission? The Landry Drake I once knew would have said strike first, ask permission later. I'm counting on my charm to get inside."

Landry laughed. "Don't bet on it. It's two hours to St. Martinville and a waste of time if they won't let us in. Maybe we should wait until morning."

Jack said, "You surprise me, you slacker. You're the one who taught me to move fast on a breaking story. Middle of the night or not, I'm going. Either I swing by and pick you up, or you can hear me talk about it on the news tomorrow."

"You know how to hurt a guy." Landry laughed. "I'll be downstairs in ten minutes." As he dressed, he and Cate talked about Wick Ambrose.

He was a guy on top of his game who raked in the dough and was one of New Orleans' most eligible bachelors. Now he was dead—hanged in his childhood home on Bayou Teche. It made no sense.

"Do you think he killed himself?" she asked, and he said he couldn't imagine it, but people's lives were never as they appeared. Who knew if Wick had demons in his mind or problems in his empire? He kissed her goodbye and said he wouldn't call unless something urgent came up. "Get some sleep," he said. "I'll be back in the wee hours."

On the drive north, Landry and Jack discussed the house. Landry opened his laptop; as part of his paranormal work, he'd created files for hundreds of locations in Louisiana that might hold possibilities. He located the folder for Merilee and opened it.

The house appeared on lists of haunted sites in Acadiana, but its story was nothing special. Landry called houses like this cookie-cutter haunted—mysterious lights appeared in the windows, eerie sounds emanated from deep within the house, and stories abounded of people who died there long ago. Plenty of rumors from kids and townspeople and trespassers, but nothing sufficient to consider a paranormal investigation. He noted that the last persons to live at Merilee were James and Maria Ambrose and their twins, Wick and Charlotte. In 2001, people in the area had reported the old mansion abandoned.

"I wasn't aware Wick Ambrose had a twin sister," Jack commented. "He's in the news a lot in New Orleans, but I never heard about her."

They crossed the huge bridge over the Atchafalaya River at Morgan City just after midnight. Even at this hour, the river had traffic; barges passed each other, moving cargo to and from the Gulf of Mexico. They took Highway 31, and at last they arrived at the historical marker. Jack had pinpointed the turnoff on GPS, but that turned out to be unnecessary; from half a mile away, the pulsating red and blue lights of a St. Martin Parish sheriff's cruiser parked on the shoulder marked the location.

Landry's heart jumped with anticipation and the exhilaration of a new case. This one already had his mind spinning with questions.

CHAPTER FIVE

The deputy examined their press IDs and radioed the sheriff, who authorized their driving on to the house. Landry Drake's name was familiar to many; over the past few years, his *Bayou Hauntings* series on Channel Nine had made him famous, and now fans eagerly awaited the launch of his new paranormal channel.

"So far, so good," Landry commented as they drove up to the decrepit two-story house. A dozen vehicles sat outside: two SUVs and the rest police cruisers. An ambulance with back doors open sat idling near the porch, and when Landry saw a state police car, he wondered if his old friend Harry Kanter was here.

Dim light from inside filtered through the windows, thanks to two generators chugging along in the yard. St. Martin Parish Sheriff Rick Angelli met them on the porch. He recognized Landry, who introduced Jack, and the sheriff agreed they could go inside if they followed orders. "Watch your step," he cautioned, pointing to rotten boards on the porch. "It's no better in there. The place is a wreck."

As they donned booties and masks, Landry noticed cops working in the expansive two-story foyer and at the top of the circular staircase. Up there in a hall, a noose hung from a chandelier. He pointed it out to Jack as the sheriff led them into a sitting room.

"Everything's off the record for now," Angelli said. "If you can't honor that, then your visit's over. If I hadn't recognized your name, I wouldn't have let you come inside at all. Right now, I'll tell you what I can about what happened here. After the investigation wraps up, perhaps I can give you more. To me it's baffling, and I'd appreciate your observations." They agreed to his stipulations.

"A 911 call came in at 9:23 p.m. Nobody spoke, so we used the phone's GPS to pinpoint the location. I was home, and my deputy handled it as a routine call without notifying me. Two of my men arrived just before ten and found the house dark and two SUVs parked outside, one with tags from Louisiana and one with Florida tags. They ran the tags—one's registered to Wick Ambrose, and the other was a rental checked out to Charlotte Ambrose of Nashville, Tennessee.

"They found the door standing open, stepped into the entry foyer and shouted, but got no response. The electricity was off, so they used their flashlights. They climbed the stairs and found a body hanging from a light fixture at the top of the staircase. They called me, I notified the state police, and here we are."

Landry said he presumed from news reports that Wick was who they found, and Angelli nodded. "There was a girl here too, lying on the floor under the body. She's Charlotte, Wick's sister. Her cellphone was in her hand."

"Is she dead too?"

"She's unconscious—not knocked out, but like in a trance. She might have experienced something traumatic. We identified her from the driver's license in a purse in the rental car."

"Where is she now?"

"The EMTs are checking her out in one of the upstairs rooms. A state police detective's with them."

"Is it Harry Kanter, by chance?"

The sheriff raised his eyebrows. "It is. You know him?"

"We worked a few cases together. He's very good at this."

"The best, and we need all the help we can get. We don't

get many high-profile cases out here in a rural parish, but finding Wick Ambrose swinging from a rope means this place is going to be swarming with activity." His radio crackled; the deputy at the highway advised him guys in two news vans from Baton Rouge wanted to come to the house.

"Looks like you two started something," he grumbled, allowing the deputy to let them through. "You need to return to your vehicle now. I'm not letting the others inside while the investigation's underway, and you need to go too."

Landry said, "We'll do it, but may I say hello to Lieutenant Kanter before I go?" Jack left to go to his vehicle as the sheriff stepped into the hall and called out Harry's name. When the veteran detective walked into the room and saw Landry, he broke into a grin and shook his hand.

"Last time we met was over at Proctor Hall in Thibodaux," Kanter said. "You were going to give the Proctors proper burials. Did you get it done?"

"I did, thanks to your help. And here we are once again. How do you always draw the cases I'm involved with? Should I check my phone for bugs?"

Kanter laughed. "I'm only a few months from retirement. You'd think they'd give me a break, but no. Old Harry gets all the bizarre cases out here in Cajun country. It's been that way my entire career. The real question is, what brought the ghost hunter up from New Orleans for a hanging? What's so spooky about this case?"

"I don't know yet. Jack Blair called me—he took my old job at Channel Nine—and he asked if I wanted to ride up with him and see what happened to Wick Ambrose. The sheriff said you were upstairs with his sister. Is she awake yet?"

"No…well, not exactly, but something happened a few minutes ago that might interest you. The EMTs took her to a bedroom and laid her on a dusty old bed so she'd be comfortable. Her breathing's steady; it's as if she's asleep but won't respond to stimuli. They've squeezed her hand, spoken to her, the whole nine yards, but she just lies there. Except for a few seconds. I was talking to her, asking her if she was Charlotte Ambrose, and one of the EMTs thought someone whispered or cried out somewhere in the house. I think I heard it too—a child's faint voice calling out to its parents for help. When it happened, Charlotte's eyes opened wide and then closed again.

"My guys and the sheriff's deputies had already given the upstairs a cursory check, but I sent them back to be sure there was no one else here. And I knew they'd find nothing. The sound—the words, if that's what they were—weren't like that. It was more like a light wind creating sounds that might be words but weren't. The EMTs and I dismissed it as nothing. Like I say, maybe it didn't even happen. We all get a little spooked in a dark old house like this. Hell, why am I describing it to you? You get what I'm talking about. This is your stock-in-trade."

Irritated, the sheriff stuck his head through the doorway and ordered Landry to go. "The news guys are outside. You should have left when I asked you to."

"I'll walk you out," Harry said. As they neared the front door, he glanced through the side glass panes and waved Landry back. "The vultures are circling. They're setting up cameras in the yard. Unless you want to answer questions about what Landry Drake's doing at Merilee Plantation, I suggest we find another way out."

Landry texted Jack, who pulled the car around to the back of the house and picked him up. "Sorry for wasting your time," Jack said as they drove toward the interstate.

"Without checking it out, we'd never know if there was a story. I learned something interesting. Harry thought he might have heard a child's voice crying for its parents. But it might have just been the wind."

They chatted about the hanging on the way back, and Landry said there was nothing at Merilee for him. He had bigger projects on his plate at the moment. As he dropped Landry at his place on St. Philip Street, Jack promised to get in touch if anything interesting developed.

CHAPTER SIX

Three months ago, Landry had left Channel Nine, the station where he'd established his "ghost hunter" reputation. For several years he'd investigated haunted venues and spooky events in New Orleans, arguably America's most haunted city, and throughout Acadiana.

Several things he encountered became episodes on a documentary called *Bayou Hauntings*. WCCY-TV aired the shows in south Louisiana at first, expanding to their sister stations throughout the south and ultimately going national through affiliated network stations. Now Landry's name and face were familiar to millions of viewers eager to see what he would find next.

When Landry got an exciting opportunity—the chance to be an owner and the star of a new cable channel called the Paranormal Network—WCCY-TV's owners supported his move and granted permission for the new channel to air Landry's *Bayou Hauntings* series. The fledgling channel picked up rights to other supernatural shows, and now that its debut was only weeks away, Landry's fans were eagerly waiting.

TPN, the acronym for their new venture, was a joint effort among Landry and two friends with deep pockets, Henri Duchamp, founder and president of the Louisiana

Society for the Paranormal, and Madison John "Doc" Adams, a prominent psychiatrist and the father of Landry's girlfriend, Cate. They rented a vacant three-story building on Toulouse Street in the French Quarter adjoining Henri Duchamp's headquarters, brought veteran cameraman Phil Vandegriff and a director over from WCCY-TV, and hired freelancers for everything else required.

Cate, the office manager for Henri's organization, assumed a similar role at TPN. Her first task was directing a work gang that retrofitted the top floor of their building into a television studio.

When Landry left Channel Nine, station manager Ted Carpenter promoted Landry's assistant Jack Blair to his position. Not only did Jack have no journalistic training, he had been a homeless addict when Landry took a chance on him two years earlier. But he was an excellent worker, smart, crafty and loyal, and once Landry departed, he and Jack stayed in close touch.

Jack's forte was research. From the day Landry put him in front of a computer at Channel Nine, he had proven himself adept at navigating the web, determining which search terms would yield the required results, and assimilating data into useful information. Jack's work immensely helped Landry, who loved working at spooky sites in the field but hated sitting before a monitor doing what he called busy work.

Although Wick Ambrose's death appeared to have no supernatural undertones, the old house fascinated Jack, and he returned to the station determined to learn more about it. He started by creating a chain of ownership.

Last night on the drive to St. Martinville, Landry had told him about Pierre and Merilee Ambrose, the cane planters who bought acreage on Bayou Teche and built the house. Jack spent the morning tracing land transfer records. He created an ownership succession list down through the years, every one named Ambrose, and the last being Wick and Charlotte's father, James.

In December 1996, James and Maria signed a deed that transferred the house and acreage to a corporation named

Merilee 1996-I LLC. It was legal for a corporation's owners to remain anonymous, but the company had to name a registered service agent, who would receive legal documents sent to the corporation. Another corporation acted as the service agent, which was not atypical but added another obstacle to finding the owners. The agent—Trust Management 1996—had a Baton Rouge post office box address.

On WCCY-TV letterhead, Jack wrote out a request to interview the owner of Merilee Plantation, put it in an envelope, and affixed a stamp. He couldn't recall the last time he'd mailed a letter in these days of electronic communication, and he wondered if he'd get a response.

Jack looked for later transfers, but there were none. Today Merilee Plantation belonged to the corporation that got it in 1996—the company whose owners were a mystery. But there might be an explanation. Perhaps in 1996 James wanted to deed the house over to his kids, who were too young to own property. Instead, he transferred it to a corporation in trust for Wick and Charlotte until they were of age. That made sense—except for why James would give his home to two fourteen-year-olds.

He recalled Landry saying the house had sat empty since 2001. Perhaps that fact meant nothing, but it didn't make sense either. The corporation got Merilee, and five years later everyone moved out, abandoning the mansion to the elements. Why would they do that to their family homestead, a nostalgic place they should have loved?

Jack wondered if James and Maria might have departed Merilee earlier than 2001, leaving only Wick and Charlotte—who would have been around nineteen—to abandon it. He switched gears into a related area of research, the backstory of Wick's parents.

Most of what little he found was in Wick's biography. He was a celebrity in New Orleans, but his parents were normal folks apparently living a routine existence. Jack learned that James once worked for a company in Lafayette called Slage Engineering, which merged with another in 2002. The Lafayette operation still existed, and Jack called the payroll department, only to be told that personnel files were confidential. No surprise there—corporations were careful with employee information these days, but he explained he was trying to find information about James Ambrose, the father of the recently deceased restaurateur, and when he would have worked for Slage.

After a pause, the woman said, "There's someone who might help you." She gave him the phone number for Daisy Poe, an octogenarian who was once Mr. Slage's personal assistant. "She may be old," the woman added, "but her mind's as sharp as ever. If Mr. Ambrose worked for the company in the nineties, I'll bet Daisy can tell you about him."

The number belonged to a retirement center in Lafayette, and in no time he was speaking to Daisy. Her voice was strong and perky, and yes, she remembered James Ambrose. "I don't think anybody who ever worked for Mr. Slage made him mad like James did that time when we all got bonuses. I'll never forget it."

She explained that in 1996 the company had completed a major project early and under budget, triggering a performance bonus that her boss shared among every employee, from mail clerk to CEO. "It was the most money I ever saw at one time in my life," she added. "Every person got three thousand dollars in cash. I was so happy I could have kissed the old codger!"

Jack eased her back to the topic. She had been in charge of vacation scheduling, and the same afternoon employees got the bonuses, James Ambrose requested ten days of vacation. As she recalled, he wanted to surprise his family with a trip to Florida, and she granted the request because he had plenty of time built up.

"What happened then?"

"The strangest thing happened. I never understood it. James wasn't that smart; he only had a job because some friend of Mr. Slage's called in a favor. He could never have made the same money anywhere else, but after his ten days of vacation expired, he never came back to work. Nobody missed him; as I said, he wasn't exactly a critical part of the operation, but it infuriated Mr. Slage that James would have repaid his generosity—the three-thousand-dollar bonus he did nothing to earn—by quitting without notice. Good thing he never came asking for his job back. I think the boss would have kicked him in the rear end!"

Jack asked if anyone at the company had followed up on James and his whereabouts.

"No, the boss said let it go. I never saw him again, but that didn't surprise me. I lived in Lafayette, and the Ambroses lived in a run-down old mansion in St. Martin Parish. It was his home place, as I recall." Jack waited for her to mention Wick's death there, but it seemed she either hadn't heard about it or hadn't connected it with Merilee.

They chatted a few minutes longer, and Jack thanked her for the information. Afterwards he called a florist in Lafayette and sent her a floral bouquet and a thank-you card.

At the office, he listed the facts he knew and the questions he had.

1843–1996: Over the years, one Ambrose after another owns Merilee Plantation.

1972: James Ambrose inherits the place and lives there with his wife, Maria.

1982: Twins Wick and Charlotte are born.

1996: James gets a big cash bonus and requests ten days off. He never returns to his menial job. Wick and Charlotte are fourteen then. In December of that year, James and Maria sign a deed that transfers the house to a corporation. It is the first time since 1843 that the owner isn't an Ambrose.

2001: Wick and Charlotte are nineteen. Merilee becomes vacant and remains so until the present day.

2021: Wick and Charlotte return. He dies, and cops find her unconscious at the scene.

Why did James quit the job he needed without notice, and what happened to him afterwards (1996)?

Why did he deed the house to a corporation (1996)? Was it to get it to his children, who were too young to own property in their own names?

Where did the four family members go when they left Merilee for the last time (2001)?

Why would they abandon their family home and acreage instead of selling it (2001)?

Where are James and Maria now?

He had to return to St. Martinville. Maybe there was nothing to all this, but he wanted to search the records at the courthouse. Who paid the taxes during the 1990s after James lost his job? Who paid them after 2001 when the house was empty? Did anything unusual happen at Merilee? Did neighbors ever call the sheriff about noise violations or trespassers or any other activity?

Going back could be a waste of time, but Jack had a gut feeling the house held secrets. He left the station, walked down Royal Street to Toulouse, turned toward the river, and entered the building that housed Henri Duchamp's Louisiana Society for the Paranormal. He needed a sounding board, and soon he, Henri, Landry and Cate sat around a wrought-iron table in the courtyard with coffees, brainstorming about the next step.

CHAPTER SEVEN

The words *BREAKING NEWS* flashed on the screen, accompanied by music and a newscaster's voice. "State police announced the discovery of a body in a cellar at the home where New Orleans restaurateur Wick Ambrose died."

Landry and Cate listened to Channel Nine's morning news as they ate soft-boiled eggs and toast at their small kitchen table. In the middle of a sentence, she stopped when he raised his hand.

"Did you catch that?" He ran to the living room, rewound the story to the beginning, and listened to his friend and WCCY-TV news anchor Ken Spearman reveal that during a search of Merilee Plantation, state police uncovered a corpse in the old mansion's cellar.

A police spokesperson said a woman's badly decomposed body was found buried in the basement's dirt floor. An officer and his partner, a K-9 dog named Brutus, had searched the house, and when cops discovered a door that led to a dark basement, Brutus sniffed out the corpse. They did not know her identity, and the spokesperson promised more information as it became available.

Landry's phone buzzed with a call from Jack, but he declined it. There would be time to speak to him. First, he wanted more information, so he called Lieutenant Kanter's cellphone.

Harry began by saying, "The story broke ten minutes ago. What took you so long to call me?"

"Very funny. So tell me what's going on."

"Off the record. Understood?"

Things Landry learned off the record often soon became public information, and when they did, it complicated his agreement to maintain confidentiality. Today he answered, "With my usual caveat. It's off the record until I get it someplace else."

"Gotcha. The dog led us to a body buried in a corner of the cellar under eighteen inches of dirt. Somebody dug a shallow grave, covered her up, and moved boxes on top to hide his work. There must have been an odor for some time, but it looks like no one's used the cellar in decades. The walls and floor are dirt, so the stench might not have been as powerful. The woman's jeans, cotton shirt, and sneakers are almost disintegrated, and the worms got to the corpse pretty good, an indication that she died years ago. No ID and no identifying marks, so we'll let the ME check her out and see if we can learn her identity."

Harry said computerized parish records went back to the mid-sixties. Over that sixty-year span, there had been no police activity at the old mansion. If the woman in the basement had died within those walls, her demise and her burial went unreported.

A few days later Harry gave Landry another enigmatic answer. According to the medical examiner, the woman, aged around thirty-five, died from asphyxiation. The contusions and broken bones in her neck were consistent with being hanged. He estimated she died and was buried in the mid-1990s, which meant the body had lain undiscovered in the basement for around twenty-five years.

Since Ambrose family members were the only people who ever lived at Merilee, the ME had a hunch. He compared the deceased woman's DNA to Wick Ambrose's and got a match.

Landry did the math. Say the woman died twenty-five years ago at age thirty-five. Wick died at thirty-nine, and twenty-five years ago he was fourteen. The woman was around twenty years older than Wick. She could be his mother.

The next step involved research. What really happened in the mid-nineties at Merilee, and did Wick Ambrose's mother, Maria, die there? The story held interesting possibilities, but Landry saw no supernatural angle. The curious tale would make a good TV crime drama, but it wasn't something for the Paranormal Network.

He didn't want the story, but he knew one investigator who'd jump on it. He returned Jack's call, related Harry's off-the-record conversation, and left it with him. Jack would make time to search for answers, because he loved researching mysteries.

CHAPTER EIGHT

Charlotte Ambrose sat with her hands folded in her lap, her eyes bright and her lips parted in a half smile. She appeared to be gazing at Barrington Clinic's colorful flower garden and thinking pleasant thoughts, but her doctors were baffled. Despite the appearance of being alert and comprehending, since sheriff's deputies had found her that night at Merilee, Charlotte hadn't uttered a word.

As the only living person there, authorities assumed she'd initiated the 911 call, but there was no proof. It had originated from her cellphone, but the caller didn't speak. The dispatcher had pinpointed Merilee Plantation's location via GPS and sent an ambulance and deputies to the mansion, where they found Wick swinging from a noose, his feet dangling two feet above the floor. An unconscious Charlotte lay below him beside an overturned six-foot ladder. She awoke for a moment, looked at the body above her, and passed out again. Two hours later, in the emergency room of a Lafayette hospital, she opened her eyes but did not respond to the doctors. They assumed she was in shock from the trauma of her brother's death, which the authorities believed she played some part in, whether witness or perpetrator.

The district attorney in St. Martin Parish wanted to charge her, but this case required delicate handling. The public hadn't known that the popular New Orleans restaurateur had a twin sister, and her unwillingness—or inability—to communicate complicated things. What if she'd seen someone murder her brother? It was possible, even though there was no evidence of another person's presence. Without charging Charlotte with a crime, a judge ordered her committed to Barrington, a well-respected psychiatric facility outside Lafayette, for sixty days of evaluation.

Ten days later experts submitted their initial report to the court. The patient's vital signs were normal. She was healthy and ate well, but she neither spoke nor seemed to comprehend when others did. She didn't react to attempts to startle her—a loud bang from behind, for instance—or to childhood pictures of Charlotte and her brother that investigators found at Merilee. In summary, despite her perfect physical health, somewhere in her mind a door had closed. Only time would tell if anyone might help her open it again.

CHAPTER NINE

Situations played out in Charlotte's mind as she sat by the window or on the veranda during the day. She didn't know where she was, nor did she care. Her brain had ceased sending the signals that run one's everyday life—the little things such as speaking, caring, wanting and wondering. She ate and drank and urinated and slept because those activities came without planning or thought. They just *happened*, and for the moment Charlotte simply *existed*.

She was aware when people tried to communicate, or talked about her, or made a loud noise, but her brain didn't take the next step. Her doctors opined that a response mechanism was disabled, and she might or might not snap out of it someday. Inside her mind nothing mattered, and her only awareness was of situations—memories, perhaps, or daydreams—that played like videos in her head.

A Christmas morning opening presents in front of the grand fireplace in the parlor. There was a beautiful tree, and she got a doll and a tricycle. Wick was mad about his fishing pole and tackle; he wanted Legos, but his father said they needed to spend more time together, and now they would go fishing.

The tremendous fight between their parents when her dad got passed over again for a raise. Slage Engineering employee wives were a closely knit group and, my, how they crowed when their husbands got nice pay increases. Everyone but James. When the fight began, Charlotte ran to her bedroom and played loud music, but she still listened as they shouted and threw things.

The boys Wick brought home to play with. Even in elementary school, he had no playmates. He never interacted with classmates or got invited to someone's house to play. His only friends, if you could call them that, were boys he met down on the bayou. Kids around his age who were fishing or hiking in the woods. His big house fascinated them, and when he invited them in to play, they would always accept.

"Tag, you're it!" she would hear them yell as Wick and some kid raced down the hallway, darting in and out of bedrooms. They left her alone most of the time, although occasionally some boy would throw open her door, race inside, see her sitting on the bed, and yell, "Oops!" as he made a hasty retreat.

The end of everything normal occurred that night they returned from Florida, where Wick seemed distraught the entire time. Not himself at all. Withdrawn, morose, angry at everyone. His foul mood made her father furious, and once he even slapped Wick in the face. It wasn't the first time Charlotte had seen James hit her brother, but it would be the last. The family came home, Wick ran straight to his room, and then her father…

Suddenly an oppressive hot flash swept over Charlotte, and she fought to suppress the next memory queuing up in her head. She recalled hazy details of what came next, and she did not want to see them. She stiffened in her chair, leaned forward with a jerk, and fell to the floor.

Where am I?

She rose on wobbly legs, sat, and looked around. She was in a spacious room with walls of glass windows that overlooked a beautiful garden. It seemed like a retirement center, but there were people younger than she, playing cards or chatting or watching TV. One girl across the room strummed an air guitar, mouthing noiseless words as she played. None of them appeared to have seen her fall. Or perhaps, like her, their minds weren't comprehending as they should.

Where am I?

A nurse wearing a white smock walked into the room and approached her. "Charlotte, how are we doing today?" she said as she pulled a noncontact thermometer from her pocket.

"I'm okay, I guess. Can you tell me where I am…"

The woman stifled a scream, dropped the thermometer, pulled a transmitting device from her pocket, and pressed a button. "Oh dear, forgive me if I startled you. You surprised me, that's all. My goodness! You haven't spoken a word until now."

What on earth is this woman talking about? "Where am I? How long have I been here?"

Before she answered, two men in white coats rushed into the room, their disruption causing others to look in their direction. When they reached Charlotte, the nurse said, "She answered me when I spoke to her. It startled me…"

"Hello, Charlotte," said a man with gray hair and a military-style buzz cut. She looked at the words stitched on his jacket. Martin Freland, MD.

"Hello, Dr. Freland. Where am I?"

"You're at a clinic in Lafayette."

"Lafayette, Tennessee?"

"No," he said in a soothing voice. "Lafayette, Louisiana. Where do you live, Charlotte?"

"Nashville. Lafayette's just down the road. That's why I thought…but wait. I'm in Louisiana? Why am I at a clinic? How long have I been here?"

He smiled, patted her arm, and said, "I'll answer all your questions, I promise. Let's find a place to talk privately." He turned to the man next to him and said, "Dr. Borland, would you mind setting up one of the consultation rooms?"

The doctor gave Charlotte a hand as she struggled to stand. "What's the matter with me?" she said, and he explained she'd spent most of the past few days sitting in a chair or lying in bed. She had gotten little exercise.

"The past few days? What do you mean? How long have I been here?"

"I'll explain in a moment." He grasped Charlotte's arm and guided her down a brightly lit hallway to a room that held a sofa, comfortable armchairs, and a coffee table, where a box of Kleenex lay. A large mirror hung on one wall, and two cameras hung on another.

"Have a seat," he said, taking a chair next to hers. "If you don't object, I'm going to record our discussion. It's important we capture every word you can tell us." The other doctor came in for a moment, adjusted the cameras, and left.

"Charlotte, you came to Barrington Clinic for observation almost two weeks ago. Something traumatic happened to you: I'll tell you all about it, but let me ask a few questions first. Some of this will seem very basic, but it appears you've experienced a loss of short-term memory, and I want to establish what you can recall."

"Was I in a wreck?"

He shook his head and began asking questions. She knew her name, date of birth, occupation and address, and appeared to recall everything before she came to Louisiana. From airline records, the police learned Charlotte had flown from Nashville to Lafayette thirteen days earlier. She rented a car, spent one night in a motel near the airport, and went to St. Martinville sometime the next day. That evening authorities received the 911 call that led them to find Charlotte and her dead brother, Wick, at Merilee.

The doctor told her about the airline flight, rental car, and motel stay, none of which she recalled. Then he asked about Wick. "When is the last time you saw your brother?"

She stopped to think. "Maybe twenty years ago. Time flies, but it was when we left Merilee for the last time. Is Wick the reason I came here? Is he okay?"

Dr. Freland paused. Although not rare, this type of situation required infinite finesse. Giving a fragile patient distressing information could exacerbate her issues, but she deserved the truth. Unless she was told what happened, she couldn't give him answers the authorities required.

He leaned forward and said, "I know this is difficult,

especially since you don't remember the recent past, but your brother is dead, Charlotte. He died at Merilee on the day after you came to Louisiana."

She stared at him as if he were from another planet. "What the hell…that's impossible. Wick's dead? I don't…I don't understand. Are you sure? How did it happen?"

"I want you to try to remember for yourself. It was night, and you were at your old house with Wick. You went inside and walked around. You both went upstairs…"

She flailed her arms and shouted, "I was there? Oh, God, did I kill him?"

"Be calm, Charlotte. I'm not saying that at all. If you can remember what happened, you can help the police. Can you recall anything about coming to Louisiana and going to your childhood home?"

Tears rolled down her cheeks as she shook her head. "How did he die?"

"That's not important right now…"

She sobbed, "It damned sure is important! Tell me, Doctor. Tell me how my brother died."

"The officers found him hanging from a chandelier at the top of the staircase."

Her voice became a whisper. "So *he* killed Wick. We should never have gone back there. *Wick* shouldn't have. I tried to tell him…"

The doctor watched her eyes as she underwent a transformation. Startled, confused, and sad before, now her eyes radiated something else.

Blankness. Opacity.

"Charlotte? Charlotte?" There was no response.

"Charlotte, please stay with me. We can help you."

He knew it was fruitless, at least for the moment. For a short time that door in her mind had opened. But the jarring disclosure about her brother's death had closed it again.

CHAPTER TEN

Lieutenant Harry Kanter might have been a few months from retirement, but that didn't mean he was beyond reproach. When he came to work this morning, he'd received an order to go upstairs and see the boss. He'd made this trip before, sometimes to brief the colonel on a case's progress, but more often when the man twenty years Harry's junior wanted to dress him down for some perceived misdeed. He had a good idea what the boss wanted today.

Harry looked through the open door into Sam Talbot's office, saw him standing behind his desk looking out the window, and rapped on the frame.

"Colonel, did you want to see me?"

"Sit down, Harry," he said without turning. He opened a humidor, removed a long black panatela, clipped and lit it, then sat behind his desk.

"You're a short-timer," the colonel began. "How long have you been a cop?"

"Thirty-five years, sir." *He already knows this.*

"Are you looking forward to retirement?"

Harry wondered where this was going. Sam Talbot didn't make small talk, nor did he care what Harry was looking forward to. "It's going to be different, that's for sure. I've worn a gun and a badge for a long, long time."

"Thirty-five years and a jacket full of commendations," the superintendent said, patting a thick file sitting on his desk—his personnel file. "An impressive career by anyone's standards."

"Thank you, sir." Harry waited for the other shoe to drop. Something was up; he hadn't been called upstairs to receive accolades about his career.

"You've become pretty good friends with Landry Drake over the past few years, or so it appears to those around you."

Now we're getting somewhere. That's what this conversation is all about. "I suppose you could say so…it's a working relationship. What I mean is, we're not social friends. We're—"

Talbot interrupted, blowing an enormous puff of smoke across his desk that encircled Harry's head and caused him to cough. "Explain to me how a lieutenant on the state police force has a—" his fingers made quotation marks in the air "—'working relationship' with a paranormal investigator. A seasoned cop who's investigated thousands of crimes and a ghost hunter who makes up sensational crap to sell to gullible yokels on cable TV."

"With all respect, Colonel, there's far more to Landry Drake's work than what you described."

"And yours, Lieutenant. There's far more to *your* work than passing along off-the-record secrets about your cases. It's clear you trust this guy. Did you know he once worked for the Iberia Parish sheriff, and he got canned for going through the boss's desk like a petty thief?"

"Yes, sir. I knew that. There's an explanation—"

"Dammit, man!" Talbot exploded. "Do you want to screw up the last few months of your career? You're running to him with every little thing you learn about the Ambrose case. I'm right, am I not?"

The boss had been keeping close tabs on him, and Harry didn't appreciate it one bit. He snapped, "Yes, sir, I've kept Landry involved. Off the record, of course, which is sacrosanct to both him and me. Always has been. I can't count the times his independent research has given us clues. And I've seen some of his cases that defy explanation to his day. May I ask how you know about my involvement with him?"

Talbot smiled, realizing he was getting to his older and more seasoned subordinate. "It's my job to know what's going on in this building. When you talk, people listen. When you take a man in another room for a private conversation, others notice. Word gets around, Lieutenant Kanter, and the word is you're too damned close to a guy who belongs in a sideshow. Ghost hunter, my ass. If you believe in that crap, you're not the officer I thought you were."

Harry forced himself to bite his tongue instead of firing back.

Talbot stood. "In a few months, I want to shake your hand at your retirement party. You and I haven't always seen eye to eye, but you're a good cop. You have been, I should say. Stay away from Landry Drake. He'll do nothing but hurt what's left of your career, and neither of us wants that. You're dismissed."

Seething, Harry waited for the elevator door to close. Instead of punching the button for his floor, he rode all the way down, stormed through the lobby, and went to the parking garage. Tires squealing as he made turns, he drove a few blocks and pulled into the parking lot of an aging brick building. One wouldn't know what was behind its run-down I except for an old neon Abita Beer sign sparking on and off in a front window.

Harry chose a bar stool and looked around. Realizing he was the only person there, he glanced at his watch. Eight fifty-two a.m.

Bit early for anybody but an alcoholic or a guy needing to drown his sorrows, he thought as he yelled, "Bud! Bud, are you here?"

A man around Harry's age came through swinging doors at the back. He wore a sleeveless undershirt and a dirty apron, and he had a mop in one hand and a cigarette in the other.

"Harry! What the hell are you doing here so early? Long night?"

"Something like that. How about a Jack Daniel's neat? Make it a double."

The man named Bud could see that Harry didn't want company, so he fixed the drink, put it on the bar, and said he'd be cleaning up in the back, and to yell if he needed anything. And with his usual insight, Bud left the bottle sitting on the bar next to Harry. Just in case.

As usual, the first swig went down like fire, burning his throat and hitting his stomach with a jolt. The rest were smoother, and after he poured another generous portion from the bottle, he sat with his hand wrapped around the glass, thinking.

Harry loved this place. It was a cop bar, a place where he and his buddies had gathered after shifts for thirty-five years. Bud had owned it the entire time—they'd all been kids when it started—and the bartender-owner knew his customers' trials and tribulations. He'd heard it all—sordid divorces, sizzling affairs, whispers about cops who took a payoff or planted a drop gun at a murder scene, football bets that paid off big time or cost a cop a month's wages—Bud heard everything and kept it all to himself. Law enforcement guys from the sheriff's office to the Baton Rouge police to the state cops congregated at this no-name bar that held their secrets. It was a sanctuary—a place for camaraderie and jokes and tears and goodbyes.

Thirty-five years on the force. Married, divorced because I was married to my job, a loner after that. I was the tough cop—the hard, no-nonsense guy who struck fear in the minds of the lowlifes who raped and robbed and murdered innocent people. I was a skeptic when I met Landry, and without realizing it, he taught me to open my mind. Things aren't always black and white or three-dimensional. Some things defy imagination. Working with him broadened my viewpoint and gave me some of the happiest and most interesting times I've experienced as a cop.

In just a few weeks, Harry's buddies were planning a retirement party for him right here at Bud's place. There would be cigars, good booze, friends, and conversation, just like a hundred other retirement parties Harry had attended.

Those parties went on until the wee hours, and they had been good times—the best, with the finest men in the world, his fellow officers on the state police force.

Bud came out to check on him. "I poured myself another drink," Harry said, gazing at the empty glass before him.

His old friend held up the bottle. "Ready for one more?"

Harry nodded.

CHAPTER ELEVEN

With only four employees at the Paranormal Network, everyone pitched in to do anything needed, from building sets to emptying the wastebaskets to picking up takeout food. Fortuitously, Phil Vandegriff, the audio-visual guru Landry had brought over from Channel Nine, answered the phone one lunch hour.

Landry, Cate, and Henri had left for lunch at Muriel's, and as Phil walked by Cate's desk, the phone rang, and he answered. He entered a message on the desktop and promised someone would return the call. When the three returned from lunch, Phil was waiting for them.

"A woman from KMG in New York wants a callback. Something about a client wanting to advertise on TPN. When she asked for our ad rep's contact info, I said someone would return the call. Do we have an ad rep?"

"Not yet." Cate laughed. "It's on the to-do list. We chose to launch the network with local advertisers, and I've gotten some lined up. KMG is a big dog. One of the biggest agencies in the country." She pulled up their website and read a partial client list. Toyota. Coke. Nike. General Foods.

"Impressive," Landry said. "What do we do next?"

Cate said she'd explore ad agencies before returning the KMG call. Landry offered the names of three companies

Channel Nine worked with, one local and two in Houston.

She called them to the conference room later that day, saying she had two important announcements. "First, the Paranormal Network officially has an ad rep. Firestone-McCauley Advertising in Houston agreed to represent us short-term while we solicit proposals from all three firms. We discussed fees, commissions, and scope of work, and they're emailing everything for our attorney to review. Which reminds me, we also need an attorney!" Everyone laughed.

"Now comes the good part. After lining up Firestone, I spoke with the KMG rep in New York. One of their clients wants to advertise on TPN. If our ad rep says the terms are fair, it'll be our first national advertiser." She paused and smiled.

"Do we need a drum roll here?" Landry asked. "The suspense is killing me."

"Here's a hint. From now on, you'll be brushing your teeth with this brand of toothpaste." She named the major brand and its parent company, a Fortune 500 conglomerate.

Henri said, "Our first national advertiser is a toothpaste company?"

"If it works out, yes. They want to buy a million dollars' worth of spots and see how it goes from there."

The news buoyed their spirits. Ad revenue represented an important step in building the network. Although nothing had been finalized, this indicated they were doing things right and their fledgling network was attracting attention.

Landry was still on a euphoric high from the good news when Cate buzzed the top-floor studio and told him Harry wanted to speak with him.

"On the landline?" Landry asked. "Why didn't he call my cell?"

"He sounds a little…off to me. Anyway, he's holding on line one."

"Hi, Harry. Is everything all right?" he began, and at once he heard what Cate had described. Harry stumbled over slurred words. Landry had never even seen the cop take a drink, but he could swear that right now, at two in the afternoon, Harry was drunk as a skunk.

"Gotta tell you something'…it's the Ambrose girl. She…"

"Harry? Are you all right? Why didn't you call my cellphone?"

"Lost my phone. Can't remember your…your number." Uproarious laughter, as if that were the funniest thing in the world. "I had my friend Bud find the number for your office." He spoke to someone else. "Yeah. Just top it off. Great, buddy."

"Where are you?"

"I'm in a place in Baton Rouge. A bar, matter of fact. Wanted to call you. The girl…something Ambrose…"

"Charlotte."

"Yeah, right, that's it. Charlotte. She woke up. Told the doctors *he* killed her brother, whoever *he* is. Said she warned Wick it was dangerous to go back to their old house. Then she…fell asleep again or something. That's a broken record. Ha, ha, I mean off the record." He broke into another fit of laughter at that comment. "Hey, buddy, I gotta go. I may come see you sometime." With a click, he rang off.

What the hell? He called Harry's phone and got voicemail. Then he called police headquarters and learned that Lieutenant Kanter was out for the day.

Thank God for that, Landry thought. The office was the last place he needed to be right now.

He returned to what he'd been working on, thought about Harry off and on, and forgot about it once he and Cate left the Toulouse Street building and walked along Chartres Street past Jackson Square to their apartment. A storm from the Gulf would come in tonight, and temperatures were falling as the wind picked up. Light rain fell, becoming fat drops and then a downpour. Missing the worst of it, they darted into their building, opted for pizza delivery, donned sweats, opened a nice bottle of Merlot, and watched a movie on Netflix. After a long day, it was lights out at ten for both of them.

Around eleven, Landry's phone rang. Cate mumbled something, and Landry said, "It's Harry. Go back to sleep."

He walked into the living room and closed the door behind him.

"Hey, Landry. I'm sorry. I guess I made a fool of myself today. And I'm sorry for calling so late, but I had to apologize."

"It's okay. Shit happens to everybody. Who am I to judge?" Landry tried to laugh it off, but Harry wouldn't have it.

"The boss jumped my ass this morning for associating with you. He told me to knock it off and called you a charlatan. Did I want to screw up my whole career in the last few weeks? That's what set me off. It pissed me off, and I went totally out of character. I drove over to this cop bar I go to sometimes, and I drank until I passed out. A beer or two, maybe three, is all I ever drink, and now I know why. Anyway, I'm sorry. Hey, on another subject, I wanted to tell you that Charlotte Ambrose woke up for a short time yesterday. Her doctor called me."

You already told me this, but you don't remember. "Did anything interesting happen?"

He recounted her inability to remember anything about coming to or being in Louisiana. The doctor said her brother died, prompting her to make puzzling comments. She had warned Wick not to go back home, and someone killed him. That was all they got before her mind shut down again.

"Any idea who she's talking about?"

"No, and it's not true. Nobody killed him. Sheriff Angelli kept the scene intact until after I arrived that night. You came later, but I can tell you the only tracks in the dust on the stairway and the upstairs hall were Wick's and Charlotte's. They had walked from room to room all over the second floor, but it was only them. If somebody killed Wick Ambrose, then it was his sister. If not, then he hanged himself."

"Which do you think it is?"

"I don't know, but I've got this gut feeling you need to go back to Merilee and check it out. Perhaps there's an explanation for all this, but I'd bet you tomorrow's hangover something strange is going on up there—something right up your alley. I'll stay out of it since you and I can't go out anymore, but keep me advised if something turns up."

Against his better judgment, Landry agreed to go back. He doubted that Charlotte Ambrose was talking about the paranormal. More likely, a person drove Wick to commit suicide—someone who wasn't present, but who had such power over the restaurateur that he took his life. Someone Charlotte knew about.

He decided against going to St. Martinville alone. Jack had been a big help, and he deserved to be part of it. Not knowing if he'd be awake, Landry texted him.

"I'm going to Merilee to look around tomorrow. I know it's Friday, but if your schedule allows, want to join me?"

The answer came in seconds. "Wouldn't miss it. See you at the usual place at eight?"

Landry agreed and tried to sleep while his mind swirled with today's crazy events. The thrill of a major advertiser for the network. Harry's drunken admission that things involving Landry spelled trouble for him at work. And now, doubts about Merilee. Did he have time to waste on a wild-goose chase? *This is it,* he told himself. *One more look around, then I'm done.*

CHAPTER TWELVE

By dawn the storm lay far to the north, and the morning brought a crisp, cool breeze off the Mississippi River. Landry and Jack met at what Jack called "the usual place"— Café du Monde on Decatur Street, a popular venue always packed with customers enjoying beignets and coffee. It had become their usual gathering place before heading out of New Orleans on a ghost-hunting adventure. From their table, they saw an enormous sign on the side of the Jax building a few blocks downriver. *Wick Ambrose's Atomic Roadhouse,* the neon letters read, a sad reminder that today they would try to unravel the mystery behind the restaurateur's hanging.

Jack took Interstate 10 through Baton Rouge and into Lafayette. After hearing what Daisy Poe had told Jack about Wick's father, and after Jack outlined the questions that needed answers, Landry agreed they should start by speaking with her. On the way up, Jack called and got permission for them to visit. After that, they'd go on to Merilee and investigate Harry Kanter's hunch that something mysterious was going on at the house.

From the passenger seat, Landry thought to himself if nothing panned out today, he'd drop the Ambrose case. He kept those thoughts to himself; there would be time to tell Jack once they started back home.

Around ten they arrived at the retirement home where Daisy Poe lived. As the only connection to James Ambrose's employment at Slage Engineering, Jack held hopes she might tell them more. A nurse led them through the facility and onto the back veranda, where they found Daisy in a porch swing. A spry lady of eighty-eight with bright eyes and a perky demeanor, she showed Jack the beautiful flowers he had sent, saying people didn't do nice things like that anymore.

Daisy laughed when Jack introduced Landry. "Oh, come now, everyone here knows Landry Drake. We watch your spooky shows on television and talk about them for days. I wasn't aware you were coming, but I'm glad you did! Before you leave, I want to show you off. My friends will be so jealous! Now tell me what brings you to Lafayette."

They talked about Slage Engineering and James Ambrose's time there. She said he didn't have a job title or description, and his mundane responsibilities included going to the post office every morning to get the mail and picking up Mr. Slage's dry cleaning. "He was a gofer, if you understand what I'm saying. The man had no ambition. We called people like him 'slow' in those days, but I don't think he had mental problems. He just didn't have the desire to learn something new. He wanted to do the minimum it took to get a paycheck."

As they wrapped up, Landry asked if anyone else might have information about James or his family. She thought a moment and snapped her fingers.

"Yes, yes there is! Presuming you can find him, Stu Pinelli might help. As I recall, Stu was the only employee James ever made friends with. He was an engineer around James's age, and he lived in St. Martinville back then. Maybe he still does. It's Stuart Pinelli—" she spelled the last name "—and if you find him, tell him Daisy said hello."

When she introduced Landry to her friends, he gave some autographs and shook some hands. Afterwards he and Jack drove to St. Martinville. At almost one p.m., they wanted a lunch place, and Landry told Jack to get ready for a treat. He knew a restaurant on Bridge Street with no ambiance but scrumptious home cooking.

He parked in front of a small tin-roofed building called Mother's, its windows plastered with Coke ads. As they walked inside, the cook peered through a window from the kitchen and shouted, "Welcome back, Mr. Landry! Hey, everybody! The ghost hunter's back in town!"

A friendly girl led them through the tiny, crowded restaurant past three tables to a fourth, the only vacant one. Four men played a rowdy game of dominoes at the far end of the room. The low prices on the menu surprised Jack, and their young server said they'd run out of everything except pork chops and shrimp creole. They chose the latter and enjoyed a nice, unhurried meal without the usual interruptions from well-wishers and autograph seekers. Nobody at Mother's gave him a second glance. They minded their own business.

When the girl presented their twelve-dollar tab, Landry swept it up with a flourish and said, "This one's on me. You can pick up the next one at Muriel's." Laughing, Jack called it unfair. Even a shrimp cocktail at Muriel's cost more than that.

Two blocks away at the courthouse, they found a clerk named CarolAnn who wanted to help Landry. She searched the property records and found the same deeds that Jack had turned up, the ones that transferred ownership from one Ambrose heir down to another. Landry asked for a copy of the one from 1996 that deeded the house and twenty-five acres to a private corporation.

Jack asked if CarolAnn had heard anything else about the Ambrose family and Merilee Plantation. She was aware Wick owned restaurants in New Orleans, and she had heard spooky tales about Merilee. People in this part of Louisiana enjoyed passing on ghost stories about the antebellum mansions that sat on the rivers and bayous.

She found the legends about Merilee intriguing because of the strange circumstances. Folks didn't understand why a family would abandon the mansion that was their ancestral home, leaving it to fall into disrepair. That odd behavior spawned yarns about supernatural sightings and terrifying encounters with malevolent spirits.

A popular legend claimed that the first Ambrose, Pierre, sometimes took house servants as his concubines. When his wife, Merilee, had had enough, she killed the girl and mutilated her husband's privates. Now Pierre's ghost roamed the house at night, moaning and groaning about his painful afflictions. The truth was that Merilee Ambrose had died at an early age from yellow fever, but Jack said after all this time, who knew what to believe?

A more recent tale making the rounds involved Wick and Charlotte. One stormy night after a row with their parents, the twins stabbed them to death and hid the bodies in a cellar. They continued to live in the house as though nothing had happened until 2001, when they abandoned the place. Locals said even today people saw the twins moving past the windows late at night, and the horrific screams as the children went about their ghastly work terrified any who heard them.

Landry didn't accept that either. If anyone back then believed it, the sheriff could have gone to Merilee and investigated the ghostly sightings. But it still might have a ring of truth, because James never returned to work after that vacation. Might that be because he was dead? If so, why was there no police report or death certificate?

The court clerk handed Landry a copy of the 2001 deed that transferred Merilee to a corporation. At the bottom were James and Maria Ambrose's signatures, along with the stamp and a notary public's stamp and signature. A thought niggled somewhere in the back of his mind about something he'd overlooked. He checked the signatures again.

Janelle Marcum, Notary ID 87038

St. Martin Parish, Louisiana

He laid the deed on the counter in front of CarolAnn and asked if she knew the notary. She shook her head.

"I've never heard of her, but it's not that unusual. I was a child when she signed that deed. She might have been long gone by the time I grew up. Tell me what you're looking for."

"I want to know if she watched James and Maria sign

this deed. That's a notary's job, but did she do it?" He turned to Jack. "Who regulates notaries in Louisiana? We've got her ID number. Let's check it out."

Excited to watch a mystery unfold before her eyes, CarolAnn said, "It would be the Secretary of State in Baton Rouge. You can use the phone on that desk over there." Landry hoped it would be simple, and he was right. In less than five minutes he had his answer.

"Notary ID 87038 doesn't exist. They're issued numerically, and so far, the state's only into the forty thousands."

When the clerk shouted, "Holy cow!" two other clerks came up to the counter to see what caused the commotion.

Landry said, "We need to find something else that has James and Maria's signatures. If they got married in this parish, would they have filed the license here?"

"They sure would!"

The clerk's fingers flew over the keyboard. She paused, stared at the screen a moment, and grinned. "Bingo! James Ambrose and Maria Helton. Married March 23, 1968, St. Martinville, Louisiana. Now let's look for that marriage license." She typed again, clicked Enter with a flourish, picked up a paper from the printer, and gave it to Landry.

The marriage license bore the signatures of James Ambrose and Maria Helton. People's signatures change over the years, but the clear, broad strokes on this document in no way resembled the messy scrawls on the deed from December 1996.

"So what does this tell us?" Jack asked.

"James and Maria Ambrose didn't sign the deed. The notary public who attested their signatures is fake. It would appear Wick and Charlotte were the only people to gain from the transfer, but they were just fourteen years old. Now Wick's dead, and Charlotte's not talking. So the question is, who owns that corporation?"

CHAPTER THIRTEEN

They needed Sheriff Angelli's permission to go back to Merilee, and at his office a block away they got what they wanted. The house was no longer an active crime scene, and Angelli had no further say in who visited or not. He warned, "Technically you'll be trespassing, but who's going to stop you? If somebody turns you in, I promise the jailers will take good care of you both. We serve chateaubriand and Merlot wine on Thursdays," he joked, asking them to let him know if they found anything.

As they drove south on Highway 31, Jack asked if the forged deed might be a sign Wick and Charlotte actually had murdered their parents. That document and setting up a corporation to own Merilee might be their work.

"I suppose it's possible, but I doubt it," Landry replied. "You have a point about one thing. If we find out who owns that corporation, it could help explain why James Ambrose disappeared."

They turned at the historical marker, parked near the house, and tore off the yellow crime scene tape that crisscrossed the front doors. Landry stepped inside and went straight to the stairs. When he and Jack had come on the night Wick died, the sheriff didn't allow them upstairs. This time he wanted to see the exact spot for himself.

As he expected, the noose and ladder weren't there—taken away as evidence, Landry presumed—and all that remained was the heavy chandelier from which the rope had hung. He stood beneath the fixture and gazed at it for several minutes before speaking.

"Jack, I'm going to tell you my thoughts about Merilee, and most of them are questions. We know Wick and his sister came back here after being gone since 2001. What prompted them to do it, and was there anything significant about the exact night they returned? Did Wick commit suicide? If so, was that his intention when he came? Why choose to hang himself, a more gruesome way to kill yourself than, say, using a gun or pills or carbon monoxide? Were the time, place, and means of his death all related somehow?

"Then there's Charlotte. Was she the only other person in the house? Did she kill her brother? Why would she do that? And how, since he's a healthy guy who could overpower her? Given that she would have to hoist him up the ladder and put a noose around his neck, I think it's safe to rule her out as the perpetrator. That makes her either a witness, an accomplice, or she was somewhere else when it happened, and she fainted beneath his body when she found him dead.

"If she witnessed his death, why didn't she try to stop him? Had they made a pact, or perhaps she was somewhere else in the house? If that was the case, then she would have heard him, come here, and found him hanging. Perhaps she fainted, knocking over the ladder. Or *he* knocked over the ladder as he swung from the noose."

Jack said, "That was a comprehensive summary—what I'd expect from the famous Landry Drake. I can't imagine a scenario you missed. For what it's worth, my theory is Wick hanged himself. I agree it's unlikely anybody else hoisted him up there. Unless he was unconscious, I guess, but even then somebody had to haul the dead weight of a grown man up a six-foot ladder and put his head in a noose without losing his balance. Perhaps several people were around to help do it, or Charlotte hired an accomplice to murder her brother. If so, why were there no other footprints? Seems to me the only person who can tell us what happened is Charlotte, and that depends on if she ever wakes up and agrees to talk."

Landry walked down the hallway toward a bedroom. "Let's check things out. This might be about a troubled man who elected to kill himself in front of his sister. But I doubt that's what happened. Perhaps Merilee has some clues for us."

Jack asked, "Do you see any paranormal aspect to this? Am I missing something?"

"No, I agree. I just outlined every possibility I could dream up, and nothing makes sense right now. Things are crazy at the network, and I don't have time to pursue this unless I see a clear supernatural connection. That's my gig, and that's what I have to concentrate on. But here we are, standing on the second floor of a decaying old mansion at the scene of a hanging. It's a perfect setting for a good ghost story, so let's poke around. If nothing turns up, then I have to let this one go."

CHAPTER FOURTEEN

Forty-five minutes later, Landry and Jack left Merilee. The house was eerie enough—many once-majestic mansions along the Louisiana bayous qualified as spooky—but room after room of decaying furniture, personal items resting on shelves where someone left them long ago, and bedroom closets filled with rotting clothing just didn't make the house haunted. Spooky, eerie, and creepy were one thing, but supernatural and paranormal fell in a different category. Something awful had happened that night at Merilee, but Landry believed the solutions to the house's unexplained mysteries lay in the world of reality, not the spiritual realm. Landry decided the time had come to let this one go.

Jack understood, even though Wick's death intrigued him. "All those questions you posed, all that wondering what happened, and you're going to walk away? What about the deed? Somebody faked the transfer. What happened to James and Maria? Did somebody kill them too?"

"That's an interesting sidebar, but those are things for Harry Kanter and the sheriff's men to investigate. Murder scenes aren't my bag, and I can't afford any more time on this project. I'm trying to build a network. We have a huge leg up since the *Bayou Hauntings* series is already a hit, but there are a million things to do now that we have our own platform. If you want my advice, you don't have time for it either, Jack. Last time I checked, they hired you to do paranormal investigations."

Jack argued, "My title is senior investigative reporter, just like yours was. Last time I checked, it didn't include the word *paranormal*."

Landry threw up his hands. "Hey, I'm not arguing. What you do is your business, but you get what I'm saying. If you want to keep after it, I won't stop you. And if the cops find something interesting, you have my number."

"What makes you think I'll call you next time? You're bailing out on me. That makes you a quitter." He shot Landry a broad grin.

As they headed toward the interstate and came to the outskirts of St. Martinville, Jack asked if he could do a quick search to see if Stuart Pinelli might still live in the area.

Landry replied, "It's a waste of time, but why not, since we're here?"

Jack parked the car in a shady spot near the old Evangeline Oak and reached for his laptop. He did a name search and found three matches in Louisiana but none in St. Martin Parish. They stopped by the sheriff's department and asked a deputy to check the county database. No luck there either. Stuart Pinelli might have lived here twenty years ago, but not today.

Back in New Orleans, Landry gave Cate and Henri an update on what he termed a fruitless trip and a project he'd quit. Although Cate wondered about the forged deed, she agreed the paranormal didn't seem to be a part of this mystery.

She asked, "Where were the parents in late 1996? Sounds like the twins forged their parents' signatures and created a fake notary to attest them. I think we all agree something criminal happened at Merilee, but it's not for us. We're the Paranormal Network, not CNN. I say leave it for the authorities to sort out. We have other things to do. Speaking of which, Henri, can we review your suggested programming schedule for the first quarter?"

As they switched gears from Merilee to the new network,

Jack sat in his office at Channel Nine and stared at his monitor. He'd learned a lot working for Landry, and one thing Landry always told Jack was not to accept things at face value. Given the facts, he saw no evidence of paranormal activity, but too much about this case made no sense.

When they'd stood under that chandelier where Wick died, Landry had enumerated the questions well. Mysteries abounded at Merilee, and Jack wanted to make sense of at least one. After the family on vacation in 1996, James never returned to work. At the end of that year, when Wick and Charlotte were fourteen, a forged deed transferred ownership of the Ambrose family home. Five years later, the house sat abandoned. What happened, when did they leave, and why?

It disappointed Jack that his old boss had quit so soon. He understood Landry had more important things to do these days, like launching a new channel. Regardless, Jack understood one thing—Landry's passion was the paranormal, and he'd be right back in the saddle if something unusual turned up.

He looked at the tax rolls and saw that every year beginning in 1997, the agent of the corporation that owned Merilee received tax bills. That made sense—it was how things should be. The taxes were never paid late, but who paid them? Who owned Merilee?

Jack listed his questions in a note folder on the computer and turned his attention to Stuart Pinelli. As James Ambrose's only friend, Pinelli should know more about the man than anyone. From his earlier search, he knew there were three men with that name in Louisiana today. Now he needed to know how old the right Stuart Pinelli should be. Daisy Poe had said Stu was about James's age, but he didn't know that either. He went with what facts he had—James and Maria married in 1972. If James was around twenty—a logical assumption for those times and this part of the country—today he would be almost seventy, and so might Pinelli.

The scant information he found on two of the Pinelli men eliminated them at once. According to his Facebook page, the first was a sophomore at Louisiana-Lafayette and a member of the Ragin' Cajuns football team. He was far too young.

The other man's photo appeared in the DeRidder, Louisiana, newspaper. Stuart Pinelli was a spry Black man celebrating his hundredth birthday in a local nursing home.

I feel like Goldilocks. One's too old, and one's too young. Will the next one be just right?

The third Stuart Pinelli served on the staff of Patton Fortier, Louisiana's senior senator in Washington. Pinelli lived in Baton Rouge and ran the senator's state office. Jack found a picture and job title—projects and grants coordinator—on the senator's website. Pinelli had gray hair and was likely in his sixties. Jack figured it should be easy to learn more about a man in such a high-profile environment.

He called Fortier's Baton Rouge office, identified himself as a reporter with WCCY-TV in New Orleans, and said he was researching a story about Louisianans who worked on Capitol Hill. The lady bought his tale and said Pinelli, a native of St. Martin Parish, was in his mid-sixties. He had joined the senator's team over twenty years earlier.

"What does a projects and grants coordinator do?" Jack asked, and she explained he worked with various enterprises in Louisiana, seeking government contracts or federal grants.

"I'm sure he'd like to talk with you," she added, "but he's traveling with the senator. He'll be back in the office on Monday. May he call you back then?"

Jack said yes and asked one last question, a long shot. "Does a man named James Ambrose work for Senator Fortier too?" No, the lady had never heard of him.

After he rang off, Jack wondered if he had the right Stuart Pinelli. If so, how did an engineer from St. Martinville end up working for a prominent national politician? So far, everything appeared straightforward, and Jack started listing questions he'd ask if he got a callback on Monday. He hoped the conversation might provide answers.

CHAPTER FIFTEEN

That evening Stuart Pinelli and Senator Patton Fortier sat on the second floor of the Windsor Court Hotel, just ten blocks away from Channel Nine's studio. From their corner table in the Polo Club Lounge, Stu scrolled through emails as his boss shook hands with well-wishers who stopped by the table. Fortier was always ready to greet a constituent, even though he grumbled about the intrusion after the person walked away.

A server brought their cocktails—a Scotch and soda for James, a mint julep for the senator—and Fortier raised his glass for a toast. "To health, wealth and prosperity for all," he said, a phrase James had heard a thousand times since he joined Fortier's staff twenty years ago. He'd long since learned that those words applied to the senator himself—the wealth and prosperity part, at least—and not the public, whom he respected only because their votes could send him back to DC.

"Anything hot on the front burner, Stu?" the senator asked, pointing to the phone. If something big came up, Stu would get the message, because Fortier didn't own a cellphone. He believed others should perform menial tasks like checking voicemail. Important people had other things to do.

"Nothing exciting, sir. There's a budget committee meeting on Tuesday, and Senator Schumer would like to see you the afternoon before to discuss strategy. The Energy subcommittee hearing on the offshore drilling moratorium is Wednesday, and Jim Morton would like to talk about it."

Morton ran Gulfpoint Well Services, a New Orleans-based company and the nation's largest supplier of offshore drilling platforms. He also spearheaded Fortier's campaign fund-raising efforts, securing millions of dollars in contributions. To say he had the ear of Senator Fortier would be a massive understatement.

"What's on the agenda for breakfast tomorrow?"

"Nothing, sir, but we need to be on the road by nine." The senator told him to get Morton on the line.

Stu handed him the phone, and he gushed, "Jim, it's been too long! How's Annie and the kids? All grown up since I last saw them, I'll bet! I got your message, and I'd like your input on the hearing. It so happens I'm in town, and I'm hoping we can meet in person. How about breakfast tomorrow at the Windsor Court?"

That meeting arranged, the senator sipped his drink and shook more hands while Stu returned to a message he'd seen earlier. A reporter from WCCY-TV here in New Orleans wanted to interview him about his job with the senator. He considered the implications. For twenty-something years he'd stayed totally under the radar, an easy thing for Patton Fortier's aide to do. The man had a gregarious personality and was never at a loss for words. When he entered a room, his commanding presence overshadowed everyone else. People hardly noticed his staffers.

But now someone—a reporter—wanted to ask him questions. Something about Louisianans working in DC.

Was that actually what he was after? It might be, but one never knew. He'd call the man—it would look odd if he didn't—but he would be very careful.

The senator interrupted his thoughts, asking if Stu thought Wick Ambrose's death would put a kink in their plans. Stu said it should make no difference, because the paperwork had been executed. The death of a party to a signed contract changed nothing. When the time came, the deal would go like clockwork.

While Fortier met his friend downstairs for breakfast the next morning, Stu ordered coffee and toast from room service. He downloaded confidential reports from overnight emails, printing them on a machine the hotel had installed in the suite's living room next door. Fortier was old school; he refused to read things on a laptop or a tablet. He wanted to hold the papers in his hands and make notes in the margins as he read.

He finished the chores and returned Jack Blair's call. On full alert, he listened as the reporter explained the story he was working on. Blair asked typical questions about how it felt to work for such an important man, what kind of long hours and days did he put in, and what did he do for downtime. Things were going fine, and Stu had opened up a little about his life on the road with a powerful man. This cordial reporter was asking all the usual questions, and Stu let his guard down.

As things appeared ready to wrap up, Blair threw him a curveball. "Years ago, you worked for Slage Engineering in Lafayette, I believe. After you left, you moved to New Orleans. Was that when you went to work for Senator Fortier?"

How the hell did he learn about Slage?
Be careful, Stu.

"I joined Senator Fortier's office over twenty years ago. I don't recall just when I left Slage Engineering, but I moved to Baton Rouge then and did freelance engineering work for a while. None of that's relevant…"

"You're too modest, Mr. Pinelli. Everything's relevant when a St. Martinville native goes to Capitol Hill. That's a success story people love knowing about. On another topic, you were close friends with James Ambrose at Slage Engineering, correct?"

Stu broke into a sweat. "Listen here. What is it you're after? What does James Ambrose have to do with my background and your story?"

Feeling the tension, Jack pushed for more. "Not long

ago, I went to St. Martinville, doing research. I learned that James never returned from work after a vacation, and someone gave me your name. They said James had only one friend at Slage Engineering—you."

"What are you after, Mr. Blair?" Jack sensed his anger and tried to keep Pinelli on the line.

"You may have heard that Wick Ambrose died at Merilee Plantation the other night. He's another Louisiana native who became a success, only he died in the prime of life. I looked into that story, and that's when I learned that his father, James—your friend—disappeared."

"Wick hanged himself. Those things happen. Maybe he had problems nobody knew about. Everybody has their secrets…"

"So far, they haven't ruled it a suicide. The only other person present was his sister, Charlotte, and at the moment she can't tell them anything."

Charlotte was there? The media hadn't reported that. He wondered why she didn't talk to the authorities, but he didn't ask. "I'm afraid I'm out of time, Mr. Blair. We seem to have drifted off the subject of your call. I knew James Ambrose long ago, but that has nothing to do with the story you claim to be working on. Goodbye."

"One more question…" But the phone was dead.

That call hadn't yielded much, but he'd found the right Stuart Pinelli. The mere mention of James Ambrose had set him off. This story might not have paranormal aspects, but it was intriguing. He'd keep digging in hopes he'd find out what made the man so nervous. Did he have something to hide about his friendship with James Ambrose? Jack turned back to the computer and restarted his search.

CHAPTER SIXTEEN

Charlotte sat by the window in her room. She looked without seeing and listened without understanding. She cooperated when someone came to take her to meals, and she used the bathroom, showered, and dressed herself when told. But she initiated nothing.

Most of the time her mind was as blank as a dead monitor. Occasional thoughts drifted into her consciousness before wafting away like dandelion fuzz on a breeze.

Her bedroom at Merilee. Her mother when she was a child. Their old Volvo station wagon. Angry words and voices. Wick. That night. Henry, her clown doll. Her teacher in first grade.

Some thoughts made her cry, and others caused her to tremble or laugh aloud. By the time she became aware of her emotions, she'd forgotten the memories.

Someone came into her room. She turned and looked into his face. This person differed from the ones who came to take her to lunch, or to ask her questions that had no answers, or to tell her it was time for bed. He was someone else, a man from long, long ago. A memory. A tear ran down her cheek, then another, and more.

Hello, Charlotte.

As he drew near, his mouth uttered whispers she heard

but did not fully comprehend.

I came to ask you about that night. What do you remember about it, Charlotte?

That night. A vague memory flitted into her mind. Something about that night. And this man. She cried out without knowing why.

Shouting became screams. Horrifying wails, over and over. When he was no longer there, she stopped.

People ran to her. The ones she saw every day. Their faces showed surprise, alarm.

Why? It seemed they all spoke at once. Words she heard but did not understand.

A man came into this room earlier—a man from a memory. Didn't he?

In her mind, Charlotte formed those words but did not say them aloud. Instead, she turned away from the people and gazed out the window. As she looked at nothing, another memory entered her mind.

The cellar. Its terrifying darkness gave her chills, and she didn't want to think about it. But these days her mind was in charge. It told her when to become lucid and when to withdraw, when to understand and when to wonder what someone meant. Her mind controlled everything.

Right now it wanted to think about the cellar.

For two reasons, houses in southern Louisiana rarely had basements. The water table in most areas lay so close to the surface that even a two-foot-deep hole would flood at once. The other issue was hurricanes; parishes near the coast experienced high water and blowing winds every season, and many houses stood up on stilts to keep the first floors dry.

Merilee Plantation was an exception, thanks to the site Pierre Ambrose had selected for its construction in 1843. Situated on a berm overlooking Bayou Teche, it sat several feet above the river, freeing it from flooding issues. And it had a cellar at the bottom of a wooden stairway accessible from the kitchen. The crude room had a dirt floor and walls, and its ceiling was the unfinished floor of the kitchen above. The room was only five feet high, and the family would have had to stoop to enter.

A few dusty bottles of wine, long since turned sour, rested on a rack at the back of the room. Crude shelves erected in the eighteen hundreds once held fruit and vegetables canned by Merilee Ambrose's servants. Tools—rakes, shovels, a pickaxe and a post-hole digger—stood in a far corner, and rotting cloth potato and flour sacks lay in a pile. A vise and some broken hand tools that might bring a few dollars in an antique shop lay on a rickety worktable.

For as long as she could remember, Charlotte had hated the cellar—its dank, musty odor, its dark corners that the electric light bulb hanging from the ceiling couldn't illuminate, and the unshakable feeling that something bad was hiding down there. Wick didn't help things; playing off her childhood fears, he taunted and teased her. He forced her to go a long time back, and many times he threatened to lock her down there—a threat that seemed less idle as she became a teen and learned his propensity for doing that sort of thing. He recounted ghastly stories of a creature that lived in the cellar, a horribly deformed half beast that came upstairs into their house at night and prowled the halls.

"I saw him in my bedroom one night," Wick said in a low voice, savoring the terror that consumed her. "I'll bet he's been in yours too. What if you woke up and…"

She would scream bloody murder, and her mother would make Wick stop taunting his twin sister. "There's nothing down there, honey," her mother would say as she held Charlotte close. "It's just a damp old room to store things in. Don't let him scare you."

But he kept at it, and his stories had just enough ring of truth to keep her away. Even today, at thirty-nine, Charlotte wouldn't have gone down those stairs for anything on earth. Because now she believed something else was there. Something so frightening it terrified her to think about it.

It all went back to that horrendous night when they'd returned from the trip to Florida. In moments everything went to hell—the dead boy in Wick's room, her mother's unrelenting, terrifying screams, and her dad's call to his work friend Stu Pinelli. Come help me fix things, he had said. She wasn't sure what needed fixing, but when that night ended, so did her childhood.

Her father forced them to wait with him in the parlor while Stu "took care of things." Charlotte almost threw up when she heard the thump-thump of something being dragged down the stairs. What was it? She knew, but she didn't want to think about it. Why did it have to be this way? She asked why they couldn't call the sheriff, but her father told her to shut up and wait until Stu finished.

After a considerable time passed, Stu came and took her dad into another room. When he returned, James told them he was leaving. Just like that, he abandoned them without an explanation, a kind word, or a goodbye kiss. Stu remained at the house a few more hours, demanding they stay in their rooms while he worked in the cellar. When he left, he said they were on their own. He'd send money now and then, and he left a number Wick could call if something big needed repairs.

"Don't bother me with little things. You're fourteen years old; you can fix them yourself," he had told Wick. "And don't tell anyone what happened here. If you do, they'll put you in prison and your sister in an orphanage. You all don't want that, do you?"

They didn't, so they obeyed. Stu had done things in the cellar, and she vowed never, ever to go find out what they were. And after the horrible thing Wick had done, she was uneasy around him. From then on, she waited until he finished in the kitchen to fix her meals and avoided crossing his path, even though their rooms were across the hall from each other.

School forced them to be together; they rode the bus to and from Loreauville each weekday morning, interacting with a bus driver and teachers, who never guessed the teenagers lived alone at Merilee Plantation. They forged signatures on report cards, sent regrets they couldn't attend PTA meetings and teacher conferences, and did well, given the circumstances.

While maintaining a façade of normalcy, Charlotte struggled with the enormity of the secret she kept. Through no fault of hers, those terrible things had happened, her father had left them, and she was alone in the house with…the words to describe him wouldn't come. In time, she labeled her brother as what he was—a twisted, warped child who played mind games with others. And worse. He scared her, and she wondered if he would kill her if she defied him.

When Wick was in the house, she stayed in her bedroom. Often she wondered about the cellar. Stu Pinelli hauled the something downstairs—she'd never forget those sounds— and before he left, he had spent hours down there in the place of her darkest fears. Just to exist at Merilee, Charlotte had to force such thoughts from her mind.

There were times she considered going down those rickety wooden stairs to confront her fears. She'd been maybe six years old when Wick had pulled her down into the dark cellar and told her about the creature, and in all the years since, she'd never mustered sufficient courage to go there.

At last, back in the Lafayette clinic, where she gazed out the window, her mind allowed her to relax. Her thoughts drifted away from the cellar to other things. Simple things that made her smile, but ones she wouldn't remember.

CHAPTER SEVENTEEN

Funerals in New Orleans are spectacles unlike anywhere else in America. The more well-known the deceased, the bigger the production. Wick Ambrose was famous in the Big Easy, an entrepreneur whose friends and restaurant patrons were as diverse as major sports and political figures, mobsters, the archbishop, celebrities, and Grammy-winning country singers.

Wick's sister and only living relative, Charlotte, was in no shape to plan a funeral or attend one, so the preparation fell upon three men, each a trusted business partner who managed one of his popular restaurants. With a little help from friends at city hall, the funeral came off like a Mardi Gras parade.

At one p.m., an NOPD police cruiser with siren wailing blocked the intersection of St. Charles and Julia. Two cops got out and stopped traffic as the streetcar came rumbling along the track toward downtown, draped in purple, green and gold banners and with its bell clang-clanging all the way. Wick's casket stood on a tall bier inside the streetcar so people lining the sidewalk could view it through the open windows. At Julia Street, the car stopped in front of Fantôme, Wick's upscale steakhouse. As several hundred spectators watched, the restaurant's staff filed out onto the sidewalk to bid their owner farewell.

Then the car clanged away down the broad avenue, rounded Lee Circle, and headed down Carondelet Street. The police car again stopped traffic when the streetcar turned onto Canal, and crowds of well-wishers and gawkers cheered as six men dressed in Mardi Gras costumes and masks carried Wick's casket to the street, set it back on the bier, and rolled it across Canal, entering the French Quarter on Bourbon Street. In the Quarter, six tuxedo-clad elderly Black men who performed at the famous Preservation Hall lined up in front of the bier. These fellows knew how to make a funeral rock, and the police car's siren wailed as the procession moved along Bourbon Street while the marching band played "When the Saints Go Marching In" and Wick's casket draped in purple, green and gold rolled through the area of New Orleans he loved best.

At St. Ann Street the parade turned left, stopping at the corner of Dauphine in front of Wick's Hideaway, one of the Quarter's most popular seafood restaurants. The band played "Just A Closer Walk with Thee," a throng of onlookers cheered, and the staff emerged to pay respects to their beloved boss just as the ones on St. Charles had done.

The revelers marched along Dauphine to St. Peter, turned toward the river, and continued five blocks toward their last stop. When the procession passed the famous Pat O'Brien's Bar, more well-wishers poured out onto the crowded sidewalk and joined the throng heading toward the Jax Brewery building.

Wick Ambrose's final stop on his French Quarter tour was at his hottest new venue, Atomic Roadhouse. Expecting a crowd, New Orleans cops barricaded two blocks of Decatur Street, and by the time the marching band and Wick Ambrose's casket arrived, there were over two thousand people shouting, cheering, and singing along to the band's lively rendition of "Do You Know What it Means to Miss New Orleans?"

The bar's staff encircled his casket, holding hands as they hailed their chief. The crowd quietened as the manager held up a bullhorn. "Nobody loved a party as much as Wick

Ambrose," he said, which set off the cheers again. "He loved you all, and he loved this great city. He'd want to buy you a drink on his special day. The fire marshal says you can't all come inside, but my staff has wristbands for the first two hundred. We'll serve everyone else out here in front. There are Abita beer stations set up on both sides of the street, and for the next sixty minutes, the drinks are on the boss's tab. Thank you all for loving Wick. He had one hell of a ride, way too short, but his legacy lives on. We're here to stay, so let's have some fun!"

Wick Ambrose's funeral was the lead story on the six o'clock news. A reporter standing in the hectic confusion outside Atomic Roadhouse compared the shouts and cheers to the mayhem of Mardi Gras revelers on Fat Tuesday. It was a fitting send-off for a well-known and respected New Orleans restaurateur whose life had ended after only thirty-nine years.

CHAPTER EIGHTEEN

The director held his hand in the air, counting on his fingers from five to one. At the end of the count, he pointed to a person sitting on a couch in what would appear to viewers as a cozy den. Above its false walls were scaffolds and stage lights, and a boom microphone hovered just above the man's head. Phil Vandegriff zoomed in the pedestal-mounted camera as eerie music filled the room. Monitors flashed the logo and name of the Paranormal Network, and the host of its premiere episode looked at the teleprompter.

"Good evening, and welcome to the Paranormal Network. This is your host, Landry Drake, and tonight we have a special treat for you. The past few years, I've investigated things that defy explanation. I've spent the night in haunted houses, seen things that scared the daylights out of me, and unraveled secrets whose answers were stranger than fiction. Tonight we're airing the first episode of a new series entitled *Mysterious America*. Over the next few months, I'll take you to some of the strangest and spookiest places in our great country. Every state has unexplained mysteries, and we'll visit familiar ones and others that may be new to you. Together we'll encounter unexplainable phenomena, explore centuries-old legends, and maybe uncover a ghost or two along the way. Get ready, because here we go!"

The director yelled, "Cut!" and Landry stood and walked off the set.

"What do you think?" he asked.

"Not bad for the first take. Forty-three seconds too long. Let's shoot it again. This time do it a little faster but watch your diction and enunciate."

"Yes, mother."

After three more tries, the director called it a wrap, and Landry gave him a high five. It was an exhilarating feeling taping the first intro to the first series that would air on the Paranormal Network. Less than six weeks from now, over two million viewers in eleven countries would see that introduction.

Cate congratulated him, and as they walked downstairs to the office, she said, "Jack asked that you call him back. He spoke with Stuart Pinelli, and he turned up something in his research."

When Landry called, Jack explained that he'd located the right Stuart Pinelli and how agitated he became when Jack brought up James Ambrose. He added, "Don't lecture me about why I should drop this story. Something doesn't make sense, and you know it as well as I do. When Pinelli hung up on me, I vowed to find out more, and I wondered where to start. James Ambrose? Stuart Pinelli? Wick? Charlotte? Merilee Plantation? I spent half an hour jumping around from place to place, and at last I landed on something interesting."

He explained that Pinelli worked for Senator Fortier. "I spoke with an aide who told me Pinelli lived in Baton Rouge before he came to DC. I did another search and found something interesting. Stuart A. Pinelli of Baton Rouge is on the board of directors of a New Orleans company."

Landry controlled the urge to snap at Jack. When Jack became enthused about his research, he had an annoying habit of stretching out a revelation for its theatrical effect that could be tiresome. Landry always let it go, giving the man credit for enjoying his work.

"I suppose that fact bears some relevance to something,"

he said. "At some point, can you tell me what it is?"

"Pinelli is a director of Atomic Restaurant Group."

Landry's heart jumped. "Wick Ambrose's company? Now that *is* interesting. What do you make of it?"

"I'm not sure. I called you the minute I found it. Are you intrigued enough to get back into the investigation?"

"The stuff you found intrigues me, but I'm a paranormal investigator. There's nothing there for me. You either, if you ask me, but I'll bet you won't let it go."

"Not just yet. The man's hiding something, and I'm determined to find out what. I'll dig deeper and then hand it off to someone else here. I'll keep you informed."

Jack left a voicemail on Stuart Pinelli's phone, saying, "I discovered something after we talked earlier today. You serve on the board of directors of Atomic Restaurant Group, the company owned by the recently deceased son of your old friend at Slage Engineering. James Ambrose never came back to work after his vacation. I asked you about him this morning, but you didn't seem interested in answering my questions. In the interest of fairness, I'd like to talk to you before we air the story. I'm on a tight deadline, so please call me by five p.m. tomorrow, or it will run without your comments."

Jack had stretched the truth hoping to get Pinelli's attention. And it worked.

In his first-class seat on an American Airlines flight to Washington, Stu saw the email as he sipped his Scotch. He glanced over and saw the boss snoring in the window seat beside him. That was good, because the email worried him.

Damn that reporter! Why's he nosing around in somebody's private life? I have to call him—it would be insane to let him air a story based on what little he knows. He has a few facts, that's all. Nothing to be concerned about.

He settled back and considered what he'd say to Jack Blair tomorrow.

CHAPTER NINETEEN

When he called Jack the next morning, Pinelli went on offense. "Listen here, Mr. Blair. I'm a busy man. I work for a United States senator, and I resent being given an ultimatum about calling you back."

Yet you did. Jack smiled. "I apologize, sir. My director's a pain in the ass when he's on a deadline. Thanks for calling back. It won't take long to straighten this out…"

"There's nothing to straighten out. I sit on the board of Atomic Roadhouse. So what? Did you notice there are six other members besides me?"

"Yes, sir, I sure did. The others make sense. Wick's attorney and his CFO, a prominent local doctor, a lawyer, and two venture capital guys from New York who I figure invested in his company—like I say, those all make sense. Then there's you. You were a friend of Wick's father, James, back in the day. Wick was just a kid, but once he grew up and started a company, he reached out to you to join his board. No offense, Mr. Pinelli, but even though you work for a powerful politician, you're not one yourself. So tell me what expertise you brought to the board that Wick needed? And how did he contact you? Had you all kept in touch through all these years after his father disappeared?"

Stu waited a moment. "Are you finished? Let's cut

through the bullshit, shall we? What do you want from me? It's not the answer to how I got on the board of directors. So what is it?"

"It's just a hunch, I guess. Something I can't quite put my finger on. I think your involvement with the Ambrose family goes way, way back, and I have questions I'll bet you can answer. Here's one—where you were on the night Wick died?"

Jack struck a nerve, and the man's voice shook with anger. "I don't have to answer your questions, you impertinent bastard. For your information, I was in Washington. I attended a congressional dinner the evening before, and I joined the senator for a breakfast at seven the next morning. Check it out if you wish. I have nothing to hide, Mr. Blair. Wick reached out to me because he wanted someone he trusted. His dad trusted me long ago, and I guess he felt he could do the same. I'm an engineer by background. I can interpret blueprints and specs, and that's knowledge that would be helpful when Wick built future restaurants. You're making something out of nothing, and I'm tired of your insinuations. Now leave me alone."

Jack waited for the click, but the man didn't hang up. So he said, "My apologies. You've been very helpful. On another subject, can you tell me what happened to James Ambrose after he took that family vacation? He never came back to work."

"No, I can't. It's water under the bridge, for God's sake. It happened years ago. As far as Wick's suicide, he had personal issues, I figure. He couldn't take it anymore, and he did what some people do."

"What personal issues did he have? You were a director of his company…"

"I was a business friend, not someone in whom he confided. I'm busy, Mr. Blair. Don't call me again."

CHAPTER TWENTY

Rick Angelli joined the St. Martin Parish sheriff's department in 2001. A gregarious, outgoing man, the new deputy listened to people's concerns and helped solve their problems. When the sheriff retired in 2018, Rick filed for the job, campaigned door-to-door, and won the hearts and votes of his neighbors.

A quiet, rural parish with just fifty thousand residents, St. Martin Parish had the usual issues such as drugs and nonviolent crimes, but few serious incidents. The department quickly solved the few murders that happened, since they usually erupted from a dispute or a botched robbery. It was a nice place—a family-oriented parish where few problems occurred.

Wick Ambrose's death was the biggest thing Sheriff Angelli had ever faced. This wasn't just a local issue; a prominent New Orleans citizen in the prime of life had ended up hanged in an abandoned mansion where he spent his childhood. No one knew who called 911. The deputies who arrived found Wick's sister unconscious on the floor below his swinging body. Over the past week Charlotte awoke only once, and she seemed to recall nothing of the event. Was she lying? What brought the two of them to Merilee Plantation?

Rick liked to solve his cases without interference, but

this time he called in the state police and their access to resources his department didn't have. The crime lab in Baton Rouge ranked among the best in the South, employing hundreds of experts in every field of criminal investigation. The sheriff couldn't have asked for a better cop on his case than Lieutenant Harry Kanter. He had great respect for the veteran detective, and he would take every iota of help the man could provide. Still, he hoped his people ended up solving the mystery, not for the glory, but because as sheriff it fell on him to solve this parish's crimes.

Calling in the state cops would help, but Sheriff Angelli had the advantage of a much smaller caseload. They dealt with major crimes all over Louisiana, while Wick Ambrose's hanging was the only big case on Rick Angelli's plate.

When Rick got his first update report from Barrington Clinic, the doctor explained Charlotte's sudden awakening and their brief conversation. She was lucid until he revealed Wick was dead, reverted to her somnambulistic state, and something unusual happened. Yesterday the staff rushed to her room after hearing her bloodcurdling screams. They arrived within seconds, but by that time she was uncommunicative. A nurse searched her room, finding nothing out of place and no one there. No one knew why she cried out.

Angelli studied the notes he'd taken. Had Charlotte been playing games, pretending to be in a trance to avoid dealing with reality? The doctor didn't think so, but Rick wondered. She emerged from the trance just long enough to learn how Wick died, and the news sent her right back. Why? He enumerated a few ideas.

She went into a trance because:

1. She killed Wick, and the enormity of her misdeed sent her into a trance. She awoke, learned it was true, and that stark reality sent her back into her catatonia.

2. She met her brother at the house and saw someone kill him. Perhaps she was an accomplice.

3. When the doctor told her what happened, it triggered a repressed memory about something else.

4. Wick committed suicide, either in front of her or at an earlier time, after which she found him.

She claimed not to have seen her brother in the twenty years since they left the house in 2001. Why did they return after all that time? *NOTE: any recent developments at Merilee?*

If she killed him, what motive did she have? *NOTE: check to see who owns the house—was money the motive?*

If he hanged himself, why did he go back to the house to do it? And why with his sister present? *NOTE: there's more to learn about the hanging. Check relationship with parents, sister, any past issues, history of violence, sexual abuse, etc.*

The questions plagued him the rest of that day and into the night. He didn't see a good ending to this. Charlotte appeared to be the only other person there. Even if she woke and cooperated, could she explain how Wick died? *Would she?*

CHAPTER TWENTY-ONE

The next morning, Charlotte emerged from her trance again. Per the judge's commitment order, Dr. Freland notified Sheriff Angelli to come interrogate her. The last time she awoke, the sheriff didn't make it soon enough to observe her brief period of lucidity. This time he did.

Landry learned all this from Harry Kanter, who offered to send Landry the video of her interrogation.

Although he appreciated the thought, Landry turned him down. "I just don't see a paranormal angle. I've got so much going on that I don't have the time. Maybe you should talk to Jack. Last time we talked, he was still interested in the case."

Kanter snorted. "Are you accusing me of wasting your time? I've only been a cop for thirty-something years, so I wouldn't recognize a paranormal angle if it smacked me in the face. Sorry I called."

There was dead silence for a long moment before Landry said, "I presume you're joking. I've never heard you joke, so I wouldn't recognize it if you were."

"Point taken, but you need to watch Charlotte's video. Then decide if there's something about this case worth your time. I'm sending it to your Dropbox account now. Call me after you look at it. Still off the record on everything, with your usual caveats. Agreed?"

Landry said yes.

Landry started the video and saw three people—a man in a lab coat who identified himself as Dr. Freland, Sheriff Angelli, and an attractive dark-haired woman wearing sweats. Seemingly relaxed, she sat on a couch, and the men sat in armchairs nearby. The doctor told Charlotte she had been in the dining room for lunch. When her food arrived, she'd said, "It must be Monday."

She hadn't spoken since her last brief episode of consciousness, and her words had startled the nurse, who asked if she had said something.

The doctor continued, "Charlotte, you told her it must be Monday, because we're having red beans and rice. You pointed to your bowl and smiled. Can you tell me why you said it must be Monday?"

She nodded. "It's a Cajun tradition. We eat red beans and rice on Monday—wash day—because the pot can simmer on the stove all day long while the chores get done."

Her doctor told Charlotte that her lucidity had startled the nurse and led to their meeting here with Sheriff Angelli before a video camera.

Freland mentioned facts from their last discussion to see if she remembered. She did—she was in Lafayette at a clinic, she did not recall coming to Louisiana or meeting up with her brother, and officers had found Wick hanging from a second-floor chandelier. Earlier talk of his death had traumatized her, while today she spoke of it without emotion.

"Who called the police?" she asked, and Sheriff Angelli said someone made a 911 call from her phone, but no one spoke. He and his deputies came to Merilee after GPS pinpointed the location.

His answer seemed to confuse her. "Was I there? In the house, I mean?"

Freland held up his hand to stop the sheriff and said, "You were there, Charlotte. The deputies found you lying on the floor at the top of the stairs."

"Just below where my brother hanged himself," she

whispered. Then she looked up. "I remember you saying earlier that I didn't kill him. Who did?"

"This is where we need your help," the sheriff replied. "We're hoping you can remember more about that night and help us find the perpetrator."

She frowned and shook her head. "It's not as simple as that."

Dr. Freland looked up from his notepad. As Landry watched, he sensed what the doctor must be thinking. This was an important development. She had knowledge about the hanging, and they must be careful with their words and actions to avoid sending her back into a trance. He held up his hand to stop the sheriff's questioning.

"Charlotte, help us understand why it's not that simple."

"Wick's not the first to hang from that chandelier."

The doctor looked up in surprise as Angelli cried, "Stop right there!"

"What do you think you're doing?" Freland snapped. "Let me handle this."

"I have to inform her of her rights."

"Not now," the doctor protested. "In her condition, I doubt she could understand her rights. And we may lose her again."

Angelli pulled the Miranda card from his billfold. "Hang on a minute, Doctor. We don't know how she's involved in all this. I have to do everything by the book, regardless." He read the rights, and Charlotte said she understood them. "Do you want to continue talking to us?" he asked.

She nodded. "I didn't kill my brother. I could never have done that."

The sheriff said, "Can you tell us who else hanged from the chandelier?"

She nodded, looked away, and mumbled words under her breath.

"Charlotte, I'm sorry. We didn't hear what you said."

"I said my mother."

Dr. Freland touched the sheriff's arm to stop him. *Let me take it from here.* "Oh my, I'm so sorry. That must have been traumatic for you. Can you tell us more about what happened and where you were?"

"She learned something so horrific she couldn't live with it."

"Are you saying she…" He paused. "Your mother took her own life?"

Charlotte nodded. "She got the rope, she pulled the ladder over to the chandelier, and she did it."

"How old were you?"

"Fourteen. We were fourteen."

Landry paused the video to retrieve his notes. Wick and Charlotte were born in 1982, so the year she was describing—the year they were fourteen—was 1996, the year of the fateful vacation. The year Charlotte and Wick's father disappeared.

Landry pressed start and heard Freland say, "Do you feel up to talking about it, Charlotte? I know it must have been terrible for you." To Landry, the doctor appeared concerned about the effect recalling those traumatic events might have on her.

She nodded. "It was the worst thing I could imagine. Horrible. But it was worse for Wick."

"In what way?"

"Because it was his fault."

The sheriff interrupted. "Did Wick kill your mother?"

Charlotte's eyes flashed with anger, and she said to Dr. Freland, "I don't want to talk to him anymore."

"That's fine. We can stop any time you say. You don't have to talk any longer."

"Yes she does," Angelli snapped through gritted teeth. "She can't stop now."

The doctor turned away from her and whispered, "We stop when *I* say so, Sheriff. This woman is my patient. I know you want answers, but her mind is in a fragile state. I'm in charge here, and I'll decide how this plays out."

Landry watched the sheriff cross his arms while Dr. Freland patted her arm gently. "Go on."

"Wick didn't exactly kill our mother. Not like you think."

Sheriff Angelli leaned forward and opened his mouth to

speak, but he backed off when Dr. Freland shot him a stern look.

"Can you tell us more about that?"

"There's nothing more to say. If he hadn't done that awful thing, she wouldn't have died. Wick knew that. So did my father. When we found out what Wick had done, things went crazy really fast, and my mother hanged herself before anyone saw it coming."

"What did Wick do?"

"I can't remember." The words came quickly, and Landry wondered if she was lying.

Dr. Freland said, "Don't worry. It's all right if you can't remember…"

Shaking his head, the sheriff interrupted. "Charlotte, what did Wick do that caused your mother to kill herself?"

Seemingly furious at the sheriff, Freland remained silent as she furrowed her brow. "I remember now. Oh, God. Why did he…my own brother…why didn't he ask for help? Because of what he did, they both died. My mother and Wick. He should never have gone back to the house. He had to know what would happen…"

Tears rolled down her cheeks. Consoling her, the doctor said the session was over. Angelli protested, but it was useless to continue, because Charlotte's eyes went blank, and her lips curled into a half smile.

She was gone again.

CHAPTER TWENTY-TWO

Landry played the video for Cate and Henri. When it finished, he said, "This case intrigues me. I still doubt there's a paranormal aspect, but I also can't stop wondering what happened at Merilee. Did Wick come back to hang himself? I showed you Charlotte's interview to get your opinions. We're all busy as hell with TPN, but should I spend more time on Merilee or let it go?"

Henri said, "How many cases have you and I worked where our gut instinct proved accurate? You're an excellent paranormal investigator, and this story has all the ingredients to whet your appetite. Antebellum mansion abandoned long ago. Father disappears. Famous restaurateur found hanged. His sister claims her mother was hanged too, and both deaths happened because of something Wick did. I think that sums it up. Cate, what do you think?"

"I agree. Let's say you check things out at Merilee Plantation and it turns out to be suicide or murder, but nothing supernatural? All you've lost is a little time, which is precious right now, but it would be exciting to launch the Paranormal Network by announcing that another *Bayou Hauntings* episode is in the works."

He threw up his arms in mock exasperation. "Okay, okay, I get it! You're ordering me to keep working on this story. My God, you two are demanding bosses!"

Landry uploaded the video to a flash drive and dropped it off at Channel Nine. Half an hour later, Jack called.

"The good fairy left me a flash drive. I know it wasn't you, since you're no longer interested in the case. Or have you changed your mind yet again?"

"Henri and Cate changed it for me after they saw the video. I've been out of the loop on all this. Can you bring me up to speed?"

"Sure, when you buy me lunch tomorrow. That's your punishment for doubting this case had merit. We'll plan our strategy then. Meet me at Acme at 11:30."

That evening at their apartment, he asked Cate to come to lunch too, and said he'd ask Henri as well. They could swap ideas like in the old days when Landry was at Channel Nine.

Cate laughed out loud. "Are you crazy? Henri wouldn't set foot in Acme Oyster House if you held a gun to his head. Could you see him sucking oysters off a half shell and chugging a beer? I can hear him now. '*Garçon*, a wine list, please. You have no wine list? Bring me a glass of Châteauneuf-du-Pape. It's a wine. What do you mean all you have is red or white? What kind of barbaric hovel is this place?'"

They both laughed at their vain, borderline-snooty friend who savored fine dining in a city full of five-star restaurants. But then Landry bet her ten dollars he could get Henri to join them for lunch. Calling it foolish, she took his bet and said she was already deciding where to spend the money.

Henri was out when Landry and Cate left and walked over to Iberville Street. By noon, folks would be lined up on the sidewalk, waiting for a table, so they beat the crowd by arriving early. Jack waved from a table near the back.

"Landry bet me ten bucks he could get Henri to join us," she told Jack as they ordered Abitas, and he got a Dr Pepper. "I knew he'd never stoop this low on the culinary scale." With a laugh, Jack said he agreed with Cate and wondered how Landry could have imagined their friend would show up at Acme.

Landry wagged a finger. "Henri's never on time, don't forget. The bet's still on, and I'm going to win."

"He can't just show up," Cate said. "He has to eat a meal too."

"Are you changing the rules on me?" Landry said with a smile. "Okay, I accept. Henri has to come here, order a meal, and eat lunch with us. Satisfied?"

She gave a smug nod and winked at Jack as if to say, "I've got this one in the bag."

Five minutes later Landry stood and waved to Henri, who stood at the front of the busy restaurant. "I'll be damned," Cate said. "He's not only here, he's the only customer in this place wearing a three-piece suit!"

He made his way to the table, greeted everyone, sat, and ordered a glass of water. Once the server left, Henri dumped the water into a nearby planter. Landry pulled a flask from his jacket pocket and covertly poured Henri a glass of red wine.

"Châteauneuf-du-Pape, my good man," he said with a flourish. Henri made a production of swirling the wine, sniffing it, and taking a taste.

"A 2006, if my taste buds don't fail me. An excellent year. My compliments to the sommelier."

"This isn't fair!" Cate cried as everyone laughed. "I can't wait to see what's next. Do you have a filet of Dover sole in your other pocket?"

"Now, now, give me some credit," Henri declared. "I'm not as picky about cuisine as all that. I'll pass on raw oysters and fried food, but I hear the seafood gumbo here is excellent. Now that you've had a laugh at my expense, may we talk about Merilee Plantation?"

Jack led things off. After watching the video yesterday, he'd spent this morning searching the internet. "Charlotte left us some tantalizing clues to consider and one fact that I could check out. In 1996, on the day that James Ambrose carted his family off to Florida, Wick did something terrible. Charlotte says when her mother found out about it, she hanged herself. To compound the mystery, Wick's own death twenty-five years later was a direct result of that awful thing he did. Charlotte said he should have known something would happen if he returned to Merilee. That's not a lot to work with, but I did learn the exact date they went on the trip."

"From Daisy Poe."

Jack laughed. "Right, Landry. You're still on top of your game. She gave me the exact date. She said she'll never forget it…"

"…because that's the most money she ever saw at one time." Landry finished the sentence.

"Right. It was June the twenty-eighth, 1996. A Friday. They got the bonus money at three o'clock, and Mr. Slage sent everyone home for the weekend. James requested ten days off, and they never saw him again."

The food arrived, and everyone dug in. Between spoonfuls of gumbo, Henri asked what else Jack had discovered.

"Nothing so far. Once I finished with Daisy, it was time to meet you all for lunch."

Landry said when he got back to the studio, he'd call Sheriff Angelli in St. Martinville and see if anything significant had happened in the parish on that day.

"I suggest you let Jack make that call," Henri said. "He's a reporter for a TV station. You, on the other hand, are a well-known celebrity whose forte is the supernatural. Let's keep you out of it for the moment. If Jack turns up something interesting, then we consider our next move."

"Good idea," Landry said. He turned to Jack. "Please call Sheriff Angelli. Don't tell him the famous paranormal investigator Landry Drake asked you to call. It's our little secret. Oh, and be glad you're the master of your own destiny. You don't know what it's like to work under the yoke of these two dictators. What I'd give to have freedom again!"

"Knock it off, you poor thing," Cate smirked. "Your life isn't so bad. Just don't go getting cocky on Henri and me, and everything will be fine."

"Yes, ma'am. I'll do whatever you say, ma'am. As soon as you pay me that ten bucks you owe me."

"Trust me, this attitude won't last long," she said to the others with a smile.

———

Eighty miles away at state police headquarters in Baton Rouge, Colonel Talbot listened to a recording. He rewound it and played it once more. About to make a consequential decision, he wanted to be sure he understood what the words meant.

"Find out where Harry Kanter is," he told his assistant. "Whatever he's doing, tell him to drop it. Get him up here now!"

Twenty minutes later Harry stood before his boss's desk for the second time in three days. Instead of instructing him to sit, Talbot switched on the recorder.

Harry heard his voice. "Hey, Landry. A few minutes ago Sheriff Angelli sent me the videotape they made, and I knew you'd want to see it too."

Talbot fast-forwarded the tape and again hit the play button.

"Just watch Charlotte's video. You can decide if there's something in this case worth checking out. I'm sending it to your Dropbox account now. Call me after you watch it. Still off the record on everything, with your usual caveats. Agreed?"

The boss stopped the tape and snapped, "That is your voice, correct? I don't want to make a mistake here. And the Landry you're speaking to—that's Landry Drake, correct?"

The son of a bitch recorded me. He bugged my office. That damned cocky bastard.

Watching Harry's face turn beet red, his boss leaned back in the chair and said, "Who are you so mad at—me or yourself? There's no privacy in this building, Lieutenant Kanter. You signed away those rights and a lot more when you put on that badge and came to work here. You and I had a talk a few days ago about Landry Drake, but here you are on tape, violating a direct order.

"I'm going to give you a break only because you have thirty-five years of service. I don't want you hanging around here three more days, much less three months, but here's the deal. You are on probation from this moment forward. You will retire in six weeks, and I'll give you the usual commendation and shake your damned hand. But if I catch you helping Landry Drake, you're fired."

He glared at Harry. "I don't like you, Kanter. This is your last shot. Blow it and your career is down the tubes. Now get the hell out of my office."

CHAPTER TWENTY-THREE

Over in Lafayette, the nurse took Charlotte's vital signs, looked at a clipboard on the wall, and said, "Honey, it's time to use the restroom. You can do that without my help, right?" With a blank look, Charlotte rose from her chair and walked to the bathroom. When she finished, she returned and sat. The nurse noted the time on her chart and said, "It's a beautiful morning outside. How about walking with me to the veranda and enjoying the warm weather?"

Charlotte stood, her lips parted in the same half smile as always, and they walked arm in arm to the porch. The nurse settled her into a comfortable chair and left. No one worried about her wandering away. A tracking band on her wrist would alert staff if she approached the perimeter fence, although with this patient, that precaution was unnecessary. The only time Charlotte Ambrose acted was at someone's direction.

The warm breeze caressed her skin. Honeysuckle vines around the column beside her chair filled the air with a wonderful scent, and she saw people sitting near a small man-made lake at the far end of the yard.

The beautiful sunshine. A breeze filled with delicious smells. Blue water lapping against the shore.

Memories.

She was in Florida, on the beach in Pensacola with her family—but Wick wasn't with them. On this special time—their first real vacation—Wick refused to take part. She felt sorry for her father, who had used his three-thousand-dollar bonus to bring them here. He and Mother tried to include Wick, but he wouldn't even take meals or go to the beach with them. At last they quit trying and let him sit in the hotel room.

What's wrong, Wick? We never hide things from one another. You know I'd never tell them. Is it something I did?

Although they shared every secret—or so she thought—Wick refused to answer her. He appeared lost in his own mind, deep in thought over something that had him more troubled than she had ever seen.

Can I help you, Wick? I will if you'll just let me.

At that remark, he spoke the only words he would say to her on the entire six-day trip.

No one can help me this time.

When they left Pensacola, her father drove straight home. In the back seat, she spent six hours watching Wick fidget, pick nervously at his skin, and stare morosely at the floorboard. When she tried to touch his hand, he jerked it away.

What did I do to make him act this way? Although she wondered, in her heart she knew this wasn't about her. She felt the vibes from her twin brother. Something really, really bad had happened, and when they got home, he would have to face the consequences for it.

Home at last, her father turned off Highway 31 and drove down the narrow lane to Merilee. Before he could even shut down the engine, Wick threw open the car door, jumped out, and ran to the porch. He pulled a key from his pocket—he and Charlotte both had keys—and bounded up the stairs to his bedroom, leaving the front door standing wide open.

Wick slammed his bedroom door. That was the end of everything. And the beginning of everything.

Billowy clouds hung in the sky above the porch as Charlotte's mind stopped replaying the memories. It was a bright, sunny day—one too beautiful for the horror to come out. And that suited her. She had relived the hours after they returned home more times than she could count. She'd had nothing to do with what had happened, but it had changed all their lives forever.

A nurse checked on her, saying words that Charlotte didn't comprehend. She looked out at the lake, her memories of that Florida trip forgotten.

CHAPTER TWENTY-FOUR

The deck of the shrimper *Jerry Boy* teemed with thousands upon thousands of shrimps the men had netted. It was a good night's catch, and now they were making for the Port of West St. Mary's Louisa dock near Cypremort. The light from a three-quarter moon on this cloudless, calm night caused the waters of the intracoastal canal to shimmer with an iridescent glow. As a faint pink glow in the eastern sky foretold the coming of dawn, the grizzled captain thought to himself nights like this made it all worthwhile.

Captain Ahern shouted to a man helping others shovel shrimp into the brine tanks. "Hey, Cliff! Check out the winch. Looked like she was slipping a little when we brought in that last net. I don't want any problems when we head out Sunday night."

Clifford Latour waved and walked to the huge winch in the center of the boat. He made an adjustment, then another, gave the captain a thumbs-up, and returned to his work.

When the boat docked a couple of hours later, the crew dumped the night's catch into freezers. The sun was well up by the time the exhausted deckhands drove away, heading home for showers and a day of sleep. As usual, Cliff waited until the others left before approaching the captain, who pulled out his wallet and handed over a wad of notes.

"You ever gonna get a bank account?" he growled, but he knew this wouldn't change. In the decades he'd been a shrimp boat captain, there had been others like Cliff—drifters who wanted to stay off the radar. He didn't care as long as the work got done, and Cliff Latour—if that was his actual name—was a good hand. Paying him in cash also made it easier for the captain—no taxes or forms to fill out. The boss didn't pry, and the man volunteered nothing about himself, which was fine by both.

Cliff walked past other shrimp boats tied along the concrete pier and up to the gravel parking lot. There wasn't much in this area; a few boats lay on their sides near the parking lot, detritus from hurricanes in the past, and oilfield trucks sat next to a block building that never seemed to have any activity. He climbed in the old Chevy van and maneuvered the dirt roads—Sunshine to Goldcoast to Intracoastal—and turned down a rutted lane that dead-ended at the water's edge among a maze of canals. There stood the decrepit fishing shack Cliff rented for a hundred and twenty a month. It stood on stilts in a marshy bayou filled with cattails.

A few people lived within a mile or so of Cliff's house—workers on the oil rigs, shrimpers like him, and a few retired guys who minded their own business and accepted people at face value. That worked fine for Cliff. He parked the van, stripped to the buff outside his house, and tossed the smelly clothes into a pile for later. Nobody noticed his nakedness because the few shacks within sight were long since abandoned.

He turned the TV on the local news, took a long, hot shower, and fixed some eggs and toast. At nine a.m. he crawled into bed and set his alarm for four. If it had been a weekday, Cliff would eat dinner and report back to the *Jerry Boy* by seven p.m. But this was Saturday morning, and he was off until Sunday night.

On Saturdays he did chores, went to the market in Baldwin, and occasionally he visited a bar on Highway 83 frequented by the Texaco guys off the rigs. He stayed to himself, but he enjoyed their noise and banter. Friends were a luxury he couldn't afford, but being around these men gave Cliff a sense of normalcy, allowing him to feel better about the life he'd chosen.

When he awoke at four this Saturday afternoon, Cliff had something different in mind. There would be no chores today. He'd heard a news story this morning on TV that set him on a mission. He picked out the clothes he'd wear, gassed up the truck, and headed north.

CHAPTER TWENTY-FIVE

The nights at Barrington Clinic were quiet and uneventful. After dinner at six, patients played cards and watched television in the recreation room until bedtime at eight, when they retired to their rooms. After a bed check, the night shift—an LPN, a security guard, and three nursing assistants—watched television. During commercial breaks, the guard walked to the front desk in the rotunda and checked the cameras. There was no reason for him to sit at the desk every minute—if an issue arose, an alarm would sound. But nothing ever happened at Barrington. Every night the place was as quiet as a tomb.

With the staff engrossed in an episode of *Chicago P.D.*, a man crept through the bald cypress trees that ran along a six-foot chain-link fence surrounding Barrington Clinic's property. He crossed the yard, slipped onto the porch, and held a plastic card to a reader by the door until he heard a click. He stepped inside, let it close behind him, and checked his watch. Nine minutes left. Plenty of time. He tiptoed down the hallway to Charlotte's room, went inside, and opened the bathroom door to allow in a little light.

"Charlotte, wake up."

She stirred, opened her eyes, and looked up at him.

A man is in my room. Not an orderly or a nurse or a

doctor. Do I know him?

As she stared, he pressed a cloth over her mouth and nose. She struggled to breathe, but in seconds her arms fell to her sides. The intruder pulled back the sheets, snipped off the tracking bracelet, and put it on the nightstand. He easily lifted her hundred-pound body in his arms and carried her down the hall to the back door. Once outside, he walked toward the trees and maneuvered her limp body through the hole he'd cut in the fence.

The man checked the time and smiled. Three minutes remained before the next television commercial. He'd be in the van and gone before the guard returned to his desk. The cameras would show nothing amiss now; only if the guard checked earlier footage would he discover an intruder. That was unlikely, but even if he did, he and Charlotte would be far away before the police arrived.

Landry was in the shower when Cate handed his phone through the curtain. He looked at the screen and said, "Harry, you're up early."

"Where are you? Sounds like you're in Niagara Falls."

"I'm in the shower. What's up?"

"Someone kidnapped Charlotte Ambrose."

"What? When did that happen?"

"Last night. The staff did a bed check at ten and found her missing. They got it all on camera. Some guy in sweats, a hoodie pulled over his face, and a mask used a stolen card to get in the building and carry her away. I learned about it when Sheriff Angelli asked me to come to the clinic."

Landry asked to drive up, but Harry refused, explaining, "My boss put me on probation for working on your cases. One more slipup and my pension and I are out the window. It would be bad enough if Talbot caught me at Merilee. If you show up too, it's curtains for old Harry."

Jack called a few minutes after eight with more news about Charlotte. "According to the Associated Press, the cops found tire tracks on a road next to Barrington Clinic's property and a hole in the fence that surrounds it. There's surveillance video of the building and the backyard, but they haven't released anything yet."

Half an hour later Harry called again to say it wasn't fair to keep Landry out of the loop. "Screw Talbot. I'm going to do this my way," he said, and told Landry everything he'd learned so far. Camera footage and an electronic entry log revealed that a person wearing a mask and hood used a stolen access badge to enter the building at 9:16 p.m. Moments after entering Charlotte's room, he carried her inert body in his arms to the door through which he entered, left the building, and crossed the yard into the trees. They found a slit cut in the fence and fresh tire tracks on a dirt road forty feet from the fence line.

"Where did he get the badge?"

"To put it bluntly, the security people there are idiots. Four days ago, Charlotte's nurse reported her access card missing at the end of her shift. We don't know how the perp got the card, but the security guard failed to disable it, so he gained access that way. The security guard is the same guy who was on duty last night and didn't see the perp come in. The guy watches TV with the staff every night after dinner. He only checks his cameras now and then, and it seems the kidnapper knew his routine. The guard station is easy to see. All you have to do is look in the front windows of the clinic and see if he's at his post or not."

"Was she alive when the perp took her away?"

"The footage shows him carrying her limp body, but we think she was alive. If his motive was to kill her, it would have been simpler to do it there and leave her in bed. Merilee is the sheriff's jurisdiction, but kidnapping is a state case. Until the boss says otherwise, I'm leading this one."

By the six o'clock news hour, the things Harry told Landry became the top story. The sheriffs of St. Martin and Lafayette parishes held a joint press conference. They outlined the facts and requested a call if anyone had observed a vehicle on the road beside Barrington Clinic last night around 9:15. Typically Harry would make a statement, but this time he declined.

CHAPTER TWENTY-SIX

Careful to obey the speed limit as he drove, Charlotte's kidnapper put his phone on speaker and hit the only number programmed into it. When the man answered, he said, "I've got her. She can't tell them anything now because I've got her."

There was a pause as he considered what the caller meant. "You've got her? I don't understand. What the hell have you done?"

"I walked into that place and took her. In and out in under ten minutes without a hitch. Nobody ever realized I was there. I'm taking her back to Merilee."

"Are you insane? This will be all over the news by morning. The FBI works kidnapping cases, and for you it means you're a dead man walking."

You unappreciative son of a bitch! "Thanks to me, she won't be spilling her guts to the cops. I called because I need your help."

"You *think*? I bailed you out once, but you're on your own now. You couldn't let well enough alone. They won't stop until they find you. You'd better sleep with one eye open from now on. Or take her back, but not even that will save you. You're dead meat when the feds find you, and they will. They always do."

"Not always. You know that as well as I do. We got away the last time…"

"*We?* Listen to me, you crazy bastard. This is all on you, and if you involve me, you'll regret it. Don't call me again."

How dare you hang up on me! Mi problema es su problema. He considered his options—something he should have done before taking her—and soon arrived at his destination. He carried her from the car to the house and upstairs.

"Charlotte, I brought you home. You're safe. Look around! Do you realize where you are?"

Although the raspy voice echoed in her mind, she didn't awaken.

He shook her hard. "Wake up. You played this game with your doctors, but you're not playing it with me. Wake up."

She took in her surroundings. Flickers of memory raced through her mind. *Home. My bedroom. I'm lying on a bed—my bed. This man—do I know him? Wick killed a boy, and then Mother left us. Daddy too. Daddy left and never came back.*

Charlotte cast a glance at her captor. *Who is he? I've seen him. Something's familiar…*

Might the grizzled, dirty creature whose eyes glistened with madness be her father? James Ambrose had been clean-shaven and neat, while this man had long, bushy hair, a mustache, and a full beard. He was older than her dad, but of course after twenty-five years, he would be.

After watching him for a moment, she decided it wasn't true. Her father had plodded through life in a dull haze of boring routine. Every step, every task seemed an effort. This crazy man moved about constantly, talked to himself, and looked as if he belonged in an asylum. If he was James Ambrose, he'd made a total transformation in a quarter century.

She turned away when he looked at her again. "Ah, you're awake. Good. We have a lot to talk about."

"Are you my father?"

"Why did you and Wick come back to Merilee,

Charlotte? You left in 2001; couldn't you just have stayed away for the rest of your lives? It would have been best. Wick's only dead because you came back. I'm sure you understand why."

"Wick said we had to come because…because *he* called. He's going to sell it. Wick was worried and said we had to come back. To be sure things were…were okay here. Wick said it would be a disaster if they found things…" Pausing, she closed her eyes as if the memories were too much to bear.

"What do you mean? Who's going to sell what?"

"Stuart Pinelli. He's going to sell Merilee, and Wick was afraid of…uh, things in the house someone might learn about."

"Stu Pinelli doesn't own Merilee. He deeded it to Wick and you when you turned twenty-one."

How does he know that? "No, he didn't. That was what you…my father arranged, but Stu didn't do it. He kicked us out one day. This isn't our house. It's his."

He muttered unintelligible words, shook his head, and wagged his finger as if having a heated conversation with himself. *This guy's a total psycho,* she thought, *and he's not my father.* So how did he know so much about this house and Stuart Pinelli?

"Who are you?"

"Name's Clifford. Cliff for short. Easy to remember, like falling off a cliff." He grinned, revealing a mouthful of stained teeth.

"Why did you bring me here?"

"I thought you'd be comfortable in your home. I have to keep you away from them so you won't tell the secrets."

"What secrets? What are you talking about? Who are you? How do you know me?"

He chuckled and muttered, "Who am I? Excellent question! How do I know you? Who really knows anybody these days?"

The man's one-sided conversation reminded her of the White Rabbit's constant reminders to himself that he was late. As he moved about, Charlotte took in her surroundings—this bedroom that had once been her own.

She cleared cobwebs from her memory and noticed the sad state of the place she once loved. *How long has it been?* She counted the years—she and Wick had left in 2001, twenty years ago. This room had sat in darkness for more years than it had been hers. The last time she had been here—the night Wick died—he had teased her about a doll named Henry.

It was hard to see the entire room because little sunlight made it through the dirty gauze curtains. She focused on a chair a few feet away and saw the doll leering at her. A crack that ran down one cheek turned the clown's porcelain grin into a twisted grimace. She covered her face with her hands, knowing Henry's eyes would follow her regardless of wherever she was in her bedroom.

"What's wrong?" the man asked, but she said nothing. Her feelings were her own, nothing to share with a stranger. Especially this one—her kidnapper. Somehow she didn't fear him; it seemed he wanted to keep her away from the doctors or the police. But why?

He watched as she got off the bed, walked to the chair, and turned Henry the clown around so he faced the cushion. At that moment there came a muffled noise—the sound of a door closing—somewhere in the house.

The man noticed it too. "Stay here," he said, walking into the hall and peering over the banister. Then she heard another voice. They argued—the words were too faint to understand, but the men were angry. In a moment Cliff Latour strode into her bedroom, followed by a man she knew from long ago. Older now, but wrinkles and gray hair couldn't hide the face she remembered so well.

"Hello, Charlotte. I came to see what Cliff has done. He made a huge mistake when he took you away from the facility, and once again it's up to me to make things right."

Once again it's up to me to make things right. She thought about what those words meant, and everything became clear. Now she understood who her kidnapper was, but what terrified her was the identity of the other man—a person who would stop at nothing to fix a problem.

Once again, awful memories flooded her mind.

Wick. That boy. This man standing before me, who came that night too, when my father asked him for help. The night when everything in my life changed forever. What this man did that night—the horrifying things he did to "make things right."

Stuart Pinelli. He's come back, and I'm going to die.

CHAPTER TWENTY-SEVEN

Landry, Cate, Henri, and Jack sat around Henri Duchamp's office conference table. Prior to the Civil War, in the days when Lucas and Prosperine LaPiere owned the Toulouse Street building, the ancient piece of furniture had been their dining table. In a *Bayou Hauntings* episode called *Die Again*, Landry had chronicled the bizarre story of the LaPiere family, the building where they now sat, and the people who died within its walls.

After their harrowing experiences there, Henri had bought the building and its antique furnishings to house his Louisiana Society for the Paranormal. When they'd created the Paranormal Network, they were fortunate to rent a vacant building next door that also once belonged to the LaPieres, and they'd uncovered long-forgotten passageways between the two structures.

This morning Landry announced he was going back to Merilee, and he was doing it alone. He wanted to experience the house—to get a feel for it and find out what it said to him. He added, "Over the past two decades, people have claimed it's haunted, but we all understand how that works. Teenagers get high, break into an abandoned mansion, have eerie sensations, and think they hear mysterious sounds. The story grows and grows until it takes on a life of its own. The atmosphere at Merilee is enough to give someone the creeps. One person died there—two, according to Charlotte—and I want to see what I can learn inside those walls."

Henri asked if Landry wanted to take the sensory equipment. In his years of paranormal investigating, Henri had amassed an array of specialized instruments, including full-spectrum low-light cameras, devices that captured sounds the human ear couldn't detect, and an array of meters to measure spikes in electromagnetic energy.

Landry passed, saying this time he'd rely on his senses. He could shoot video with his phone, but he doubted he'd need it. By now, he'd written off Merilee as just another ancient, abandoned mansion. Two members of a family had hanged themselves there, but deaths didn't make a house haunted. Far more gruesome tragedies had occurred in houses that weren't inhabited by spirits.

Cate found his skepticism odd. "You're always the one who goes in expecting the paranormal. From your description, it sounds like at the very least, Merilee's a spooky place. Harry Kanter said a child's voice echoed through the house. Sounds right up your alley."

Jack agreed and asked to come along, saying an extra set of eyes and ears might pick up even more.

Landry wouldn't have it. To Jack he said, "Believe it or not, there was a time before you, before Cate, and before Henri when I was a simple guy—an Iberia Parish sheriff's deputy—and I explored paranormal stuff on my own. Now I have more help than I can handle." He smiled. "Thanks for your offer, but I'm going alone."

"And of course you'll be going in the dead of night," Cate said, and he nodded.

"Tonight, as a matter of fact. In Paranormal 101, I learned spooks love the darkness!"

Landry arrived at Merilee a few minutes before eight that evening. This time he didn't call Sheriff Angelli for permission, because he doubted anyone would be around. And he was correct—the house sat silent against the deepening shadows of nightfall, its gables reaching toward the sky. Down on the bayou, frogs croaked as if speaking to each other, and a gator splashed around, nabbing its dinner. Off to his right, Landry caught sight of something that darted into the trees nearby. It startled him, and he stood for a moment, watching and waiting, but he saw nothing. It might have been a deer, or perhaps a fox, alarmed to see a human here at night.

The front door gave a mighty creak as he pushed it open, signaling anyone—or anything—that an intruder had entered. He dropped his backpack on a dusty chair in the entry hall, turned on his flashlight, and walked up the circular staircase. He was most interested in the second floor—where the hangings had occurred—and when he reached the top of the stairs, he looked over the banister to the foyer that extended to the ceiling above him. Moonbeams filtered through the oak trees outside and shone through the old mansion's grimy windows, creating moving, ghostly shapes on the walls and floor but providing little illumination to the dark hallways and rooms of Merilee Plantation.

As Landry played his flashlight around, something flew from the ceiling straight at him, and he almost lost his balance as he stepped backwards. Inches from his face, two bats whizzed by and disappeared into the darkness. He caught his breath and directed the light to the opposite end of the wide hall. On both sides, doors opened into the bedrooms he and Jack had seen earlier. He walked to the nearest one and listened closely.

Mommy. Daddy. Please, someone, please help me.

The plaintive whisper of a terrified child echoed through the house like a scent on the wind. Urgent, eerie…and lost. He realized it had been disastrously I to write off Merilee as just another old house.

I'm afraid. It's so dark in here. Please help me.

Landry's muscles froze. Without realizing it, he had taken a few steps, and now he was standing directly under the chandelier. A sense of dread came over him as something lightly brushed his neck.

Another bat? He thought, swiping his hand to drive it away, but it delicately swept past his ear. Sensing something above him, he wanted to turn, run down the stairs and out the door. He should leave this place now…before something happened. But his feet wouldn't move. He couldn't will himself to run. He shuddered, and his sweat-drenched hand dropped the flashlight. Knowing, sensing, steeling himself for what was coming, he lifted one arm and stretched out his fingers. Something was up there in the dark, swaying slowly. He couldn't see it, but his skin prickled with fear. There was something—he *sensed* it was there. He reached out and connected with something hard and rubbery, like the bottom of a shoe.

Dear God, another person is hanging up there.

There was movement behind him, and he felt something touch his face. Waves of nausea swept over him, and he collapsed in a heap onto the floor.

When he started this line of work, Landry and Cate had made a pact. If he was off on a case, he would check in every two hours unless they agreed otherwise. Depending on circumstances, it might be nothing but a thumbs-up emoji, but it would signal that things were fine.

He had left home before six p.m., and she got a two-word "I'm here" message at eight. When ten came and went, she lay in bed, staring at the ceiling and waiting. At some point she fell asleep, and at twenty minutes past one, she jerked awake and grabbed her phone.

Nothing.

Landry had missed two check-ins, and something was wrong. She called Jack, whose dull *hullo?* Showed he hadn't stayed up worrying. He was on full alert when she explained, because he understood how important the check-ins were to Landry and Cate.

"I'm going up there," he declared.

"Wait a minute. We need to call the sheriff first. He can get there a lot faster than we can."

"Call him! I'll be on the road in ten minutes. Do you want to come?"

She began crying. "No. I'm afraid, Jack. This time something's really wrong. It's just a feeling, but I don't want to find him." She paused. "Just call me as soon as you can. Don't leave me wondering."

She called the sheriff's dispatcher in St. Martinville and stared at the phone in her hand for thirty-four excruciating minutes. She refreshed it often to be sure it was turned on, unmuted, and she hadn't missed a text. At last it rang. Unknown number. She punched the button and answered.

"What have you found out?"

Sheriff Angelli's voice held a tenseness that scared her. "Landry's Jeep is here, Miss Adams, and his backpack was sitting in a chair in the entry hall. The deputies have made an initial search, and so far there's no sign of him. There are fingerprints everywhere. If they're his, we should know soon."

Sobbing and scared, she snapped, "An initial search? Why don't they tear the place apart? He's missing, Sheriff. Where is he?"

"Miss Adams, I understand your concern, believe me, but his disappearance isn't all we're dealing with here. FYI, I called Landry's friend Harry Kanter at the state police, and he's headed this way. We need all the help we can get."

"All the help you can get? What do you mean? What's going on up there?"

"Please be patient, ma'am. We…uh, there's more to this than you realize. We have a situation here."

"What situation?" she cried as she shook off a wave of nauseating fear.

Sheriff Angelli paused. He couldn't tell her everything. This was an active crime scene, and at the moment he wasn't sure himself what was going on. They didn't train officers at the police academy to deal with things like this, and this situation baffled him.

"When we arrived, we found another body hanging from the chandelier where Wick Ambrose died. It's not him. That's all I can tell you right now. Please be patient, and we'll do everything we can to find Mr. Drake." He disconnected the call.

CHAPTER TWENTY-EIGHT

Jack was halfway to St. Martinville when he got Cate's call. After hearing what the sheriff had told her, he knew he'd never get inside the house, but he wanted to be there if they found Landry. He also called the night desk at Channel Nine and asked for a cameraman. At some point this story would break, and Jack and WCCY-TV would scoop the competition on tomorrow's big news story.

Inside the mansion, the medical examiner worked under powerful lights run by generators in the yard. After he arrived, deputies removed the body of an adult female from the noose and put it in a sheet on the floor beneath the chandelier. Sheriff Angelli knew who she was because he'd seen her driver's license last time. He told the ME she was Charlotte Ambrose, Wick's sister.

Charlotte died just as her brother had done. The ladder and noose were different because Harry Kanter had taken the ones from Wick's death to Baton Rouge. But the method and the result were identical. Unlike Wick's, this death had a strange and enigmatic twist. The famous paranormal investigator Landry Drake was high on the suspect list. Right at the very top. This case had the potential to blow wide open and expose this quiet parish and its sheriff to enormous publicity, and that was why Angelli breathed easier when

Lieutenant Kanter and another state police officer walked through the door. If anyone could make sense of all this, it might be Harry Kanter.

Harry listened as the sheriff enumerated things so far—the call from Cate, their arrival at a dark, empty house, finding Landry's SUV and backpack, a body swinging from a noose, and several sets of fingerprints, one of which Angelli bet were Landry Drake's. And last but not least, the prime suspect, Detective Kanter's good friend, seemed to have fled the scene.

Mommy. Daddy. Help me.

Kanter's head snapped up. "Did you hear that?"

Angelli nodded.

A deputy at the railing upstairs shouted down, "Sheriff, we heard a voice up here. There's someone in the house!"

"We heard it too. Which room did it come from?"

"I can't say. It was echoing through the hall. It might have come from anywhere."

"Go room to room and check it out. Take someone with you."

Harry said, "It's a waste of time, Rick. They won't find anything. An EMT and I were upstairs with Charlotte the night Wick died. We heard that same voice and the same words. They didn't come from a person."

"Not a person? What do you mean? I heard the words just like you did."

"I think it's the reason Landry Drake came back here."

"You don't believe he killed her. That doesn't surprise me."

"He didn't do it. I've done homicide investigations my entire career, and I'll bet my pension Landry didn't kill her. He's a victim too, and I hope we find him alive. Let's do a walkthrough and get the lay of the land. Stay with me, Sheriff. We'll start at the top of the stairs."

Jack arrived at the turnoff to Merilee, expecting to find a cop, but no one was there. He drove to the house and found the yard filled with state police and sheriff's cruisers, the medical examiner's van and, closest to the house, Landry's Jeep. He made it to the front porch before a deputy asked who he was.

"I'm with Channel Nine in New Orleans," he answered, hoping the truth would get him inside. "I work with Landry Drake. He and I came here after Wick Ambrose died. Landry's family is worried, and I'm here to find out where he is. Is Sheriff Angelli here?"

The man told Jack to stay put, turned, and yelled through the open doorway, "Sheriff, got a minute?"

Angelli stepped onto the porch, looked at Jack, and snapped, "Get out, now! You have no business coming here."

Astonished at the sheriff's attitude, Jack explained he'd come to check on Landry. As a friend, not a reporter.

"I'm ordering you to leave! Get off this property, or I'll throw you in jail." He told the deputy to arrest Jack in five minutes if he was still around.

Jack said, "Sheriff, hold on one second. Cate Adams says you found another body hanging from the chandelier. Can you tell me who it is?"

If looks could kill, Jack would have been lying in the yard, waiting for the coroner. Without a word, the sheriff turned on his heel and went inside.

Jack asked the deputy why the sheriff seemed so uneasy. "I met him earlier when I came up here with Landry Drake. He seems solid as a rock, but he's agitated as hell now. What's going on in there?"

The deputy said he'd lose his job if Jack didn't hightail it off the property.

He gave it one last effort. "Is Lieutenant Kanter here? The state police detective?"

"Two state guys are here. Younger guy and an older guy—he's a plainclothes detective."

"That's Harry Kanter. He can vouch for me."

The man shook his head. "The sheriff doesn't seem too interested in having someone vouch for you. Did you hear him order me to arrest you if you don't leave? I gotta obey orders. You go now or I cuff you."

As he left, Jack called the station's night desk again and got the cell number for the cameraman who was on his way.

He told him there was a story breaking at Merilee, but not to go there. If Channel Nine's news van drove up now, the sheriff would have apoplexy.

"I'll meet you in Lafayette," he instructed. "We'll find an all-night coffee shop there and wait until the story breaks. We'll be twenty minutes from the scene, and maybe we can still scoop the other stations." The next morning, when news broke about Charlotte Ambrose's death by hanging, Jack would be the man reporting from St. Martin Parish.

On his way to Lafayette, he called Cate, who was growing more frantic by the minute. It was almost four in the morning, eight hours after Landry's last check-in. Jack told her about his trip to Merilee and that he and a cameraman were remaining in the area in case a story developed.

"He was at Merilee. But now he's disappeared. Pray, Jack. Pray to God he's alive."

CHAPTER TWENTY-NINE

When he opened his eyes, Landry's first sensation was a massive headache. He sat on a hard floor, his back against a pole with his hands tethered behind it. A piece of duct tape covered his mouth, and he fought the instinct to gulp in breaths of air. He must remain calm and breathe through his nose.

Everything around him appeared to be made of rusty metal—the floor, ceiling, walls and even two bolted-down tall stools nearby. Grimy windows lined the walls on all four sides. The entire room tilted to the left, and debris and boxes lay in disarray where they had slid to one wall.

I'm in the wheelhouse of an old boat. Could be a derelict trawler. But why? How did I get here? He looked down, realized there was a chain around his torso, and vainly struggled. There came a sound—a swishing noise—but when he tried to shout, his words came out as muffled snorts even a person ten feet away wouldn't pick up. The swishing stopped, and there came a series of knocks, a tap, tap, tapping on metal. He looked up through the front window and saw a pelican tapping it with its beak. The bird noticed him, peered inside, and cocked its head, as if it too wondered what Landry was doing there.

Should I try to make noise? What if my abductor is

somewhere nearby? He opted for the former—what did it matter if his kidnapper found out he was yelling. The person would learn it soon enough anyway when he returned. *If* he returned.

What if he doesn't come back? What if I'm miles from anywhere and I die like this?

Landry raised his legs and brought the heels of his boots down hard. The metal floor resounded with a dull clang that seemed loud enough to attract attention. He did it again and again, pausing to listen after each try until at last he heard the sound of heavy footsteps ascending a metal stairway. Someone was coming, and he hoped it meant help, not harm.

The metal handle on the wheelhouse door turned, and the door creaked open. A large, barrel-chested man with an unruly mop of black hair and a thick beard and mustache stepped into the room. The man wore overalls and rubber boots, he reeked of fish, and he looked across the room at Landry.

"What have we here? You're in somewhat of a pickle, aren't you?"

Landry gave his best imploring look, but the man stayed far away. Landry mouthed words—*Umm, umm*—in hopes the man would take off the tape. That seemed to work; he walked close enough to see the restraints. He bent down and gave the chain a tug as if to confirm it was doing its job.

The man's cautious because he doesn't know why I'm here. He thinks I might attack him. As big as he is, I wouldn't stand a chance. Help me! Help me, please.

Landry cried aloud as the man grabbed the tape and jerked it off his face.

"Start talking, my friend. What's your story?"

"I…I'm not sure. I can't remember anything. Where am I?"

"Cypremort. You're on an old trawler that ran aground in the canal ages ago. I'd never have heard you if my place wasn't nearby. How'd you get here?"

Cypremort? He knew the place was near the Gulf around an hour south of Merilee Plantation. How the hell *did* he get here?

"I can't remember. I was at a house miles away from here, and somebody kidnapped me. Can you help me get loose?"

"Not right at the moment. Gotta find out more about you first."

"I'm an investigator. Landry Drake. You might know my name. I'm no threat; please help me get free. He tied my wrists behind this pole."

The man looked behind the pole and nodded. "He sure did. Used those plastic tie things. They work pretty good, seems like."

"Please just get me loose. I can pay you…"

"You've got a locked chain around you. It would take bolt cutters to get you free, and I don't have the time right now. I have to go to work."

"Okay, just call the police. My phone…I think my phone's in my jacket pocket. You can call Harry Kanter with the state police. His number's programmed in my phone."

The man rose and walked a few steps away before turning. "Folks around here don't much care for cops nosing around. Especially if somebody has the state police's number programmed in his phone."

As he walked to the door, Landry cried, "Please help me. Don't just leave me here."

"That reminds me," he said, returning to where Landry sat. "Gotta make sure you'll be okay 'til I get back." He pulled a roll of duct tape from his pocket, cut off a piece, and smacked it over Landry's mouth. As he was leaving, he said, "By the way, your phone's not in your jacket." He reached in his overalls, pulled Landry's iPhone out, and held it up. "It's right here, and it's been ringing off the wall ever since I brought you here." The metal door slammed with a resounding clang, and the metal steps rang with the sound of boots descending.

His abductor had left him alone. For now.

CHAPTER THIRTY

Landry looked up, realized he'd been asleep, and tried banging the floor again. No one came this time. He learned that with some effort, he could scoot his legs underneath him and slide up the pole to a standing position. Although securely bound, at least the circulation in his legs was better. There was no way to tell how long he'd been here; his only indicator was the sun, which had shone through one set of windows when the man was here but through the opposite ones now. Morning to evening, he assumed, and now his stomach rumbled from hunger. He was thirsty too, but he forced himself to concentrate on something else. In his predicament, obsessions wouldn't help anything.

Now he stomped his feet on the metal floor, which vibrated even louder than before, but it seemed no one was around to hear him. When the sun set, the wheelhouse became dark, and he slid back down on his butt and dozed.

Sunlight streamed through the left windows—the east ones—and Landry stood again, this time with more difficulty. His legs throbbed, his arms ached, and his jeans were damp from urinating at some point. He heard the heavy footsteps again, and the burly man stepped through the door. He glanced at Landry and began unloading a grocery sack he'd brought. Landry's stomach growled as he looked at cold cuts, cheese slices and, best of all, bottled water.

The man pulled away the tape and said, "I'm gonna feed you now. If you don't want to eat, that's up to you. But this is your only chance for today."

"I need to pee."

The man ignored him and brought the water. He uncapped it and held it to Landry's lips, allowing him to swallow. "More," Landry said over and over until he'd drunk the entire bottle.

"You're gonna need to pee now for sure," the man muttered, opening the meat and cheese. In his dirt-encrusted fingers, he held slices of ham and American cheese to Landry's mouth. He bit off chunks and almost gagged once or twice. It wasn't from the food, which tasted wonderful despite the man's grimy hands. It was the overpowering stench of shellfish on his captor's overalls. Landry figured he worked on a shrimp boat. Most who chose this isolated area to live either worked on boats or the oil rigs.

"Who are you?"

"Cliff Latour. Nice to meet ya."

"Why did you do this? They'll find you…"

"Nobody says I did anything, Mr. Landry. You're jumping to conclusions because I had duct tape and your phone. Maybe I abducted you, and maybe I didn't. Let's leave it at that."

"But why? What do you want from me? I'll do anything you want…"

"Before long, I suspect you'll do that, for a fact. When a man gets desperate enough, there's almost nothing he won't do. Are you finished eating, or do you want some more?"

"Water, please. I need more water."

As Latour brought another bottle to Landry's lips, he jerked his head forward and tried to bite the man's finger. Latour pulled back before it happened and looked at Landry in surprise.

He muttered to himself, "What the hell did you do a fool thing like that for? Don't know how you figured biting me would help you. Talk about biting the hand that feeds you. No more food or water for today, Mr. Landry." He taped

Landry's mouth and left. A third bottle of water and the rest of the food sat on the floor ten feet from Landry—ten feet that might as well have been a mile.

Why did I do that? When it happened, he knew it was a mistake, but it was the instinct for survival kicking in. The timing was lousy, because he desperately needed more water. For now, he busied himself by standing now and then, stamping his boots on the floor and hoping against hope somebody would hear. After hours of stomping with no results, he decided he must be someplace far from houses or people.

Over long hours, the sun moved from one set of windows to the other and at last disappeared. Landry's captor had kept his promise—no more food or water for today. He sat in the darkness, struggling to create a plan but coming up empty-handed.

Heavy footsteps on the outside stairs awakened him. He realized it was morning when Cliff Latour opened the steel door, flooding the room with sunlight. Landry's heart jumped when he noticed another grocery sack in the man's hand. He was ravenous and parched with thirst.

"Are you going to behave this morning?"

Landry nodded. *I'd bark like a dog for food and water.*

Latour pulled away the duct tape and held the water bottle as Landry gulped swallow after swallow. Because he was starving, the stink of shellfish didn't bother him as much. He ate several slices of bologna and cheese and half a package of Oreo cookies.

The man put yesterday's trash and today's into the sack and took a seat in one of the bolted-down chairs. "Got a dilemma on my hands," he said, talking to himself as much as Landry. "I have to decide what to do about you."

"You can let me go. I promise…"

"Don't feed me bullshit. That sounds like something from TV. 'Let me go, and I promise I won't tell.' And they always go straight to the cops. Just like you would."

Landry had nothing to lose by keeping him talking. "What's your dilemma?"

"My job. Starting tonight, we're going out for three days

straight. By the time I get back, you'll either be dead or almost. So either I have to kill you or figure something else out."

"Why did you kidnap me? What do you want? Are you asking for ransom?"

"Ransom," Cliff mused, as if that concept hadn't occurred to him earlier. "No, it's not about that. I need you out of the way. You've stuck your nose in too many places it shouldn't be."

"Are you talking about Merilee Plantation?"

The man looked into Landry's eyes. "You think you're pretty smart, but you'll never figure that one out."

So that's what this is about. I'm not surprised.

Landry slid up the pole into a standing position. "I need to use the bathroom. Not peeing, the other way."

Still working on his dilemma, Cliff ignored him for a moment. Then he said, "Number two, huh? Hmm. I hadn't considered your needing to do that."

"You're new at this kidnapping thing, I guess. Am I your first prisoner, or did Charlotte have that honor?"

Cliff cursed, got up, and walked to the door. "You're a smart guy, aren't you? Ask a lot of questions, kinda rub people the wrong way, that kind of thing. I'm half a mind to leave you tied up for three days and find out what happens."

Landry had pushed too hard. "Help me out here. Please. I have to go to the bathroom."

When the man walked out of the wheelhouse, Landry hyperventilated. He'd played too many cards, and now he was going to die. But in a moment Cliff returned, carrying a fifteen-inch piece of metal pipe. "We're going out on the deck." He brandished the pipe. "See this? I'll knock the hell out of you if you try anything."

"I won't do anything," Landry promised. The man took a key from his pocket, opened a padlock, and removed the heavy chain. He used a pocketknife to cut one of the plastic ties on Landry's wrists, stood, and backed away. He slid the knife across the floor to Landry and said, "Cut the other tie off and slide the knife back to me."

As Landry obeyed and massaged his aching arms to get

the circulation flowing, he searched for ideas how to overpower his captor. Cliff was bigger and stronger than Landry, and he had a weapon. Still, he'd be on alert for a chance.

"Go out on the deck and turn left. I'll be right behind you. Any funny business and I'll coldcock your ass."

Blinded by the sunshine for a moment, Landry's eyes adjusted, and he looked around to determine where he was. They were on a wide canal. Half a mile away, he saw other boats tied up along the shoreline, but none were close enough. A hundred feet away was a fishing shack up on stilts to protect it from hurricanes. Next to it was a beat-up old van.

This old trawler listed a few degrees to the right with its bow jutting into the riverbank, and its stern lay partially submerged. Rusting and grimy, it looked to have been abandoned for a very long time.

On the bow, Cliff pointed to a rusty bucket. Landry would have to do his business out in the open, but there wasn't another soul within sight. The kidnapper had chosen a good place to hide his prisoner. As he dropped his pants, he looked over the side to find out how far it was to the ground. Around twelve feet—not that far, but there wasn't time to defecate, buckle his britches, climb over the rail, and drop to the ground on unsteady legs before Cliff popped him with the lead pipe.

"Do you mind turning around?" he said as he squatted, but Cliff stayed only a few feet away, watching him and poised for any sign of trouble. Unable to escape, Landry finished up, stood, and led the way back to the wheelhouse. As he walked, he noticed ripples in the water down below. Something was moving, maybe someone was there, and he had to yell.

He looked at Cliff and took a chance. Instead of shouting for help, he stopped, turned toward the man, and raised his voice.

"Cliff, is that your shack right over there?"

The man brandished the pipe. "What the hell are you doing? Get inside."

Cliff took another plastic tie from his pocket and tossed it to Landry, ordering him to tether his left wrist to the pole. Landry complied, and as the man moved behind him to secure the other one, they heard something. A noise—footsteps clanging up the metal stairs. Someone was coming!

"Dammit to hell," he muttered, glancing toward the open door. A face appeared—a teenaged girl's—and it was impossible to tell who was more surprised.

She stepped inside, confusing Cliff, who paused a moment. As he did, Landry swung with his free arm and grabbed the pipe from Cliff's hand. Landry swung before Cliff could react, and the girl screamed as the makeshift weapon connected solidly with the side of his head. The kidnapper fell to the ground, unconscious.

"Shit, mister! You killed him!"

She turned to run away, but Landry yelled, "Help me! He tied me to this pole. He kidnapped me!"

Unsure of what to do, the girl paused, and Landry screamed, "Look in his pocket. There's a knife there. Give it to me so I can free my hand!"

She looked at Cliff, then at Landry, and decided what to do. Using just two fingers, she felt for the knife in the unconscious man's pocket. She kicked it toward him and ran across the wheelhouse and out the door. In seconds she was down the stairs, running away as fast as possible.

Landry cut the tie, moved Cliff's body to the pole, and secured him with more ties from Cliff's pocket. He wrapped the chain around him and snapped the padlock shut. He went through Cliff's other pockets, searching for a key to the old van outside. It wasn't there, but he found a wallet with Clifford Latour's driver's license and a wad of cash, mostly fives and ones. He stuck the wallet in his pocket, felt Cliff's wrist for a pulse, confirmed he was alive, and left. Landry scampered down the stairs, jogged to the fishing shack, and opened the door to the truck. He hoped the remoteness of this place meant the keys were in the ignition, and he got lucky. Now before he left, he needed one more thing.

As he expected, the door to the shack was unlocked, and he stepped inside a dark front room filled with shabby furniture. Trash and debris lay strewn about everywhere. On a rickety kitchen table he found what he wanted—his phone. He grabbed it, ran outside, and jumped in the van.

"Hey! Hey, there! Stop where you are!" Some distance away, the teenaged girl and an older man with a gun—most likely her father—were running toward him. Landry had another quick decision to make. These people didn't know if he was friend or foe. It was better to get out of here and find help than try to explain it to an armed man whose neighbor Landry had coldcocked with a pipe.

The engine sputtered twice before engaging, and as he pulled away from the house, Landry glanced in the rearview mirror and watched the man raise the shotgun. He revved the motor for all it was worth and drove away, thankful that when the rear windows exploded into a million pieces, the shot and shards missed him.

CHAPTER THIRTY-ONE

Landry pushed the van hard, putting miles between himself and Cypremort. He wasn't sure what parish he was in, and he doubted he could make it home to New Orleans, but he'd go as far as he could. The gas gauge was either dead empty or not working, and Landry worried that the kidnapper might come after him. He turned on his phone and saw eight percent power and two bars of signal. *Should be enough.* He called Cate.

"Landry, thank God! Are you okay? Where are you?"

"I'm in a truck I stole from the guy who kidnapped me. I'm down near the Gulf, and I have to get as far away from here as I can. Hang on—I see a sign. I'm eight miles from Franklin. Tell Harry I left a guy unconscious and tied to a pole in an old trawler at the Port of West St. Mary canal near Cypremort. C-y-p-r-e-m-o-r-t. My phone's about to die too. Come get me or ask Jack to come. I'll try to make it to Franklin and go to the sheriff's office there. Gotta go for now." He clicked off his phone to conserve power.

Landry kept a watch through the rear mirror as the pickup sputtered its way east. He got on Highway 90 at Baldwin, headed south, and was doing a respectable thirty-eight miles an hour when his luck ran out. Maybe it was an empty fuel tank, or maybe the truck simply gave up the ghost, but three miles outside Franklin, he coasted to the shoulder and stopped. Moments later he saw flashing blue lights in his mirror. As he opened the door, words came from a loudspeaker behind him.

"Do not exit the vehicle! Stay where you are! Close the door and put your hands out the window!"

That guy with the shotgun called the cops on me for stealing the truck, he thought as he complied. In a moment two troopers approached the pickup, one on either side. They had their sidearms drawn and aimed directly at him, one through the passenger window and another three feet from his face.

"Open the door slowly and step out of the vehicle. Keep your hands where we can see them."

He did so and complied when the officer asked him to turn around. Seconds later he was on the ground with a knee in his back and his face kissing the asphalt. He felt cuffs on his wrists and lay still until the cop turned him over, and they both hoisted him upright. He looked at the cop car—these guys were with the St. Mary Parish Sheriff's Department.

"I can explain," he said. "I'm Landry Drake. Call Lieutenant Harry Kanter on the state police force. He'll vouch for me."

The officers ignored him; one held a gun on Landry as the other searched his pockets and found Clifford Latour's wallet. He opened it and took out the driver's license. Just then a message crackled on the radios attached to their shirts. It was the dispatcher, reporting the vehicle was registered to Latour.

"Where's your ID, Mr. Drake, and who's Clifford Latour? You have his wallet, and you're driving his truck. And your back window's blown out. There's glass all over the cab. What's going on?"

"Latour kidnapped me. I got away in his truck, and somebody shot at me. I told you I'm Landry Drake. Do you know who I am?"

"Yes, sir, we're aware of who you are. A citizen called in a stolen vehicle report. We didn't expect to find you driving it. Every cop in Louisiana's been looking for you since they found that girl hanged in St. Martinville and you disappeared. I'm going to read you your rights now."

"What girl? Are you talking about Merilee? I don't remember…"

"I'd suggest you stop talking until you get an attorney, sir."

After he had Landry cuffed and in the back seat of his cruiser, the cop radioed in the situation. In a moment the radio crackled again. It was the sheriff, instructing them to bring the prisoner directly to his office.

Ten minutes later, the deputies brought Landry to the sheriff. It surprised them when he said, "Take off his cuffs. You men handled this by the book, but this isn't what it seems. Mr. Drake, come with me to the conference room. Lieutenant Kanter's waiting to speak with you."

"May I have my phone back?" Landry asked, and the sheriff asked one of the arresting officers to bring Landry his belongings.

The deputy handed Landry a clear plastic bag. "Sheriff, the wallet in here belongs to a Clifford Latour, who also owns the stolen truck Mr. Drake was driving."

"That's the guy who kidnapped me. Listen, my friends are on the way here; can I tell them where I am?" The sheriff agreed, and Landry made a quick call, adding a request at the end. Cate said they were only twenty miles out, and they'd be in Franklin soon.

After he disconnected, the sheriff said, "I've sent some deputies to bring Latour in for questioning. He should be here before long. By the way, Harry Kanter has great regard for you. Despite the St. Martinville Parish sheriff putting a BOLO out, and despite your stealing the pickup, Kanter claims you're not a criminal. He asked if we'd FaceTime him once you got here."

The video call connected, and Landry thanked Harry for vouching for him. Because of that, he was in a conference room instead of a cell. He added, "The deputy said they were looking for me because a girl was found hanged. What's that about?"

"That's about Charlotte Ambrose."

The color drained from Landry's face. "Charlotte? She's dead too? What happened? Was it…did I have something to do with it?"

"We aren't sure what happened. She was hanging from the chandelier just like her brother. Your prints were all over the place."

"Right. I wanted to see if there were paranormal presences in the house. I heard the same child's voice you and I heard earlier. I walked up the stairs and stood in the hallway. Bats flew at me, and I stepped backwards. That's when…okay, I remember it now. That's when I touched something in the air, and I felt something brush my face. Next thing I recall, I woke up tied to a pole. He must have knocked me out."

Harry hoped to learn more when Latour arrived at the sheriff's office. "Here's where things stand right now. You didn't check in with Cate, so she called Sheriff Angelli, and he drove out to Merilee. Your Jeep was there, and Charlotte was hanging from the fixture, but you weren't around. Angelli notified me, and he issued a BOLO—be on the lookout—bulletin for you as a person of interest in a homicide. I didn't want to believe you were involved, and I still don't, but the facts speak for themselves. Your prints were everywhere—not exactly where it mattered most, like on the ladder or her body—but many other places. You were there and so was Charlotte. She died, and you disappeared. So far everything points to you, and I can't say what will happen when you go back to St. Martinville. Whether voluntarily or not, you have to go see Angelli and clear things up."

Kanter listened as the St. Mary Parish sheriff questioned Landry about the last two days—waking up chained to a pole, confronting his abductor, learning he might die, and how he got free. "I asked the guy why he kidnapped me. He wouldn't say much, but when I mentioned Merilee, he said I'd never figure that one out."

The sheriff asked Harry if he wanted to come down and assist with Clifford Latour's interrogation. Kanter declined but asked to be kept in the loop. Landry understood why he wasn't coming. Since he was on probation, even today's FaceTime call could have gotten him fired.

Unsure if Rick Angelli might want to send deputies to bring Landry to St. Martinville for questioning, the sheriff asked him to sit in the conference room until he made a call.

"No problem. I have to wait for my friends anyway. If I get to leave, they're my ride." While he waited, Landry borrowed a phone charger. Soon Cate and Jack burst through the door. She cried and hugged him for a moment before pulling back, holding her nose, and saying, "God, you're filthy. You stink too, like you need a bath."

He laughed. "I love it when you talk dirty to me. That's what two days chained to a pole peeing in your pants will get you. Enough talk. Did you bring what I asked for?"

She held up a Burger King sack, and he tore it from her hands, ripping it open and devouring the double bacon cheeseburger and fries. "This is way better than meat and cheese stuck in my mouth by a man with dirty fingers," he said between rapid bites as a sympathetic clerk brought him a cup of coffee. "Never thought I'd say it, but this burger tastes like it was made in heaven."

As Cate held his hand, he explained everything, adding he might have to go to St. Martinville. In a moment the sheriff joined them and explained what would happen next.

"You owe your friend Lieutenant Kanter a drink. He convinced Sheriff Angelli you aren't a flight risk. You'll have to go to his office to get your Jeep keys, but for now you're a free man, except Angelli said don't leave the state without calling him first. One last thing—my deputies will be here with Clifford Latour in five minutes."

Exhausted, Landry said he wanted to be gone by then. As he, Cate, and Jack got into her car, they watched a sheriff's cruiser pull in. "That's him in the back seat. That's the guy who held me captive," Landry said. Cate commented that with his unruly black hair, beard, and mustache, he looked like one of those guys who used to make moonshine up in the hills somewhere.

"Didn't you want to talk to him?" Jack asked, and Landry said it wouldn't have gotten him answers.

"No way the sheriff is going to let me ask him questions and potentially screw up the case. I want the guy behind bars, and I'll do whatever I can to see that happens. I'd love to be a witness at his trial a few months from now."

Landry got his keys at Angelli's office in St. Martinville, and they drove to Merilee to pick up his Jeep. Crime scene tape still hung from the doorway, and his was the only vehicle there. Jack drove it home, and Landry rode with Cate. Back in their apartment, Landry stripped down, took the longest, hottest shower he could stand, and fell into bed. Cate checked on him now and then, but he was dead asleep when she came to bed around ten. He slept until morning and awoke ravenously hungry again.

CHAPTER THIRTY-TWO

Henri met Landry and Cate for breakfast at Café Beignet on Royal near the office. Cate asked Jack too, but he couldn't come. His boss, Ted Carpenter, had ordered him to do his own business and quit taking time off to work with Landry. "He said it with a grin," Jack explained, "but he was dead serious. I'll lie low for now, but this doesn't mean we stop communicating. Please keep me updated on developments." She promised they would.

His head clearer today, Landry recounted every detail of his trip to the old mansion, losing consciousness there and waking up on an abandoned trawler near the Gulf outside of Cypremort. Henri pressed him for his opinion, and Landry said he figured Cliff Latour had killed Charlotte. "Maybe he drugged her like he did me. Otherwise, how did he hoist her up the ladder without a struggle? I guess when I arrived at Merilee, I interrupted him in the middle of his work, and he had to eliminate me too. I guess I'm lucky he didn't hoist up another noose and do it then and there."

Cate wondered if there were two of them. That might explain how they got Charlotte up the ladder. She said, "From your description of him, he sounds like a caveman. How smart is this guy, anyway?"

In Landry's opinion, Cliff Latour was no dummy. His

size and facial hair gave him a fearsome appearance, but he used good English and seemed to understand the gravity of what he'd done. "His only dilemma was having to leave me alone for three days. If that hadn't happened, there's no telling how long he'd have kept me chained inside that old boat. If he was going to kill me, why go to all that trouble?"

Henri asked what motive the man had to kidnap Landry.

"He said I was nosing around places where I shouldn't. I mentioned ransom, and it was obvious the thought had never entered his mind. I think he killed Charlotte, and he was going to kill me too. I want to find out what his role in all this is."

Landry's phone dinged with a text from Jack. Four brief words.

Call me. Important news.

They joked that even with the boss breathing down his neck, Jack was helpless to resist working on this case.

"Henri, is there a payroll slot open?" Cate laughed. "If Ted finds out what he's up to, Jack may be over here looking for a job."

Landry said, "Seriously, he'd be a great addition. He's the best research guy I ever saw, but I hope it doesn't come to that. He needs to stay put. His job title is investigative reporter, and if he can learn to report as well as he investigates, he'll have a great career at WCCY. He needs to stand on his own and sever ties with me. We can't keep working with him since it could cost him his job."

Henri agreed, suggesting Landry speak to Jack, because cutting communication with no explanation wouldn't be fair after all he had done. He was a friend, after all. Landry agreed.

Another ding. "He's texting again." Landry read the message aloud.

Did you get my text? This is about Clifford Latour. Call me. Important stuff you need to know.

Henri smiled. "You're going to call, aren't you? He's got you on the line, and he's reeling you in."

"It won't hurt to hear what he's found."

Henri raised his hands in mock resignation. "You just

said it was dangerous to communicate with him. Don't let him burn his bridges, Landry."

"It's not going to come to that," Landry said as he entered Jack's number. "From now on, we'll be careful, and we'll be fair to Ted and the station. Jack too. He doesn't work there twenty-four seven. He can talk to us when he's off."

Cate chuckled. "Sounds like you and Jack are going to be friends with benefits from now on. None of the serious stuff, all the fun."

But Landry wasn't listening. He had the phone to his ear, hearing what Jack thought was so urgent.

CHAPTER THIRTY-THREE

Landry tried to go first, saying he had something to say to Jack, but it didn't work. Eager to reveal what he'd found, Jack insisted on talking first about Clifford Latour. "The only piece of information I had to go on was Latour's driver's license. He applied for it twenty-five years ago, using a street address in Baton Rouge and a post office box as his mailing address. The application required a social security number. Over the years, he's renewed that license three times."

He paused and so did Landry. Once again, Jack was playing the suspense game for all it was worth.

At last he asked, "Do you want to know more?"

"Jack, you're on the job. Ted's going to can you unless you stop working on my stuff."

"I'll take that as a yes, so here's the kicker. The street address in Baton Rouge doesn't exist. The mailbox does; it's in one of those off-site mailbox-to-go storefronts."

"How did you find out what was on his application for a license?"

"A little bird down at the DMV told me. Give me some credit; I'm good at research. Even the great Landry Drake once admitted he admired my work."

He laughed. "Okay, so Latour used a fictitious home

address. Maybe he was hiding something."

Jack said, "Duh. His social security number is interesting. Clifford Latour lived in Monroe and died in 1957, so this is a case of stolen identity. There's no more information on the man who kidnapped you. No bank account, no credit cards, no credit history—nothing. He used a dead man's identity to get a license, but that was it."

"Why go to the trouble just for a license?"

"It isn't that much trouble, and obviously he needed one. The DMV doesn't cross-check social security numbers. You find a deceased person and you use their information. As long as you aren't going for the gold—credit cards, a bank loan, or a job—you can stay under the radar. I figure he needed ID, and that's what he got."

Landry was silent for a moment. "You just mentioned a job. This guy had one. He worked at night, and he said he was going out on a job for three nights straight. That's when he talked about killing me. So he was working."

"Did you expect I'd stop my research before I finished? The fake Clifford Latour—your man—works on the *Jerry Boy*, a shrimp boat out of Cypremort. Like lots of drifters, I'll bet he takes his pay in cash. That saves the captain time and paperwork, and Clifford doesn't need a bank account. As long as nobody spills the beans, everything's fine."

"Good job, Jack. Excellent work. You've given me a lot to ponder. Have you told Harry?"

"That's something for you to do."

When Jack finished, Landry broached his subject. It was time to talk about distancing themselves from him, and Jack listened without interruption until he was finished.

"So does this mean you're breaking up with me?" Jack said. "I thought we had something special between us, and you don't even have the guts to do it in person? Did you learn *nothing* from dating in high school?"

Landry laughed out loud. "At least you didn't say what Cate did—that from now on we'll be friends with benefits!"

Jack guffawed at that.

"We're all worried about you. You haven't had that job for long, you have big shoes to fill—mine—" another laugh

"—and Ted's an easygoing boss. If he thinks you're taking advantage of him, or that your loyalty lies with me, you may never see the end coming until he gets the balls to can you. A firing won't look good on your résumé."

"I agree, and I've figured it out. I'll get my work here done on time and to the best of my ability. There's nothing wrong with my helping you on the side."

"Not necessarily true. It all comes down to what Ted believes. Just be careful, that's all. I don't want you living back on the street."

Jack chuckled. "Trust me, I'll never put myself in that position again. Now what's next with our Mr. Latour?"

"A call to Harry. I'll keep you advised. After hours, of course."

CHAPTER THIRTY-FOUR

Four fifty-inch televisions mounted on Stuart Pinelli's office wall displayed newscasts all day long from CNN, MSNBC, Fox News and the ABC affiliate in Baton Rouge. Stuart was on the phone with a major donor from Shreveport when he saw a news flash on the local station.

Baton Rouge Man Faces Kidnapping Charge. Above the large black letters was a mug shot provided by the St. Mary Parish Sheriff's Department. Stu paused the broadcast, got off his call, and turned up the volume. He listened to the entire report before muting the TV.

Son of a bitch! Things were bad enough before, but what the hell was he thinking? Kidnapping a celebrity and threatening to kill him?

Clifford—after all these years, Stu had become accustomed to using that name—always stayed under the radar. He wasn't one to take risks, because he understood the consequences of getting caught. He took Stu's advice, used his new identity to create a different life, and until recently, when things started going crazy, they hadn't communicated in years. Now Cliff was in a real mess, a situation that might involve Stuart as well.

Perhaps he won't tell the cops anything. Before the words were out of his mouth, he knew how ridiculous that statement sounded. Law enforcement people took classes on interrogation techniques, and kidnapping charges meant involving the state cops, who had master interrogators. Cliff would talk whether he intended to or not. Which meant Stu had to stop him before he did.

Since Stuart worked for one of the most powerful men in the Senate, he considered using Fortier's name to pull strings, but if it backfired, he'd lose his job…and a lot more. He had to get Cliff out on bail, but how? Realizing it was a long shot, he called a local attorney who was one of Senator Fortier's big donors, furnished details and instructions, and wired funds to his account.

That afternoon the St. Mary Parish sheriff got the call. He and Rick Angelli were interrogating Latour when a clerk called him to the phone. A lawyer said Cliff Latour was his client and demanded the interrogation stop until he arrived to speak with his client.

The call surprised them. The prisoner had made no phone calls, had waived an attorney when they read him his rights a second time, and his new lawyer worked for a well-respected Baton Rouge firm. This was no ACLU lawyer defending an indigent's civil rights. How did attorney Robert Turner find out about this case, and who'd be paying his not insubstantial legal fees?

With that call, the interrogation ended. Back in his cell, Cliff wondered what was up. Two hours later, a deputy returned him to the same room. A man waited there for him, and Cliff learned he had a lawyer.

"I'm Robert Turner," the man said. "I'm your attorney. Have they been interrogating you?"

"Hold on a second," Cliff said. "Who hired you? I don't have the money…"

"I heard about your case. I'll represent you pro bono—that means on the house—because I believe everyone deserves the best defense they can get."

"Did Stu hire you?"

"Stu? I have no idea who that is."

"Stuart Pinelli. Did he hire you?"

The attorney's voice turned hard. "I told you why I came.

Mr. Latour, you're facing a serious charge. You might go to prison for the rest of your life…"

He muttered, "I won't be the only one."

Turner leaned in and raised his eyebrows. "What did you say?"

"Nothing. Go ahead."

"I'm offering you a lifeline—your only chance. Tell me everything about you and the crime you're accused of committing. What have you given the officers so far?"

"Nothing of any consequence. My name, where I work, and that I live down on a canal near the Gulf. There was some noise on an old trawler that ran aground years ago, and when I went to look, I found a man inside tied to a pole."

"Have you admitted any involvement?"

"No. They keep asking, but I said I didn't do anything. If they say I did, they're liars."

The attorney said, "From now on, don't talk to anyone, not even other prisoners. If the cops ask more questions, demand to talk to me. Not a word to anyone. Do you understand?"

Cliff nodded. "Can you bail me out?"

"I'm going to try. That's all I can promise."

"Who'll pay my bail?"

"If it happens, I'll pay it."

This is Stu Pinelli's doing, Cliff thought as they took him back to his cell. *Maybe I shouldn't hope for bail. I might be safer behind bars.*

CHAPTER THIRTY-FIVE

Landry told Harry what Jack had learned about Clifford Latour's identity, and Harry's first question was to ask what Landry himself thought about what they'd learned. Harry was a veteran cop with decades of investigations under his belt, and even though Landry's investigative career was young, Harry could see he had a knack for intuitive reasoning.

"He told me a few things while he held me captive. He abducted me from Merilee, and from his reaction when I mentioned Charlotte Ambrose, I'm certain the house plays into this somehow. We learned he used a fake social to get his driver's license. We need to find out who rented the postal box the license renewals go to."

Harry said he'd handle that. If the box had been in a government post office, the renter's name would be confidential. It would take a warrant to find it out, but a storefront postal facility was a different matter. A state police detective could wrangle information from the owner of a mailbox-to-go operation.

Landry continued. "Jack says he got the license—his new identity—twenty-five years ago, and he's renewed it several times. Other than that, he's stayed off the radar. Think how hard it is these days to avoid things we all take for granted, like bank accounts and income taxes and credit cards."

Harry said, "Latour lives a simple life. As long as you live frugally, a cash existence can work. It's when you need credit that the problems arise, and apparently he didn't."

Harry went to work finding information about the postal box. An hour later he called to say that Clifford Latour had rented the post office box in 1996. He'd listed the same fictitious street address and used his new driver's license for identification. It was as simple as that, and the information revealed nothing new.

After thinking it over, Landry exclaimed, "Hold on! Why didn't we all see this earlier? Jack said Clifford Latour applied for a license twenty-five years ago. I just put two and two together. He rented the post office box in 1996. That's twenty-five years ago, and that's our connection."

Harry didn't follow the logic, and Landry said, "Let me rephrase it. In 1996 James Ambrose got a big bonus, took his family on vacation, and never returned to work. His wife killed herself around then, and James dropped off the radar. In that same year, Clifford Latour rented a post office box in Baton Rouge and got his first driver's license. Latour and James Ambrose are the same person."

The logic made sense to Harry, and after their call, Landry texted Jack to call him after work, while Harry contacted the sheriff in Franklin to reveal the new developments. "Don't release him without advising me," he ordered, but the sheriff said he was an hour too late. The lawyer had showed up with a court order allowing Latour to go free on twenty thousand dollars' bond, which the attorney posted.

No bail hearing, no chance for the prosecution to present a case, and now, no Clifford Latour. All it took was a signature from a judge who'd known Senator Patton Fortier for forty years. Not only friends, the two were fishing buddies, and the judge owed Patton a favor. Many of them, as a matter of fact. And Stu Pinelli kept a tally of them all.

"Are you taking me back to Cypremort?" Cliff asked as he climbed into the passenger seat of attorney Robert

Turner's luxurious BMW 7 Series sedan. The man didn't reply, but the direction he turned out of the parking lot answered the question. The lawyer headed north on 90, and when he took Interstate 10 eastbound in Lafayette, Cliff was certain who had hired the lawyer.

They were on the way to Baton Rouge, and the only person Cliff knew in Baton Rouge was Stuart Pinelli, a man he hadn't seen in twenty-five years.

CHAPTER THIRTY-SIX

Rodney and Myrna Beecham sat down for dinner. Their shotgun house stood in a rural part of northern Iberia Parish, just a stone's throw from Bayou Teche. Tonight the front and back doors stood open to capture the evening breeze.

It was a sad, special time of remembering for the Beechams. On the night of October 3 every year, Myrna set an extra place at the dinner table to remember their son, Cody. Rodney and his wife held hands as he prayed, "Dear Lord, please look after Cody and keep him safe. If it is in your will, God, give us a sign. That's all we ask. Amen."

"Happy birthday, son," Myrna whispered, squeezing his hand before letting it go and picking up her fork. "How old is he today?" she asked Rodney.

He thought a moment. "I guess he would be thirty-seven."

"Don't say that! Say 'he is thirty-seven.' He's not dead, Rodney. We can't lose hope."

He smiled and nodded. This conversation occurred every year on Cody's birthday. The husband, once as lost and despondent as she, had somehow moved on. He couldn't say when it happened. Maybe it came on gradually. But after twenty-five years without a word, a man had to accept reality.

Myrna hadn't. She kept his bedroom just as the day he left—a shrine to a little boy of eleven who would be an adult now. If he walked through their door, he'd be a man whose face they might not recognize.

For Rodney Beecham, getting past it didn't mean losing hope. He simply allowed the years of grief and misery to become a dull ache that arose whenever he thought of his son. Time didn't heal his wounds, but the passing years allowed them to fade.

He'd never say so to Myrna, but deep in his soul, he'd known for years that Cody wouldn't be coming home.

CHAPTER THIRTY-SEVEN

As he rode to Baton Rouge, Cliff struggled to devise a plan. He considered one scenario, then another, then a third, but each had a flaw. He must escape before this man delivered him to Stuart Pinelli, because he had an idea Stu had plans for him. End-of-life plans.

Pinelli wasn't a big shot himself, but the guy he worked for was one of the biggest. He pulled strings and got things done like few other men and women could. After working for the senator all those years, Stu was in a position of authority, and he made things happen by riding the boss's coattails. A word here, a request there…on behalf of the boss, of course…and people did what he wanted. Senator Fortier never knew about Stu's occasional maneuverings for his personal benefit.

Cliff knew all that about his former friend Stu, but the other day when he'd called to say he'd kidnapped Charlotte, Stu got all pissed off and yelled at him for no reason. Kidnapping her had been the smart thing for both of them, but Stu didn't get it. At the end of that call, Stu had said he'd never help Cliff again, yet he sent a lawyer to bail him out. Had he changed his mind and decided to help solve the problem, or did he have another motive—like eliminating a nuisance called Cliff Latour?

After twenty minutes without conversation, Cliff said, "You're taking me to Stuart Pinelli, right?"

The man kept his eyes on the road ahead. "I have instructions where to take you."

"From whom? Who's behind all this? Somebody hired you to spring me. I want to know who it is."

"I've done my job, and once I drop you off, we'll never see each other again. Stuart Pinelli hired me, which means Senator Fortier asked him to do it, because Pinelli never acts on his own. Why Fortier wanted you out of jail is beyond me, but our firm is proud to represent Senator Fortier, and when his people call, we act. My instructions are to drop you in Baton Rouge. Stuart Pinelli will meet us and pick you up. You owe him a lot. Now shut up so we can get this over with."

Somewhere near Henderson, traffic slowed to a crawl as cars merged, moving to the right shoulder to get past a three-car crash. When traffic came to a standstill for a moment, Cliff made his move. In one burst he unbuckled the seat belt, opened the car door, and rolled out and down a grassy embankment. He heard shouts, but he never looked back as he hit the tree line and disappeared.

Cliff had nothing but the clothes on his back and his somewhat fearsome mountain man appearance. He had to put some miles between himself and the interstate. He headed south through the trees until he came to the Henderson Highway. When he saw a sign with a big left-pointing arrow and the words *Cajun Catfish Hole, 2 miles*, he smiled, because now he was certain where he was. His stomach rumbled as he turned on Highway 349 and walked past the Hole, a place where he'd bought many a pound of fish to take home to the family…back when there had been a family.

Another mile or so down the road, it seemed safe enough to try hitching a ride. Traffic was sparse, and the vehicles that passed didn't stop for a formidable bear of a man with his thumb out. He continued south, extending his thumb when he heard approaching traffic, and at last a horn honked. He turned when a pickup as old as his pulled to the shoulder.

"Where ya headed?" asked the old man behind the wheel.

"Saint John Bridge Road on 31. Near Levert." Not exactly true, but close enough to walk a few more miles.

"You're in luck, feller. I'm headin' that way myself. Hop on in."

Cliff glanced at the ancient dashboard and breathed easier when he found no radio. If the cops issued a bulletin, he had a little time. He expected conversation on this quick fifteen-mile trip; people were friendly in Cajun country, and their questions weren't nosy so much as genuinely interested. He'd make up a story and leave it at that.

As it turned out, Cliff didn't have to fabricate much at all. He gave a fictitious name and said he worked on a shrimp boat out of Delcambre. The old man liked to talk, and most of the trip all Cliff did was ask questions. He raised rabbits on a farm near Loreauville and sold the meat to markets in the area. He'd been to Henderson to buy feed—eighty-pound bags of pellets and bales of hay filled the back of his truck— and Cliff got an earful on how to run a commercial rabbit operation.

As the pickup drove away, Cliff walked along the highway, thinking about the consequences of his actions the past few days. For twenty-five years he'd lived a safe but solitary, lonely life as Cliff Latour, deckhand. But for one unfortunate decision, he'd still be there.

For as long as he'd been calling himself Cliff Latour, he had nightmares. Not every night, and not all night, but often enough to give him insomnia. Sleep frightened him because of what might invade his mind. That voice—that infernal, lilting voice—drove him crazy. At last Cliff decided the only way to stop it was to confront the source. He had to go back to Merilee and find the kid who cried, *Mommy! Daddy! Please help me!* In his dreams. In doing so, he'd started a chain reaction that continued to this minute.

As he reached the turnoff that led to his old home, James Ambrose shed his false identity, just as he would shed his locks and facial hair as soon as possible. Whatever happened from this point, he would confront it as the man he once had been. He wouldn't spend the rest of his life in prison—that much he knew—but other than that, henceforth every move he made would be in reaction to the moves of others, just like a game of chess.

He left the main road and walked down the lane that led to Merilee, his childhood home and the place where he'd raised his own children, up until that night. Oddly, he felt at peace despite knowing very soon he faced judgment for his transgressions. He neared the house, grateful to find no one around, and walked inside. Just enough daylight remained for him to look around a bit before collapsing into bed.

Without electricity or running water, some creature comforts would have to wait. As darkness descended on the old mansion, he walked through his home, climbed the stairs, and went to the master bedroom. Exhausted mentally and physically, he hoped for slumber uninterrupted by the child's plaintive crying. A shiver of apprehension ran down his spine. This time things would be different, because James had come home. Home, where it all happened.

When would he be required to face his worst nightmares, to answer for his misdeeds and face his atonement? It was coming soon. Would it be tonight?

CHAPTER THIRTY-EIGHT

Sheriff Rick Angelli was incensed that an alleged kidnapper had disappeared in his parish. Baton Rouge attorney Robert Turner sat in the sheriff's office, getting what folks in these parts called an old-fashioned ass-chewing.

"I've got enough trouble with the deaths at Merilee Plantation," the sheriff ranted, "and then you come along and miraculously arrange bail for a kidnapper who miraculously escapes from your moving car while you're on an interstate highway in my parish. Sounds almost too good to be true. Why don't we go over your story one more time, and perhaps all of a sudden it'll make sense to me."

The lawyer repeated his story. He had no incentive to help Clifford Latour escape. He had been hired to represent a client, and that was what he did. While he was transporting the man, traffic slowed for a wreck, and Latour leapt out.

"You didn't restrain him, right? No handcuffs, nothing."

"I'm not a police officer, Sheriff. I don't own a pair of handcuffs, and the St. Mary sheriff didn't loan me a pair. To tell you the truth, I never thought about it."

Angelli shouted, "To tell you the truth, I think you're lying. And I'm about to throw your ass in a cell for obstruction of justice. One last time. Who hired you to get

Mr. Latour out of jail?"

The sheriff's ranting was so vociferous that a clerk walked across the room and eased his door shut. That helped to muffle the yelling, but only a little.

"No disrespect, Sheriff, but as I told you more than once today, I'm bound by attorney-client privilege."

"I understand attorney-client privilege, Mr. Turner. Until today, it meant not disclosing confidential matters between you and your client. Never in my career has a lawyer refused to say who his client is."

"St. Martin is a small parish, and perhaps you do things in a different way. Here's how it is. If you want to get a judge's order to force me to talk, then bring it on. Until then, I have things to do. I'm going back to Baton Rouge."

Angelli left the room and called Harry, saying he had tried everything but couldn't get any information. "Think you can convince him to tell us the truth?" the sheriff asked.

"Put him on the line," Kanter said. Angelli went back, handed the phone to Turner and left his office, slamming the door behind him. In almost no time, the lawyer opened it, asked the sheriff to come back in, and handed Angelli the phone.

Harry asked to be put on speaker and said, "Sheriff, Mr. Turner wants to answer your questions. I'll hang on and listen, just to be sure he and I agree on what the word *cooperation* means. Are you ready, Mr. Turner?"

The lawyer was not happy. He snarled, "Stuart Pinelli hired me. He asked that I represent Mr. Latour and try to get him released on bail. I accepted the case and accomplished my client's goals."

"Who's Stuart Pinelli, and what's his connection with Latour?"

"I've known him for several years. He works in Baton Rouge, as do I. I don't know his connection to Mr. Latour, nor did I ask."

Kanter interjected, "Is it typical of your firm to accept cases without asking what your client's interest in them is?"

"I wouldn't say it's typical…"

Harry said, "Let's talk about your friend Mr. Pinelli. I

just did a quick web search. Were you planning to tell us he works for Senator Patton Fortier, or did you consider that irrelevant?"

That news surprised Sheriff Angelli. He watched the lawyer fidget, gathering his thoughts as attorneys were trained to do.

"I'm aware that Mr. Pinelli works for Senator Fortier. The senator is a client of the firm."

"Don't be modest, Mr. Turner," Kanter said. "I'm looking at a contribution list on the web. In the last election, your managing partner was one of Fortier's largest donors. I'll bet if I dig deep enough, I can find your name on a donor list somewhere too."

Kanter's needling achieved the desired effect. "So what of it? That doesn't mean I set Clifford Latour free."

"Oh, I'm not even interested in that part anymore. Are you, Sheriff? I'm convinced now that you were nothing but a pawn in a much bigger game. Fortier's the big fish here. I want to know his connection to Clifford Latour. That's the big question, isn't it? And I'll bet you know the answer."

That was enough for Robert Turner. "I won't take any more of this. I have things to do, so if you want to ask more questions, arrest me. Subpoena me. Do whatever you want. I have nothing to hide." He stood.

Harry got in one last punch. "You're right, sir. Now that Fortier's involved, there's likely nothing more we need from you. Your only concern should be what happens when Fortier finds out you talked to us and the shit hits the fan. Get what I'm saying? Let him go, Sheriff. I'll call you later." He disconnected.

At the front door, the lawyer turned to Sheriff Angelli and said, "Be careful. You seem to be a rational person, unlike Lieutenant Kanter. Patton Fortier wields more power than you can imagine. People in south Louisiana—even right here in your parish, Sheriff—they love him and treat him like he's a god. He gets things done for his constituents. If that's a crime, then lock him up. But don't poke the sleeping bear unless you're prepared for the consequences. You're an elected official like Fortier. His endorsement—or lack of it—can make or break a candidate. Don't let some hothead state cop cost you your job."

CHAPTER THIRTY-NINE

In the twenty-one years since Stuart Pinelli had landed a job as a project coordinator for Patton Fortier, he had proven himself invaluable. His engineering background allowed him to assess proposals submitted by Louisiana businesses seeking federal government contracts, and the more successful he was in obtaining funding, the more votes his boss garnered at election time.

Over time, Senator Fortier came to appreciate another rare quality Stu possessed—he had a knack for playing fast and loose with the rules, while keeping his—and his powerful boss's—noses clean. A Fortier supporter and CEO of a New Orleans oil company donated a million dollars to a certain political action committee, and a few months later his twenty-one-year-old daughter went to work at a federal power plant. Despite holding a degree in philosophy and knowing nothing about the industry, she received a six-figure salary.

In another situation, a farm equipment dealer in Monroe ordered his employees to work nights getting out the vote, and soon afterwards he won a contract to sell ninety enormous tractors—a year's worth of sales for him—to the Department of Agriculture.

Quid pro quos were such an ingrained part of

Washington politics that nobody raised a fuss when a fresh-faced college graduate got a job that should have gone to a forty-year-old with a stellar résumé, or a small-time implement dealer knew what number he should bid to win the tractor sale. It was like those days when quarterbacks at major universities drove Cadillacs because the local car dealer was one hell of a donor to the school's athletic program, hobnobbed with the coach, and entertained guests in a suite every season.

Stuart Pinelli was Senator Fortier's fixer—the man he called to get things done. The list of projects Fortier assigned him never slowed, because there was a constant need for money. Campaigns cost a fortune these days; so did lining the pockets of a senator and his powerful friends.

Back in 1996, on the night of that fiasco at Merilee Plantation, Stuart had hadn't an inkling that a few years later he'd be working for Patton Fortier. Back then he'd been a fixer too, and that night in a quid pro quo he traded his talents for something that might give him a big payoff down the road. Then came the job with Fortier's team, in the years when the senator was methodically building his power base. Fortier couldn't pass out favors back then; years would pass before he became Louisiana's senior senator and one of Washington's most influential insiders. Stu hung in, did what he was told, and proved himself both loyal and trustworthy.

The year Fortier won his fourth six-year term, his party gained control of the White House and Congress, and he became chairman of the powerful Senate Appropriations Committee. Stu had over ten years in service to Fortier by then. Already a dependable confidant, he snagged an important job running the local office for the state's most powerful politician.

Stuart couldn't recall the first time he crossed the line. Was it a deal he brought to the boss, or the other way around? There had been so many over the last decade—big ones and small—that they ran together. And it wasn't as though he could look back at a list—the things Stuart the fixer accomplished weren't recorded for posterity. They were swept under the rug with all the other dirt in DC.

One date he wouldn't forget was when he first mentioned Merilee to Senator Fortier. Almost eight years had passed—the blink of an eye relative to the speed at which things got done in Washington. Now at last it appeared the deal he made back in 1996, and his patience since then, would provide a windfall for Stu.

Merilee Plantation and its twenty-five acres of bayou frontage lay near the line between Iberia and St. Martin Parishes. It was five miles from St. Martinville and the same distance from New Iberia, two beautiful, historic towns along Bayou Teche that drew thousands of visitors for their Cajun culture and food.

Almost every town along the Teche had a visitors' center, and chambers of commerce vied with each other for tourist dollars that buoyed the economies of charming Acadian communities. Stuart Pinelli had a grand idea to consolidate tourism—a federally funded Wilderness Area Heritage Center that would unite the Teche parishes from St. Landry to St. Mary. Steamboats would haul visitors up- or downriver, docking at historic points along the way and stopping for lunch, afternoon tea, or cocktail hour at the beautiful new heritage center. Children would watch crocodiles from a viewing station, families could visit a museum of Acadian history, and an IMAX theater would present the heritage of the area and its people.

The most important aspect of Stu's dream was location. The massive heritage center costing tens of millions of dollars in federal money would be built along the Teche, on Merilee's twenty-five acres. After an extensive renovation, the antebellum mansion would become the centerpiece of the entire project. Tour groups would explore its nooks and crannies, see period furniture and clothing, and listen to ghost stories about the spirits that might still roam Merilee's dark halls at night.

Fifty million dollars was a pittance by Washington standards, but it was a big deal for southwestern Louisiana. When Stu had first pitched it to the boss on a flight from DC to New Orleans eight years ago, Fortier gave him the go-ahead to work on it. Although he didn't ask, he presumed his wily subordinate had a personal interest in the project. And Stuart knew what he had to do to keep Patton Fortier's attention—make it worthwhile for the senator as well as himself.

From time to time Stu brought up the project, keeping the idea alive among senatorial committee members and lobbyist friends. The man's patience had surprised Fortier. Most people wanted immediate results and found the slow-moving wheels of DC power frustrating, but the senator noticed that after twelve years working the system, his man had become a master at it.

Once Patton Fortier became chairman of the Appropriations committee, everything changed. Pipe dreams and grand ideas could now be accomplished. The impossible became reality, and federal dollars flowed like water from a spigot.

One afternoon after a key vote, Fortier had returned to his office to find his aide from Baton Rouge waiting for him. "What brings you to town?" he asked, and Stu's answer caught him by surprise. The Teche-Merilee project was underway at last. Using Fortier's name to open doors once closed to him, Stu had secured interagency promises for contracts and funding and construction. He had meticulously compiled everything into a thick three-ring binder. There were letters of agreement, property surveys, Google Earth shots of the property, demographics on everything imaginable involving the Teche parishes, and an option to purchase the key twenty-five acres where the heritage center would be erected.

"Pour us a drink and let's talk some more," the boss said, impressed at Stu's ingenuity and fortitude. His aide had bided his time for years, and now he had created a comprehensive proposal for his pet project.

They talked until seven, adjourned to the National Democratic Club for more drinks and a steak dinner, and by eleven Patton Fortier was on board to create a multimillion-dollar project in Louisiana that would bring jobs and economic stimulus to rural parishes.

THE ATONEMENT

Stu spent every spare moment completing deals that would make his dream a reality. As always, he dealt favors to Fortier supporters, arranging for the services of fifty different companies as various phases of the project began. The first money spent would go to acquire the mansion and twenty-five acres from the private corporation that owned it. Soon afterwards would come a widely publicized groundbreaking ceremony complete with earthmoving equipment on the scene to kick things off.

After so many years, it was going to happen at last. There were times he hadn't believed it would, but now a bright future lay ahead for Stuart Pinelli and his boss, who would reap their covert rewards soon.

CHAPTER FORTY

In his opulent office at the Hart Senate Office Building, Patton Fortier reclined on a sofa with his feet propped on a coffee table. The end of his Cuban cigar glowed red in the darkened room. Night had fallen, and other than the cigar, the only light came from a Tiffany lamp that sat on a table some distance away. He had a problem—a big one this time—and he wondered if he'd be able to pull one last rabbit out of his hat. He'd been doing it in DC for thirty-nine years. Surely there was one more left.

Fortier's constituents sent him back to Washington over and over, giving him over sixty percent of the vote each time. He repaid them by funneling billions of dollars into projects that benefitted the people of Louisiana. Over the years Patton learned politics by studying the habits of penultimate power brokers such as Lyndon Johnson and Ted Kennedy and the Kingfish, Huey P. Long. He allied himself with his party's leaders, bartered his votes for promises to be paid in the future, and in time Patton became one of the most powerful too.

When he'd run for reelection three years ago, he told the faithful this would be his last term. He'd return to Washington for six more years and retire on top of his game at seventy-eight. Now, in the twilight years of an illustrious career, something threatened to destroy everything he'd built.

Even though old man Slage in Lafayette was the root cause of all this, Patton knew it wasn't fair to blame him. Slage had supported the senator back when he ran for office the first time. He gave money, knocked on doors, held rallies, and introduced Patton to influential corporate leaders all over southwestern Louisiana. As Patton's power grew, he rewarded his old friend by sending government contracts to his engineering firm. Someone had to design bridges, highways, interchanges, and parks, and when it was time to open bids, Slage Engineering almost always won. His competitors complained—some even accused Slage of bid-rigging—but there was never any proof, so nothing changed.

Slage got rich, and in turn Fortier got rich as well. Between campaign contributions and cash under the table, it was a marriage made in heaven. Then one day Slage called to recommend one of his engineers, Stuart Pinelli, a man looking for more opportunity than he could find in Lafayette. Slage called Stuart bright, energetic, crafty and blindly obedient to doing what he was told—wink, wink.

It was perfect timing. The senator needed a projects coordinator to identify areas where federal funds might be spent in Louisiana and to select which friendly firms should get the contracts. From Stuart's first weeks, he proved himself up to the task, traveling the state and helping wealthy contractors and businessmen understand the expedience of donating big money to Senator Fortier. The campaign coffers overflowed with contributions as Stu did his magic.

Every staffer for a US senator used his or her boss's name to pull personal strings. It was a perk of the gig, allowing them to skip lines at trendy nightclubs, snag last-minute reservations at a popular restaurant, or bypass a waiting list to get their kid into the right school. As long as they were discreet and didn't get drunk and play the "do you know who I am?" card to a bouncer or a cop, the senators ignored it.

Stu Pinelli pulled a lot of strings from his office way down in southern Louisiana, and Fortier knew it. He noticed it every time they went out for dinner or drinks back in his home state. It wasn't just the expected and deferential "Welcome, Senator." There was always more—equal deference to a senator's aide who'd done nothing to earn the respect. "Mr. Pinelli, it's great to have you back again, sir. Your usual table?"

Patton took another puff of the fine Cohiba and a sip of Johnnie Walker Blue from a Waterford glass. Life was good, but his man Stuart Pinelli had created a problem. A state cop named Kanter called earlier today. It seemed Stu hired a partner at one of Louisiana's most prominent law firms and implied that he was acting on behalf of Senator Fortier. As a result, an alleged kidnapper went free on minimal bail— thanks to a judge who believed he was doing Fortier a favor—and that suspect escaped. Patton called the firm himself—this was too important not to verify—and everything the cop said was true.

It was time to rein in his eager protege. He drained the last of the Scotch and pressed a number on his phone. Stuart answered, listened, and offered feeble excuses for his transgression, but Patton told him to shut up and listen. When he finished, Stu understood his orders. He would submit his resignation by eight in the morning. He would find Clifford Latour and return him to the authorities, and he would explain that he acted on his own. Patton Fortier was not involved. If he did all those things quickly, he might survive with only a blemish on his record and his reputation.

"I'm sorry, Senator. I never expected—"

"I'm not finished," Fortier interrupted. "There's one more thing you're going to do." He explained what he wanted.

Shocked and unable to respond for a moment, Stuart stammered, "A deal's a deal…"

Fortier laughed mirthlessly. "Haven't you been in DC long enough to quit believing in fairy tales? The strong survive, my friend, but you are history. You'll do as I say, and you'll keep your mouth shut, because you understand better than anyone what will happen if you don't." Fortier hung up.

Stuart's hand shook as he laid down the phone. He'd gotten the axe just as the project to which he'd devoted a quarter-century of his life was coming true. Rage and resentment surged through his mind. And although he had the goods to crucify that asshole, he didn't dare. He'd witnessed what happened to people who crossed Patton Fortier. Nothing that might be traced back to the senator, of course—just coincidental, tragic accidents.

CHAPTER FORTY-ONE

James opened the master bedroom's closet door, pushed aside the musty, tattered rags that had once been his clothes, and rummaged through a dozen shoeboxes sitting on a shelf. Surprised that the one he wanted was still there, he opened it, tossed tissue paper and shoes on the floor, and removed a pistol that lay in the bottom. He put it on the nightstand and crawled into his bed.

He burrowed beneath tattered and dusty bedcovers, as excited as a child on Christmas Eve. For longer than he cared to recall, his bed had been a cot in a fishing shack, and tonight's dust motes and musty odors were a small price to pay for sleeping in one's own bed again at last. He arranged the pillows just as he liked them, lay back, and relaxed.

The house creaked and moaned as if it were alive, but the sounds were familiar ones. James Ambrose inherited Merilee from his father, who did the same from his, and although he hadn't slept a night there since that day in 1996, he felt a sense of peace lying in the bed he and Maria once shared, letting the house speak to him. They would come for him—cops all over the state must be looking, and eventually someone would think of his coming home to Merilee—but he hoped to rest just for one night. He wouldn't let them take him into custody again, but he would deal with that later.

When he saw them coming, it would be time to end all this.

There were side effects to his being back home. Along with euphoria came a flood of gut-wrenching memories. He recalled Maria and that day when the family returned from their Florida vacation. James took responsibility for what happened, although the real blame for the horrors of that afternoon rested on the shoulders of another. In this eagerness to surprise his family with the bonus money and a trip to the beach, he demanded a spontaneous departure. No time to pack—throw some clothes in a duffel. No time to think or plan—this is our spontaneous vacation. And no time to wonder about his son, Wick, who'd resisted leaving Merilee as hard as a fourteen-year-old with secrets could do. He'd wanted just five more minutes, but James had demanded he leave.

On their six-day trip, he had written off his son's moodiness and distance as a teenager's payback for his father's demands. He never thought…how could he? No one could have dreamed what chaos the spontaneity would cause, nor the consequences he and his family would suffer forever afterwards.

James forced the thoughts from his mind, thinking of better times ahead. Times of retribution and settling scores. He slept.

An unfamiliar noise aroused him from a bad dream. *What is that?* A scraping sound, perhaps, muffled by his closed bedroom door. Now there was nothing, and James wondered if it was part of the dream.

But then it came again. A scraping sound, and that haunting voice.

Mommy. Daddy. Please help me!

Faint words firmly etched in his mind because they invaded his dreams every night for twenty-five years. He was home at last, but coming home meant dealing with the past, confronting fears and errors in judgment that could have prevented the tragedies. Returning to Merilee meant atoning for one's sins.

Once James heard the voice, he understood where to go. As apprehension swept over him like a shroud, he crawled out of bed, picked up the gun, opened the door, and walked down the hall. Breathing deeply to steady his shaking hands, he grasped the knob and turned it. He took a few steps inside and heard the scratching sound. It was distinct now, echoing through Wick's bedroom as if from every direction at once.

The closet door was closed. Of course it was—he secured it himself before he left Merilee years ago. But Wick and Charlotte had lived here long after he left. Maybe Wick had unscrewed the long, heavy bolts.

He wouldn't have done that, not for anything in the world. I'll bet he never even slept in this room again.

James tiptoed to the closet door and looked at the frame. Moonlight filtered through the windows, allowing just enough light to see yet creating an aura of foreboding menace. He crept forward and ran his hands over the wood until he felt the heads of the screws. Six, seven, eight. They were tightly in place, as they should be. As he'd left them.

Mommy. Daddy. Don't leave me here! Please help me!

The mournful words resounded throughout the room. James, already skittish and wary, jumped backwards, hit the bed, and fell onto the floor. He lay there a moment and listened to a soft, grinding sound, then a clunk as something hit the floor. He gripped the bedstead for balance, rose to his feet and crept back to the door.

Clunk. There it went again. Then a grinding noise. A familiar sound. The sound of…

Oh God, I have to get out of here. Oh God, I shouldn't have come back.

Although terrified, he was gripped by a ghoulish fascination. He stood inches away from the door and watched a screw begin to turn ever so slowly. It took time—he'd used ten-inch deep-thread wood screws—but in a moment the screw finished unwinding itself and fell to the floor.

Clunk.

Five long screws lay on the floor. As the sixth began unscrewing by itself, James sprinted toward the hallway. In seconds Wick's bedroom door slammed shut, trapping him inside.

Please don't leave me. Play with me. Let's play a game!

James babbled as tears streamed down his cheeks. "I didn't know. I swear I didn't know. Please believe me."

Clunk.

He twisted the knob right and left, and he hit and kicked the door, but he remained a prisoner in his son's childhood bedroom.

Grind, grind, grind. The eighth screw was removing itself from the door frame. In a moment he heard it hit the floor too.

He watched in horror as the knob began to turn very, very slowly. Then the door creaked open.

Dear God, I didn't mean for anything to happen. Please believe me.

Mommy. Daddy. Is that you? No longer muffled by the heavy wooden door, the voice echoed throughout the room.

The door stood wide open. James couldn't see inside, but he knew the time for atonement had come at last. He wrapped his arms around his chest and took one slow step after another until he stood in front of the yawning opening into the pitch-dark closet. He stepped across the threshold and entered, turning to watch as the door closed behind him.

Grind, grind, grind. He heard the now-familiar sound. The screws were going back in place, securing the closet door as tightly as James himself had secured it long ago. There would be no escaping now. James ensured that when he'd bolted it himself years ago, but now he was the prisoner. And he wasn't alone.

CHAPTER FORTY-TWO

Jack called Landry on Friday afternoon. "I'm at Café Pontalba having a late lunch and wondered if you'd give me an update. You don't call. You don't write. I'm beginning to think there's someone else."

"Just saving your hide, buddy." He told Jack what Harry had learned from the lawyer, and the identity of the man who'd bailed out Clifford Latour.

Jack suggested from now on they call Latour by his actual name—James Ambrose. "So Pinelli works for Fortier. Why would a prominent politician want this guy sprung from jail?"

Landry said, "That's the real question. Harry thought it might be personal. Perhaps Pinelli had a reason for helping the guy, and Fortier didn't know it. He knows now, though. Harry called his office in DC, and Fortier returned the call. Harry asked him if he got Ambrose released, and the senator denied any knowledge of it. He did know the law firm— some of its top partners are friends and heavy donors to his campaign. He brushed it off as one of his aides doing someone a favor. Happens all the time, he said. But Harry could feel the tension in his voice. The senator was not pleased with Mr. Pinelli's activities."

Jack snorted. "Bet you the senator's in on it too. An

accused kidnapper gets out on ridiculously low bail and promptly disappears. Yeah, like that happens every day. Hey, I'm going back to Merilee tomorrow. It's Saturday, so don't jump my ass for stealing the station's time. I want to look around some more. I have to go because last time you went, you screwed everything up by getting kidnapped. As a gesture of friendship, I'm willing to forget we broke up. You may come along if you wish."

"Okay, but if you want to kiss me, it damned sure won't be on the lips!"

———

Saturday turned out gorgeous—warm with a light breeze and barely a cloud in the sky. Merilee looked less forbidding on a day like this, and after checking in with Cate by text, Landry led the way to the second floor to restart his investigation. He would examine each room, keeping his phone and Jack's at hand to capture anything unusual. Before things got underway, there came loud noises. Not the mournful cries of a child, but a thump-thump from a room.

They determined the sound came from a middle bedroom and rushed inside. Thump-thump, like someone or something banging on a door.

Landry shouted, "Hey! Is someone in there?"

A muffled reply. "Help! Help me. I'm trapped in here! The door's screwed shut."

They saw the screw heads positioned all around the door frame. Jack bounded down the stairs and out to his car to get tools, and Landry shouted, "We'll have the door open in a minute. Who are you?"

Indistinct words came through the heavy door. "Please help me. It's so dark in here."

Within minutes they removed the screws, opened the door, and found a long, narrow closet. Someone stood in darkness at the back.

"Thanks. I owe you," he said as Landry recognized his voice. He tried to slam the door, but James moved quickly. He stepped into the room, grabbed Jack from behind, and held the .38 pistol to his neck.

"Good to see you again, Mr. Drake. If you do everything I ask, you and your friend will leave here alive. But believe me, I'll kill him in a second if necessary. I have nothing to lose. I'm not going to prison, but I have a score to settle, and you're going to help me do it."

"Who…who are you?" Jack gasped as he tried to be still with a gun barrel pressed against his skin.

"This is James Ambrose," Landry replied.

He smiled. "So you figured out who I am—or used to be. It doesn't matter. Like I say, I have nothing to lose. Now take your phone and call the number I say aloud. Keep the phone where I can see it. I don't want you doing something stupid like calling 9-1-1." He called off ten numbers and told Landry to place the phone on speaker.

You've reached the voicemail of Stuart Pinelli. Please leave a message.

"Stu, this is James. I'm calling on Landry Drake's phone, and he's my hostage at Merilee. Call me back in two minutes, or you'll regret it."

The return call came much sooner than that. James ordered Pinelli to come to Merilee at once. When he resisted, James said, "I'm wrapping everything up. It's all over, Stu. Can't you see that? Either you come here and face the truth, or I'll tell Landry Drake the entire story—every little detail. Your goose is cooked either way, my friend. You might as well get it over with. It's ten minutes past eleven. If you're not here by one o'clock, I tell everything and I ruin you. I hope you don't come, Stu. I can't wait to bring you down."

When the call ended, James pushed Jack into a chair and ordered Landry to sit beside him. Keeping the pistol on them, he took a seat ten feet away.

Landry asked what was next.

"Now we wait."

"Can I ask questions while we wait?"

"Ask away. I'll answer if I want."

"The other night when I came here, I realized someone was hanging from the chandelier. I passed out, and next thing I knew, you had me tied up miles from here."

"I used chloroform. Made it myself. I learned how from

a book in the library, and it was pretty simple. You had fainted, so I kept you sedated until I got you down to the Gulf."

"Your daughter Charlotte's body was hanging up there. Why did you kill her?"

He bellowed, "Kill my own child? What kind of monster do you think I am? She was the last of the family. First Maria, then my son, Wick, and at last my beloved daughter. After my wife died, he never rested—for twenty-six years he waited for Wick, and then he got the chance to take Charlotte too. It was my fault for bringing her here, but I thought she'd like being back home again. He shouldn't have killed Charlotte. She had no part in what happened, but he wanted atonement. Revenge. From all of us."

A wistful, faraway look came over his eyes. "Everything was just fine until the day I made the family go on that trip. I shouldn't have insisted…how could I know what Wick did…he might have said something, but he was afraid he'd get in trouble. He confessed later it wasn't the first time, but things never went wrong before. He was only fourteen, for God's sake. I would have forgiven him."

Jack started to say something, but Landry put a hand on his arm and whispered, "Let him keep talking."

"The minute we got home from Florida, Wick ran upstairs. I unloaded the car and yelled for him to come get his stuff, that I didn't intend to carry it up for him. He came out of his room and walked down the stairs in a trance. He babbled nonsense about how he didn't intend it to happen, and he was so, so sorry. I shook him hard and demanded he tell me what was going on. But Wick couldn't. He was only fourteen, and he was involved in something so horrible he couldn't form the words in his mind. Wick just stood in the hallway, pointing up the stairs."

James fought back a tear and whispered, "As hard as this is, I must confess now. Forgive me, Father, for I have sinned." Then he continued.

"Charlotte was the first to realize what had happened, because she knew he'd done it before. She ran to Wick, grabbed his shoulders, and shook him hard. "Take us there," she told him, and he led us upstairs to his bedroom. This room, right where we are now."

He paused and gasped for breath as he unloaded what was on his conscience. Then they heard something.

Mommy. Daddy. Please help me.

The words, clear and crisp, from the lips of someone very nearby.

CHAPTER FORTY-THREE

The words came again. A child's singsong voice, trembling with fear. *Mommy. Daddy. Help me.*

Other words followed, echoing through the house, strong and evil and laced with venom.

You *help me. You promised.*

James answered, "I'll help you, like I said I would. We have to wait now." Then he resumed the story, pointing to the closet from which Landry and Jack had rescued him.

"This is Wick's bedroom. That afternoon Wick led us over to that closet. The door was wide open, just like it is now. He couldn't talk. He just stood there transfixed, staring into the darkness. The first thing I noticed were the huge scratch marks on the inside of his closet door. They were deep gouges, almost like someone took an ice pick to the wood, but soon we all realized they represented something far more horrific. Someone had clawed the wood as they struggled to escape. I saw a body in the closet—a boy younger than Wick, curled up on the floor. He'd died from thirst or starvation or both, after being imprisoned in the dark closet for six days."

Landry whispered, "Wick did that?"

James nodded. "There was something wrong with him. He wasn't wired like other people, if that makes any sense.

It wasn't about cruelty—he didn't torture animals or anything like that. But he'd go down on the bayou and find boys fishing or walking along the bank, and he'd invite them to come to the house and play. It always happened in the summer when school was out. I went to work every day, so I didn't learn about it until Maria told me one day that Wick had brought a new friend home, and they were upstairs playing in his room. That was the first and only time I heard of Wick doing something like that.

"I walked upstairs to find out what they were doing, and when I opened Wick's bedroom door, he reacted like he'd been caught red-handed. 'Where's your new friend?' I asked, and he ran over and unlocked the closet. 'We were just playing tag,' he said as a bawling little kid emerged, whimpering, 'He locked me in the dark. I want to go home.'

"The kid left, and I sat Wick down for a talk. I wondered if he was doing something sexual, like making them pull down their pants, but that wasn't what Wick wanted. He had a thing about domination. Wick didn't hurt them—not physically, at least—but he would lock them in his closet in the dark. It embarrassed him to talk about it with me, and I told him never to do that again. To be honest, I didn't want to talk about it any more than Wick did. I just figured it was some kind of weird game he had played, and he'd stop now that he got caught."

"Did it happen again before that day you took your trip?" Jack asked.

"Maybe. Probably, but we didn't know. He brought other boys to his room, but if anything went on, Maria never saw evidence of it. Wick was twelve that first time, and he was fourteen when we went on vacation. Maybe that was only the second time he locked a boy in his closet, and maybe not. What difference does it make now?"

"Who was the boy?"

"I never found out. Didn't want to. Just wanted to make it go away."

A wisp of smoke, an ethereal plume of mist so fine it was barely visible, took shape near the closet. Engrossed in James's confession, neither Jack nor Landry noticed.

Landry said, "When we found you in the closet a moment ago, the door was secured from the outside with long screws. Who did that?"

"He did." James nodded toward the shadowy outline of a child—a boy dressed in a T-shirt, shorts, ball cap, and tennis shoes with laces untied. Freckles peppered his cheeks and nose, and shaggy bangs hung over his forehead. Landry thought of Tom Sawyer's friend Huck.

"He's a child…and a spirit. How would he lock you in the closet?"

"He didn't. I went inside willingly. It's my atonement. I came home to confront him—to pay penance for the sins I've committed. I heard his wails last night, and I came to Wick's room. He unscrewed the screws, I walked in to face my atonement, and the boy did the locking up. With his mind, I guess. It doesn't matter how. I was content to die there until I heard noises and realized someone had come. You two, as it turned out.

"That night we found this boy's body—the awful night I learned my child had taken a life—I sealed off that closet door with those screws so it wouldn't happen again. I know it was a stupid idea, because if Wick wanted to do it to another boy, he'd pick somewhere else. But it was important to me."

"Did you leave the body inside that closet?" Landry asked, but before James responded, a man holding a pistol stepped into the room.

"Drop the gun!" he shouted to James as the shadowy figure near the closet disappeared.

"I'll kill this man, Stu. I swear it! You drop *your* gun!"

Pinelli laughed. "You won't kill him because you're weak. You always have been. I stood outside in the hall and heard your confession. You came back to Merilee to atone for past sins, not to add more grief to your already miserable life. Do what I say. Drop the gun, now."

As James let the pistol drop to the floor, Pinelli said, "Now we're getting somewhere. Gentlemen, finding your bodies inside Merilee's walls will mark the end of tragedies for this house. Have you heard what Fortier's doing to the place, James? Before you know it, there will be tourists tramping up that stairway, gawking at the place where your entire family was hanged, and coming right into this bedroom to see where the ghost child once lived."

"What…what are you talking about? You can't…"

Pinelli had some confessing of his own to do, it seemed. Spurned by his nefarious boss and seeing his comfortable life ending, he intended to make things right in his own mind. "You're right, James. I can't. Not anymore. I owned this house for a while. I forged your and your dead wife's names and made up the notary to attest the deed in 1996. After a while I let Senator Fortier in on the deal—gave him fifty percent of the corporation so he could profit someday when we sold Merilee. Thanks to you—thanks to my hiring a lawyer to bail your sorry ass out of jail—Fortier fired me. And he made me sign over my half of the corporation. He owns Merilee now, even though no one will find out because the corporation's iron clad. Layer after layer of ownership. He'll make millions when the government buys this place for a visitor center."

"I don't want that," James cried, and Stu broke into a grin.

"Of course you don't, but you're all going to be dead in a few minutes. It doesn't matter anymore what you want."

Stu raised the pistol. Words echoed in the room.

I *don't want that.*

"Who…what's going on? Who said that?"

Now the freckle-faced boy stood near the hall doorway behind Stu. He glanced over his shoulder and said, "What the hell…"

Tell them. Confess what you did. Tell them you threw me in the bayou.

Stu looked confused. He had three men to kill and an alibi to create, but now he had another issue—a specter floating inches off the floor behind him. The boy whose body he'd carried off that afternoon when James called him for help.

"I…you were already dead. There was nothing I could do…"

You didn't care. You threw me in the bayou. You buried her in the cellar.

James glared at Stu. "Maria? You buried her in the cellar? I never knew…"

"Enough of this bullshit," Stu shouted. As he raised his weapon toward James, the placid, freckled face of the boy mutated into a maggot-infested skull, its grotesque cheekbones protruding as worms crawled through dark eye sockets, feasting on the flesh that once covered its face. An animal had gnawed off the nose and ears—the same creature whose claws tore away skin from the face and arms and turned an eleven-year-old boy into a leering, grinning skeleton.

Here's how I look now, the specter cried. *The gators ate me. Now it's your turn.*

CHAPTER FORTY-FOUR

In a flash the horribly mangled phantom flew across the room and swirled madly around Pinelli's head. Stu's arms flailed as he tried to remove the thing that was attacking him, and his weapon crashed onto the floor. Landry scrambled over to swoop it up while the swirling vortex of misty horror engulfed Stuart from head to toe. His screams bore evidence of what he was enduring inside the opaque cloud, and he tore at his face, as if removing it might ease the pain.

Within seconds it was over. The mist evaporated, and Stu fell to his knees, clutching his face and sobbing. "Why didn't someone stop him? My face. It hurts! God, it hurts. What did he do to me?"

He lowered his hands and raised his head. Landry and Jack gasped—the man's face was a mirror image of the child's, its flailed skin and cheekbones protruding like a monstrous Halloween mask. Huge gashes marred his cheeks and forehead, and an eyeball hung loose from its socket.

"We have to call 9-1-1," Landry yelled, but James said it was too late.

"Stuart's going to die. It will happen before help can arrive, and we're going to leave him as he is. He receives his atonement now, as I have received mine." He looked at the man writhing on the floor, the shrieks almost too much for other humans to bear.

James knelt beside him. "I confess to you, Stuart Pinelli, that I hate you. I have hated you since I asked for your help when Wick killed the boy. I thought you were my friend, but you betrayed me. You sent me into exile and promised you'd take care of my children, but instead you took everything for yourself. For all these years, I've dreamed of seeing you in this house, dying on the floor in front of me. This is your absolution, Stu—the atonement."

Moaning in agony, Stu clawed at his face and cried, "Kill me! Kill me!"

Kill him.

The child's voice echoed in the room, eerie and harsh.

Kill him.

There was a single gunshot, and Stuart Pinelli received his release from pain.

Landry and Jack spun around and saw James holding the pistol he'd dropped earlier. He said, "It's over for him, as it is for me. It won't be long now."

Exhausted and resigned, James collapsed into a chair. Landry called Harry, who said he'd contact Sheriff Angelli and be there as quickly as possible. "Don't let Ambrose get away," he cautioned.

"Give me the gun," Landry cried, but James shook his head and gripped the pistol more tightly.

"No. It's over."

"It can't be over until you tell us why everything happened. If you…if you're not here to explain everything, then your atonement will mean you're forever labeled a mass murderer—a deranged, sadistic killer who hanged your own wife and children. Is that how you want to be remembered? If Stuart killed them, like you told us earlier, then confess. Tell the world that he did it."

James broke into a feeble smile. "You don't understand. No one could; I hardly understand it myself. Stuart Pinelli didn't kill them. The boy did it—the ghost of a child my son, Wick, left to die in his closet."

Sirens wailed in the distance as Landry kept James talking. "But you don't have to die. You've carried guilt for twenty-five years, but your crime was taking your family on vacation. How could you have known, when Wick didn't reveal that he kidnapped a boy? Don't blame yourself." He extended a hand. "Give me the gun. I'll help you tell your story to the authorities. You don't have to die."

"They'll never understand," he whispered as he passed over the pistol.

Seconds later the front door crashed open, and a voice cried out, "Landry! Landry Drake! Where are you?"

"Up here! In the bedroom!"

Sheriff Angelli and his deputies bounded up the stairs, assessed the situation, and cuffed James.

"Go easy on him," Landry said. "He's a victim too."

"Holy shit, Sheriff," a deputy said as he knelt beside Stuart's body. "Check this out. Look what he did to this guy's face. It's like he took a razor to him. You can't even tell who this poor guy is."

Landry said, "James didn't do that. He fired the shot that killed him, but he did that man a favor by putting him out of his agony. That's Stuart Pinelli. He works—worked, I should say—for Senator Fortier."

Angelli said, "Okay, and you say Ambrose killed him. He already faced kidnapping charges—your kidnapping, as a matter of fact—and now he's killed someone. Facts are facts, Mr. Drake. You say you witnessed a murder. Are you now asking to retract that statement?"

Landry said, "Can we speak for a moment?" Sheriff Angelli had seen the supernatural events at Merilee, but if the deputies learned that Pinelli's horrific wounds were the work of a ghost, there would be no keeping it quiet.

The sheriff sent his men downstairs to wait for the medical examiner but refused to allow Landry to say anything else. "You saw him fire the shot that killed Stuart, yet for some reason you're defending him, saying he did the decedent a favor by killing him. That makes no sense, but it's time for you to stop talking, especially in front of Mr. Ambrose. If you and Jack will follow me back to headquarters, I'll take your statements there."

He escorted James downstairs and put him in the back

seat of his patrol car. In the other squad car, two deputies surreptitiously shot photos of Landry with their phones. They had recognized the ghost hunter immediately, and here he was at a bizarre crime scene in an old mansion.

By nightfall, the pictures would be all over social media. By morning Jack Blair would be interviewed on Channel Nine's Sunday news show. Along with famous paranormal investigator Landry Drake, he saw Senator Fortier's senior aide in Louisiana murdered at Merilee Plantation. Jack's sensational revelations raised a furor of interest, causing Landry to spend the next few days dodging reporters.

CHAPTER FORTY-FIVE

With a deputy monitoring his moves from ten feet away, James Ambrose sat on the bunk in his cell at the St. Martin Parish Correctional Center. Facing two capital crimes—manslaughter and kidnapping—the chance he'd ever be free again was slim.

In another part of the building, Landry, Jack, Sheriff Angelli, and Harry sat around a table in the sheriff's conference room. A recorder captured answers as Landry and Jack described what had happened at Merilee. The bizarre story of a ghost demanding retribution from Senator Fortier's aide stunned the sheriff. Harry understood his fellow lawman's puzzlement, because he'd also been a skeptic before he met Landry. After working cases with the man dubbed Louisiana's ghost hunter, Harry realized the supernatural existed. Without accepting the reality of paranormal activity, many things simply defied explanation.

Although Merilee Plantation was in St. Martin Parish, this was a state case because it began as a kidnapping—a crime that fell under the state's jurisdiction. That posed a dilemma for Harry, who was under direct orders to stop working with Landry. Without revealing that fact to the sheriff, he told Angelli to take the lead in the investigation. Harry would figure out how to deal with jurisdiction when he had to.

Landry explained that Wick Ambrose had left with his parents for six days rather than confessing he'd locked a boy in his closet. Jack added, "Sheriff, when I spoke to you earlier, I asked if anything significant happened in the parish on June 28, 1996. That was the day they left for Florida. Charlotte told us her brother did something so awful that their mother hanged herself over it. You told me the parish records showed nothing significant happened on that day."

"That's right. No kidnapped kid, no missing persons report, nothing like that."

Harry said it made no sense his parents wouldn't report him missing. Unless they were involved, which none of them considered a possibility.

Landry said, "But it makes sense if the boy lived in another parish."

"But that doesn't add up either. You said the ghost is a child. How old was he?"

"Ten or eleven, I'd guess." He glanced at Jack, who agreed.

"How did a little kid get to Merilee? Did his parents drop him off for a play day? No, because they would have come back to get him. Did he hitch a ride? I doubt it. No self-respecting person would pick up a child hitchhiking and not find out what was up. So how did he get to the house? Did he walk several miles?"

Angelli thought maybe not, explaining, "Merilee Plantation sits just north of the Iberia Parish line. The kid could have walked there and also lived in a different parish. I'll call Sheriff Barbour and see what his records show about that day."

As he waited for his counterpart in Iberia Parish to pick up, Landry told Harry and Jack he needed to confess something.

"The first job I ever had was as a deputy for Willie Barbour. He caught me going through his desk. It's a long story, but I was trying to get back some notes he took from me, and I got canned for the first and so far the last time."

Harry grinned. "What a jerk, firing you for going through

his desk. Sounds like simple breaking and entering to me. Or maybe burglary or petty theft. Lord, Landry. You pushed the limit even way back then. Out of curiosity, why did he take your notes?"

"I wasn't very good at obeying orders. He wanted me to patrol the back roads of the parish all night, and I wanted to check out paranormal events at an old insane asylum. I did some extracurricular research, and he confiscated it."

"You're talking about the asylum in Victory!" Harry exclaimed. "I worked that case, remember? That's where you and I met."

"It is. I remember it well. You were a gruff bastard then. Now you're a gruff old bastard." Harry grinned.

Sheriff Angelli put down his phone and said with a smile, "Willie said to tell you hello, Landry. He said you used to work for him and asked if you still defied authority or if you'd grown out if it. How long were you there?"

"Just long enough to get in deep trouble," Landry quipped. "Did you find out anything interesting?"

"Sure did. Willie checked his database for that day in 1996 and got a match. An eleven-year-old named Cody Beecham went out to play on the bayou like he did most summer days. When he didn't come home that night, his parents filed a missing persons report. I didn't tell Willie Barbour we had a ghost on our hands."

There was no question the missing boy was also the specter that haunted Merilee Plantation. That meant the parents had to be informed as soon as possible. They talked about whether Sheriff Barbour in Iberia Parish should meet with the parents, since the missing child lived there. But his death had occurred in St. Martin Parish, and the visit to the Beecham home fell in Rick Angelli's lap.

Late that afternoon, the sheriff asked when Harry wanted to transport James to the state holding facility in Baton Rouge. This was the state's case, after all. Tomorrow was Sunday; the sheriff said if Harry wanted to take him now, he'd meet them tomorrow in Baton Rouge to continue the interrogation.

It was confession time for Harry, because piling one lie

on top of another always ended up in disaster. He explained that his close association with Landry had gotten him in trouble with the boss, and he was under strict orders to drop this case or face losing his pension. He explained, "My retirement's only a few weeks away; I could leave now, but I'd rather go when I planned. That said, I refuse to quit working the Merilee case. It's too damned interesting, and I want to know how things turn out. So this needs to be our little secret."

Angelli exploded with laughter. "Harry Kanter going rogue? Who'd have thought? I know Sam Talbot, and I'm glad you work for him and not me. I need your expertise on this case, so you scratch my back, I'll keep your secret!"

Harry knew the St. Martinville Parish jail was as secure as the one where James Ambrose would have spent the night in Baton Rouge, and he said he had no qualms about leaving the prisoner in Angelli's hands.

Rick also thought things would be fine. "We'll keep Mr. Ambrose on suicide watch. Someone will be watching every minute. Let's meet here tomorrow at nine. Landry, can you come back too? We have a one-way mirror set up where you can observe. Your insight on the paranormal aspects can help us ask the right questions."

Jack wanted to come too, but Angelli refused. "Landry's an expert, and his insight may come in handy. No offense, but you're a reporter. There's no way you can be present."

The next morning, Jack's boss, Ted Carpenter, watched him on the set as his live interview aired, and afterwards he ushered his investigator into his office. "We talked about your staying out of Landry's cases," Ted began. "I like you, Jack, and I want you to succeed here, but you're trying my patience. Tell me how you two ended up together and help me understand why you disobeyed a direct order."

And to his credit, Jack did just that. He knew Ted was a reasonable man and that he respected Landry very much. Jack told the truth—on a Saturday he'd asked Landry to ride with him for one last look at Merilee. It was two friends, not people working a case together. It was personal business, even though it turned out to be the biggest news event of the day in southern Louisiana.

———

"We need to go see the Beechams," the sheriff said. "Landry, I'd like you there too. I've done more of these visits than I want to recall, but never one where I have to explain that their son who's been missing for twenty-five years haunts an abandoned mansion just upriver from their house. At least you believe in ghosts. I'm not ready to go that far just yet."

Harry said, "Rick, I hear you loud and clear. This stuff is hard to believe, but it's true. In my thirty-five years as a cop, I've seen a lot of crazy stuff. I thought Landry was a lunatic when I met him at Victory, but I saw things there I still can't explain. Not logically, I mean. If you follow Landry Drake around long enough, something will happen to make you a believer too."

Landry agreed to go with Angelli and asked when he wanted to do it. Should they go immediately, which meant putting off James's interrogation for half a day? Harry suggested they keep going. The boy had disappeared twenty-five years ago; one more day wouldn't matter, especially since their prisoner was cooperating.

Angelli agreed. At present, James was talking without benefit of counsel, and he could decide to stop at any moment. If he did, they might never learn everything that happened at Merilee. The interrogation would continue, and the minute they finished, Sheriff Angelli and Landry would go to see the Beechams.

It had been a long day for everyone. As Landry and Jack headed back to New Orleans, Jack grumbled about being snubbed. "Did you hear the sheriff? 'No offense, but you're a reporter,'" he mimicked. "And we all know reporters are like dog shit, except smellier."

Landry glanced over to make sure he was kidding and promised he'd fill him in off the record. Jack admitted he understood the sheriff's decision, but he didn't have to like it.

That evening back at Landry's apartment, Cate let him

take a long, hot shower before asking if he felt like talking about what had happened at Merilee.

He laughed. "I feel better than I deserve. Let's go over to Muriel's for dinner. We can talk there."

They walked to Jackson Square and entered Landry's favorite restaurant. Their friend Claude manned the front desk as usual, and after warm greetings he took them upstairs to a quiet corner table. When they walked through the dining room, several patrons recognized Landry from his ghost-hunting documentaries on television. A few people glanced their way and pointed, but tonight it was a blessing that no one approached his table for an autograph.

He recounted their harrowing moments first as captives of James Ambrose, then of Stu Pinelli, and what they learned about Wick's awful crime so long ago. He said, "There's much more to learn from James. I appreciate Sheriff Angelli's allowing me to observe the interrogation."

CHAPTER FORTY-SIX

Back in St. Martinville on Sunday morning, Landry sat in a dark room and peered through a large window. He watched James Ambrose, Harry, and Sheriff Angelli enter a cramped room containing a table and three folding chairs. From their side, Landry's window appeared to be a mirror.

Through a speaker, he listened as Angelli read James his rights once again. They confirmed he did not want an attorney present and that no one coerced his answers from him. At 9:04 a.m. the questions began.

The first part of the interview established background. He told them about his marriage to Maria, the birth of their twins, his job at Slage Engineering, and how he never got a raise or a promotion. If he hadn't inherited it free and clear from his father, they couldn't have afforded to live at Merilee Plantation. He and his family lived a modest life on Bayou Teche, minding their own business and cultivating no friends.

James allowed only one outsider into his life—Stuart Pinelli, a single man close to his own age who was an engineer at the firm. James assisted him on projects now and then, and he became the closest thing to a friend James could claim. Sometimes they went for hamburgers at lunch, and he listened as James ranted that no one at Slage appreciated him. As he talked, they realized James cared about being friends far more than Stuart. Harry made a list of James's personality traits—unambitious, antisocial, a man with a chip on his shoulder about the cards life had dealt him.

When the questions turned to Wick's childhood, James had little to say. Women ran the household and cared for the children, he said more than once. A man should go to work, bring home a paycheck, and do whatever he wanted after hours, unimpeded by his wife or children. He spent lots of his free time in a little pirogue on the bayou, fishing or just drifting along. If the children got in trouble, or needed help with homework, or wanted advice or a shoulder to cry on, they went to their mother. If Wick occasionally locked little boys in his closet, James wouldn't have known or cared, Harry realized, adding *self-centered* to the list of traits.

After a brief lunch break, the interrogation continued. Harry asked about June 1996, and James recalled his excitement at the three-thousand-dollar cash bonus he'd brought home. There wasn't a spontaneous gene in his DNA, but he loaded up the family for the fateful six-day trip to Florida. Wick resisted going, but his father insisted. He was sullen and morose the entire time, never joining the family for meals or swimming with them in the ocean, but James admitted he ignored his son's actions.

"Teenagers," he told the cops. "They love you; then they hate you. In my mind, I was doing a great thing by taking them on vacation. We only took one or two vacations ever, and never to the beach. Wick repaid me by being an ass. At least that's what I thought until…well, you know. Until we got home and everyone found out what he'd done. My wife, Maria…" He paused and took a deep breath. Harry noted this was the first sign of emotion he'd exhibited since they began.

"Something snapped in Maria. I don't know what—there was no time to find out. I was downstairs with Wick and…and that kid's body was up in his bedroom…and next thing I know, I heard a bang. That was the ladder hitting the floor when she kicked it out from under her. Poor thing, she fashioned a noose, climbed the ladder, and put the rope around that huge old light fixture. Then she was gone." He looked away, lost in a memory but with no sign of sadness or regret.

"Let's take a break," Sheriff Angelli said, but James asked to keep it short, explaining that atonement included confession, and the sooner he did it, the faster he would pay the price for his sins.

A deputy led James to the restroom while Harry and the sheriff got Landry's take on their progress. He gave them his thoughts and added, "James said something before he shot Stu. He said Stu betrayed him. Something to do with Wick's killing the little boy. He believed Stuart was his friend, but he betrayed James. We need to find out what he meant by that. One thing's certain—Pinelli disposed of the bodies. He tossed the kid into the bayou and buried Maria Ambrose in the cellar."

When James returned, Harry said, "Landry Drake told us you hated Pinelli for betraying you on that day in 1996. What did you mean?"

"Everything went crazy all at once when we got home from the trip. My mind whirled around. My son had killed a boy and the body lay upstairs. Charlotte was screaming, I tried to decide what to do, and then…dear God, my Maria hanged herself without even a goodbye. I collapsed on the floor and looked at her body up there while a hundred crazy thoughts went through my head at once. *How do they execute murderers in Louisiana? Do they still use the electric chair, or is it lethal injection? Would they do it to Wick, who's only fourteen? Or me? Will they think I killed my wife? What do I do with the body? Should I call the sheriff? What happens to Charlotte if Wick and I go to prison?*

The crazy, disjointed things spun in my brain until Charlotte moaned, "Daddy, please help her. Please get my mother down from there."

He paused and drank some water. Harry asked if he needed another break, and he shook his head.

"I decided I had to call somebody smarter than me. Stuart Pinelli was an engineer and the smartest man I knew at Slage. He was also my best friend, and I believed if anyone could help us, it would be Stu. So I called him. Looking back, it was the worst thing I've ever done, but I couldn't think straight, like I said. I needed someone—another man— to help me figure this out."

"And Pinelli came to help?" the sheriff asked.

"Yeah, he got there in around fifteen minutes, since he only lived a few miles away in St. Martinville. All I told him on the phone was that something awful had happened and there was a dead body at my house. When he got there, he listened to me, scoped out things, and then he said something like, 'Pardner, you've got yourself a big problem here. That body in there is someone's kid. Every cop in the area's going to be looking for him, and when they find out what happened, Wick's a goner. They try teenagers as adults all the time, and he'll get the death penalty for certain. Premeditated murder. That's my prediction.'"

Ambrose shook off a chill that the memories brought, and he continued. Stuart said nobody would believe Maria climbed a ladder and killed herself. Women just didn't do gruesome things like that. "I can barely accept it myself, even though you're my friend. They'll put you in a room and grill you night and day until you crack," James recalled Stu saying. "It's like the Gestapo. They'll deprive you of water and sleep until you're so exhausted, you'll admit to anything. Then your ass'll fry too."

Landry felt sympathy for the man's plight. He'd become a pawn in another man's sick game. Every terrifying word Stu Pinelli uttered brought James more and more under his spell until James could do nothing but accept his predictions as truth and turn the entire matter over to Stu for resolution.

"Stu asked me if I wanted his help. He said he would do it, but he was taking a huge risk, and I had to trust him implicitly. If things went wrong, he could lose his career and his reputation. They could even charge him as an accessory to murder. He had a plan, but I had to agree to it and never look back. I said yes, yes, I wanted his help. And I would do anything he said. I didn't want Wick to go to jail for a stupid, tragic mistake. I begged him, and he said, 'It'll cost you.' I heard those words, but they didn't sink in. I would have given everything I had to make it all go away. And that's exactly what he took from me. Everything."

It was nearing four o'clock, and James needed rest after his harrowing day in the confessional. They called it quits and sent him back to his cell, where he remained under suicide watch.

After spending six hours in a cramped, dark room, Landry appreciated that the interrogation ended. They spent only a few minutes reviewing the afternoon's answers before he left. They'd all meet again at nine tomorrow.

CHAPTER FORTY-SEVEN

The next morning, the jailer ushered James back into the interrogation room. Sheriff Angelli asked if he had gotten much sleep, and he moved his hand in a seesaw motion. Not much. As Landry watched, Harry looked at the notes he'd taken and began.

"When we left off, you were explaining how you'd asked Stuart Pinelli to solve your problem. You said you'd do anything he asked. Is that a fair assessment of what you expected from him?"

James nodded, and the sheriff reminded him to verbalize his answers for the recorder. "Yes. Stu was smarter than I was, and he told me he could make everything go away."

"Did you consider that might make things even worse?"

James rarely looked either lawman in the eyes, averting his own to his lap or fixating on a spot across the room. This time he raised his head and looked straight at Harry.

"My wife was swinging from a noose, and the child my son killed was in his bedroom. There could be nothing worse than what was happening at that very moment. I believed my life had ended, and that turned out to be true."

"What did Mr. Pinelli do?"

"He told Wick, Charlotte, and me to wait in the parlor while he took care of things. It was surreal sitting in a room with my twins, repulsed at the thought of touching them or allowing them to touch me after everything that had happened. Nobody spoke. We just sat and listened to noises—banging, bumping on the stairs, doors opening and closing—and some time after that, Stu came in and took me out in the hall.

"'You're going to leave Merilee tonight and never come back,' he said to me. I didn't understand; my children were only fourteen. I asked where we would go.

"What he said next struck me like a blow to the head. 'Not *we*, James. *You*. I'll take care of the twins. You're going to start a new life. I'll help you figure everything out, but you will leave now and never come back. You will never see your children again. It must be this way; do you understand me?'

"No, I didn't understand him, and I said so. I asked where the bodies were. Maria and that boy. Gone where no one would ever find them, he answered. I ran out into the hall and up the stairs. Everything was good again. No noose and no ladder, a clean floor in the closet—it was like none of it had happened."

Landry considered it difficult to listen as the man described ending life as he had known it. Pinelli's plan required James to disappear, leaving his teenaged children in the care of a virtual stranger—a friend from work. Stu promised he'd keep tabs on them, and he told James to sign documents that transferred ownership of the house to a corporation. That was for James's and the children's benefit, he said. If anything came up, nobody would take the house away from them because technically the Ambrose family didn't own it anymore—a corporation did. And that corporation belonged to Wick and Charlotte. Or so he said.

"He told me nothing but lies. The corporation belonged to him and him alone, and the moment I left St. Martin Parish, he told Wick and Charlotte they were on their own. They could live in the house until he decided otherwise. We had no friends or neighbors, so the kids fended for themselves. Charlotte told me when someone began asking hard questions, they said their parents left on a short trip. Stu kept enough money in a bank account to buy food and clothing, and he paid for minor upkeep on the house.”

James broke into a rueful smile. “How nice of him to do that, since he owned the damn place. The kids did okay, I guess. They must have finished high school, because I learned Wick went off to college. I moved down on the Gulf and assumed a new identity, and I never saw my children again. Not in person, that is. I saw Wick on TV now and then when he opened a restaurant or somebody interviewed him. And I saw Charlotte the other day when I brought her home to Merilee, but I never imagined he’d kill her. I hate myself for bringing her back.

“Stu helped me get a license using a dead man named Latour’s ID. I took his name too. For the next twenty-five years, I lived as a shrimper named Clifford Latour. I drew my pay in cash, lived like a hermit on the canal, and spent every spare minute regretting the tragedy I’d created and how I’d abandoned my own children to save my life.”

He broke down in tears, and they allowed him time to compose himself. Regardless of the man’s tragic life and regrets, he was a kidnapper and a murderer. There would be no leniency, and the questions that had to be asked would cut him deeply.

Harry started in again. “You claim your wife committed suicide after learning what Wick did. The only other persons in the house were your children, both of whom are also dead. Let’s talk about their deaths. First there was Wick. Where were you on the night he died?”

“Out in the Gulf on the *Jerry Boy* for thirty-six hours straight. Captain Ahern can confirm it. I didn’t kill him. I didn’t even hear about his death until I got home, and I cried until there weren’t any more tears. Losing a kid—even after everything—it’s just horrible.”

“The authorities found Charlotte unconscious below his body. Sheriff Angelli here interviewed her later on, but she remembered nothing. After that, the judge committed her to a psychiatric facility in Lafayette, and you kidnapped her from there.”

James shook his head. “I didn’t kidnap her. She was my

daughter. I wanted to help her…"

"What did Charlotte tell you about that night Wick died?"

"Nothing, but I understand why it happened. The boy drove him to do it."

"The ghost? You keep blaming him, but you say you spent years out on a shrimp boat, so how can you be sure of that?"

"Because I know. Wick left Merilee in 2001 and never returned until that night. He should have stayed away forever, because the boy waited for him all that time. Retribution. Atonement. Don't you see that's what all this is about? Payback for past sins. Wick's. Mine. Stu's. Even Charlotte's, poor child. All she did was keep quiet, but I guess she had to pay for that sin of omission."

The sheriff snapped, "No jury's going to believe your cockamamie story that a ghost drove people to commit suicide. But that's the only answer you have. What really happened to your family, Mr. Ambrose? Why don't you tell us the truth this time?"

Landry carefully considered James's answer. He'd been waiting to hear about this case's paranormal aspects.

"Once, a long time ago, I returned to Merilee. What I experienced scared the life out of me. The boy calls for his mother and father. The words resound throughout the house. And he cries—dear God, the wails will tear your heart out. He sat locked in the dark all that time until…until he died. No one can imagine the horror he endured, all alone and scared out of his mind.

"He wants retribution. Mostly from Wick, for obvious reasons. But he wanted revenge on the rest of my family, because none of us tried to save him. When Wick and Charlotte came home to Merilee that night, the child would have taunted him in that eerie voice. He would have pushed and pushed until Wick killed himself."

Angelli shook his head. "Charlotte conveniently passed out while Wick killed himself, or so you made it appear. I say you killed Wick, used chloroform on your daughter like you did to kidnap Landry, and left her to take a fall for murder."

"Like I've said over and over, I wasn't there. We'll never know what she saw that night. I'll tell you one thing—when I returned that one time, it scared the hell out of me. He started in on me, tearing at my conscience and my sense of morality and decency. He began picking me apart until I felt like a sadistic creature who let a little boy die. I was lucky that night. I ran outside and escaped his spell. Wick wasn't so fortunate. The boy drove Wick to madness and forced him to seek atonement by taking another life—his own—as he'd taken the child's life many years ago."

Break, came the one-word text from Landry on Harry Kanter's phone. "Let's take five," he said, and Angelli summoned a deputy to take James down the hall for a break. Harry and the sheriff went the other way and met Landry.

"He's telling the truth," Landry said. "You hear of so-called 'vengeful spirits' in Acadiana folklore. A person dies in a bizarre or cruel way and bides his time in the same place where he died, waiting to seek retribution against his murderer. This boy died a most unnatural death and never received a proper burial. When Wick returned to Merilee, the ghost seized the opportunity to avenge his own death. James called it atonement, and he's right. Wick Ambrose paid the price for his sins."

CHAPTER FORTY-EIGHT

When the interrogation resumed, Angelli asked, "How often did you see Stuart Pinelli after you left Merilee in 1996?"

"Never. We spoke sometimes; he gave me one of those old flip phones to use, and it rang three or four times a year when he called to gloat over some accomplishment or milestone in his life that I'd never experience. He'd talk about Wick and Charlotte—mostly lies—but his motive for calling was to reinforce how he controlled me like a puppet master. I could never be James Ambrose again if I wanted to be a free man. Telling the police what happened would send me to death row. He told me that so many times that I believed it myself. And I guess he was right, because both of you think I'm lying. Twenty years ago he joined Senator Fortier's staff, and after that no one would ever imagine he was involved in the horrors at Merilee. Stu became a powerful man—too powerful for me to buck. So I did as he said. I lived my life as a shrimper named Cliff Latour."

He described how Stu controlled Wick and Charlotte, leaving them to fend for themselves alone in the house from age fourteen. Thank God they had the good sense to go to school and continue life without ending up in the child welfare system, he said. They went to college on scholarships and were nineteen in 2001 when Stu Pinelli kicked them out of the house for good. James didn't know why Stu had picked that time to do it; maybe he had plans to sell the property. Whatever the reason, the house had sat abandoned from that day forward.

James followed Wick's success through occasional news stories. He graduated with a degree in restaurant management and landed a job with one of New Orleans' best-known chefs, a man who owned three of the city's most popular restaurants and hosted his own show on the Food Network. Wick learned the business and, like chefs under tutelage by the masters often do, he left to create his own restaurant empire.

James said, "Wick Ambrose. The guys down in Cypremort would talk about him, and I'd want to say, 'That's my boy. I raised him.' But I wasn't Wick's father anymore. I was Cliff Latour, so I kept quiet. Stu would call now and then to needle me. He'd tell me Wick wanted to incorporate, and how he formed the company and was on Wick's board of directors. I wondered then if Wick realized how manipulative Stu was. I hoped my boy could make it in life without getting trapped like I did."

"Let's talk about Charlotte. You kidnapped her from Barrington Clinic and took her to Merilee. Why?"

"To bring her home. I thought she'd be happy back at home. But Stu Pinelli came. I guess that was my fault. When I took her away from the clinic, I called him. I was helping him out by keeping her from talking, but he acted like an ungrateful bastard. He took everything from me, and then he took Charlotte too."

"What do you mean?"

"He came there. He told me I shouldn't have taken her away. That the cops would find me, and I'd tell them about him. He worked for a senator, and he said he'd take care of things like he always did."

"What did he do?"

"He knocked my little girl out, and he hanged her from the chandelier. 'Serves you right,' he told me. Both my kids died in that house, and both the same way. The bastard…"

He broke down for the first time, and tears streamed down his cheeks. "The bastard took away the last thing he could from me."

After a few more questions, Harry and Sheriff Angelli consulted with Landry. If something new surfaced, they'd call James back for more questions. For now, the interrogation was finished.

CHAPTER FORTY-NINE

Sheriff Angelli called the next morning to advise the Beechams there was news about their son, Cody. The sheriff and Landry took separate cars to their house; when they finished, Landry would go directly back to New Orleans. When Angelli knocked, a woman opened the door and invited them inside.

"Rod, they're here," she called, glancing at Landry once, then again.

"Have I met you before?" she asked him. "Your face looks so familiar…"

"That's Landry Drake from TV," her husband said as he strode into the room. "What's this all about? What are you doing here?" Rodney Beecham had been a tall man once, but today osteoporosis and the burdens of his life weighed on his stooped frame. He wore a flannel shirt, overalls, and work boots, and when he shook hands, Landry felt the calluses that proved the man worked hard all his life.

They declined Myrna's offer of coffee, and as they sat on furniture that had seen better days, Rodney told the sheriff he wanted to hear their news about Cody.

"It's best if Landry explains what we've learned," Angelli said. "He's experienced it firsthand."

The man wasn't having any of this. "Hold it right there.

We've been wondering what happened to Cody for twenty-five years. Sheriff, you called us yesterday and teased us by saying there was news that you had to give us in person. Now you show up with a ghost hunter, and you want him to do the talking. What the hell's going on? Is Cody…" He stumbled on his words as a tear rolled down his cheek. "Is he alive or dead or what? Don't tease us anymore. We don't deserve this."

"He's dead, Mr. and Mrs. Beecham," Angelli said. "He died soon after the day he disappeared in 1996. I'm sorry to have been evasive, but once Landry explains, I hope you'll understand why I wanted him to be here. You'll have questions that he's far better qualified to answer than I."

Rodney and Myrna hugged and cried. "You knew it all along," she sobbed. "You knew Cody wasn't coming home, but I couldn't let him go. I had to keep believing." She looked up. "His bedroom is still exactly the way he left it that day. I clean it every week, but I never changed a thing."

"I'm so sorry," Landry offered, but the woman pulled away from her husband and gave a dismissive wave.

"Like a silly old fool, I held on to hope for twenty-five years. Go ahead, Mr. Landry. Tell us what you came to say. It's time for this to be over."

Over the next forty-five minutes, the Beechams learned everything the authorities knew about Cody's abduction and death. They grilled Landry about his appearances at Merilee Plantation in the afterlife and were stoic as Landry explained his theory about atonement and retribution. Landry told them nothing about Maria Ambrose's suicide that night, or how James abandoned his house and children.

At the time Wick Ambrose's hanging made the news, they had no reason to connect it to their child's disappearance. Nor did they think of their son Cody when Wick's sister, Charlotte, died in the second hanging a few days later at Merilee. Today the Beechams learned of another—the third hanging, when Wick and Charlotte's mother had committed suicide after learning her son had killed Cody Beecham.

Rodney took his wife's hand. "You're saying our boy

exacted retribution against that family. I used to be a religious man back in the day. But when you lose a child, sometimes you lose faith too. You wonder how a loving God could allow you to go for twenty-five years without hearing a word. Know what I mean?"

When he paused, no one said a word.

"The boy—the ghost, I guess I should say, although he's still my boy—he somehow scared those people into hanging themselves. I hope they were terrified out of their minds. I hope those sons of bitches were horrified, and I hope they suffered."

Myrna gave a violent shake of the head, a sign Landry and the sheriff mistook as an objection to her husband's harsh words. In a moment they heard her whisper, "I'm proud of Cody. Good for him. An eye for an eye. Retribution. Atonement, like Mr. Landry says. Good for you, son."

Rodney looked at his wife. "Call me crazy, but I want to go there. I want to see where they…where Wick Ambrose locked my boy up and left him to die. It's something I have to do, Myrna." He smiled when she said she understood and wanted to go too.

"I'm okay with it," Sheriff Angelli said. "See any issues, Landry?"

Landry cautioned the Beechams that things might not go well. "The ghost isn't your son anymore. He retains the appearance of a young boy, but for years he's been consumed with a desire for revenge. There's much we don't understand about spirits—do they think rationally, retain human capacities for love and tenderness, and can they remember every detail from their pasts? What I'm saying is that Cody may not accept you as his parents, because your son died twenty-five years ago."

Rodney and Myrna rode with Angelli as Landry followed. At the historical marker, they turned down the narrow lane and came to the old house. The state police had boarded up the first-floor windows and doors after Stu Pinelli's murder, and yellow signs nailed to the boards warned trespassers this was a crime scene. The plywood over the front door had hinges, a hasp, and a padlock to allow easy entry.

Angelli opened the lock, and they walked into the dark entry hall that was gloomier than before, since no light came through the downstairs windows. Landry led them to the staircase, concerned how things might play out. As they climbed the dust-covered risers, he wondered if bringing the Beechams here was prudent.

Doubts filled his mind as they walked up the staircase. What if things turned out terribly badly? Although this spirit appeared in the form of a child, it was a vengeful, hate-filled phantom that demonstrated earlier what harm would come to those it hated. The parents had done nothing wrong; they had waited for twenty-five years. But what if the spirit saw it differently? What if they should have looked for him while he was still alive? What if he blamed them for his fate?

The answers came quickly as they reached the top of the stairs and heard a mournful cry.

Mommy. Daddy. Where are you? Please help me! It's so dark.

CHAPTER FIFTY

"Listen, Myrna! Did you hear that?"

She grabbed her husband's arm. "Yes, yes, I did."

She cried out, her voice echoing down the long hallway. "Son! Cody, we're here! We came to find you!"

The intensity of what happened in milliseconds astounded them. A light brighter than a thousand-watt bulb appeared in Wick's bedroom door, blinding them as it flooded the hallway with light. Her eyesight restored, Myrna stifled a scream and pointed. A few feet from them stood the ethereal shape Landry had seen before—a floating, wispy child wearing a T-shirt, shorts, and a ball cap.

"Cody! Cody, that's you, isn't it?" She ran toward the figure, looked down at his feet, and smiled. "You never could keep those shoelaces tied, could you?"

"Be ready to help if necessary," Landry whispered to Angelli as Myrna reached the phantom and attempted to wrap her arms around it. They passed through the misty cloud, and it dissipated and reformed. They watched the spirit shimmer in the light, its shadowy face looking up into hers. Tears rolled down her cheeks as she broke into a wide smile.

As soon as he saw the spirit's face, Landry knew that the couple was in no danger. Instead of the macabre skull with its skin ripped away, they saw their son's freckled face, tousled bangs, and turned-up nose. This was their boy—their son, Cody, as he had looked the day he left home for the last time.

"You came! You came, Mommy." In a flash the phantom swirled around her, spinning wildly as it had around Stuart Pinelli, but this whirling dervish was spinning with love. Where there had been horror and screams before, this was a touching moment of reunion. The spirit engulfed her tightly in a loving hug between a long-dead child and the mother who had grieved for him.

Landry wept, and even the sheriff, in a rare display of emotion from a veteran cop, dabbed at a tear. Rodney Beecham walked to his wife and son, and the child's wispy arms caressed his mother's face while he pressed his head against his father's broad chest. It was as beautiful a moment as it was bizarre, an experience that would be indelibly etched in the minds of Landry and Rick Angelli.

CHAPTER FIFTY-ONE

After signing his confession and with corroborating statements from eyewitnesses Landry Drake and Jack Blair, the police charged James Ambrose with the murder of Stuart Pinelli. Both that and the kidnapping charge were capital offenses, and the court-appointed attorney who met with him found a client who refused to cooperate.

"We can try insanity," the lawyer suggested. The case was rife with ghosts and haunted houses, hangings, and other mayhem. They'd get jurors who scoffed at the supernatural. If James believed, it would be easy to find a psychiatrist who'd pronounce him insane.

But James would have none of it. He intended to offer no defense, even though he was signing his death warrant. "I don't care," he told the lawyer. "Death is what I deserve. This is atonement for my sins."

At last, his attorney accepted his client's wishes and entered a plea of nolo contendere—no contest. During the pretrial phase, James cooperated, but not in the way his lawyer expected. He handed prosecutors the nails for his coffin, one by one. He answered every question, although the answers entwined him more and more tightly into a web from which his only escape was by lethal injection.

Deemed a suicide risk, James lived in solitary

confinement for two months at the state holding facility in Baton Rouge. During that time, he was cordial toward the guards and had a positive attitude about every aspect of the twenty-three-hour-a-day lockdown in a concrete room, showers twice a week, and no television.

As he awaited trial, the prison psychiatrist evaluated James once a week, and after the fourth positive report from his meeting with the prisoner, he recommend James be transferred to the general population. He still had a cell to himself, but he could interact with others, something the doctor thought would be good for him.

Guards marched him from the solitary unit across the yard to another block of cells at three forty-five one afternoon. James walked into his cell and sat on the bunk. The moment they left, he ripped the bedsheet into long strips, and tied them together. He tested them for strength, decided they were satisfactory, and tied one end into a noose, which he looped around his neck. James climbed on the bed and threw the rope around a sprinkler pipe that ran along the ceiling. He prayed it would do the job, and it did.

At fifteen minutes after five, the dinner gong clanged throughout the cell block. A guard walked down the run to open the cell doors and found James hanging from the pipe. He had left solitary confinement less than two hours earlier, and at last he had both the means and the opportunity to accomplish what he'd intended to do all along.

Atonement. Retribution. For James, the long, hard journey was finished at last.

———

Cate and Landry wanted to provide the wretched man a proper send-off. With everyone in his family dead, there remained no one to consult about arrangements or burial. Online, Jack Blair located the Ambrose family plot in one of St. Martinville's oldest cemeteries, and Landry called a funeral home to pick up James at the prison, prepare his body, and bring it to St. Martinville for burial in the family crypt.

Landry called Father Paul Broussard, a former priest

with whom he'd worked on another case and asked him to officiate at James's brief service. Six people attended—Landry, Cate, Jack, Henri, Lieutenant Kanter, and Sheriff Angelli. This was the lawmen's first time to attend a funeral for an accused criminal and a man they barely knew, but they agreed with Landry. A man paid the ultimate price for a crime not his own. He deserved honor and respect at the end of his life.

CHAPTER FIFTY-TWO

No matter how one tried to sugarcoat it, the fact was that Harry Kanter got probation for associating with Landry. Colonel Talbot had minced no words: if he caught Harry working with the ghost hunter again, he and the pension he'd worked three decades to build were history.

Harry's opinion was he got screwed, blued, and tattooed, and he was pissed. He and the boss's animosity went way back, and Landry's crew agreed that Harry didn't deserve the humiliating punishment Talbot dealt him. He was on probation, forced to walk on eggshells for the next few weeks to get a few more shekels in the kitty for retirement.

They were understandably surprised when Harry walked into the Toulouse Street studio one morning. "It's the middle of the week," Cate said. "Aren't you supposed to be working? Did Talbot…"

"He hasn't had the pleasure just yet. I'm officially on vacation. I had twenty-one days built up, and I submitted a time-off request for the next three weeks. When I go back in, I'll have only three weeks left to work for that rat bastard Talbot."

Henri asked if Harry felt safe being around Landry, even on vacation. What if the boss found out and fired him, even though theoretically Harry's free time was his own?

"I doubt he'd do that. I talked to the union steward; if something happens to my pension after thirty-five years, they'll go to bat for me. And it'll be in the media—the steward's been waiting for something to hang Talbot with, and this would be perfect. I may be a guinea pig, and I came down to help you guys."

While they appreciated his offer, Henri, Cate, and Landry were up against a hard deadline to launch in just five weeks. Teaser ads were already airing on cable networks, but holes in the programming lineup remained to be filled. They were so busy no one had time to assign Harry tasks. He tried to be productive, pitching in to help move furniture on the set and finding odd jobs to do, but he felt like a fifth wheel instead of a team member. This veteran lawman couldn't visualize himself doing that for the next three weeks, but he damned sure didn't intend to sit around Bud's Bar with a bunch of cops.

It only took a day of piddling around for him to devise a plan. The next day Cate and Landry took a quick lunch break and invited Harry to join them at Desire, the Royal Sonesta hotel's Bourbon Street oyster bar. Harry considered it perfect timing; he had their attention for forty-five minutes, and he offered to become their unpaid, unofficial investigator. There was more to learn at Merilee, and he experienced the paranormal there himself.

He laid out his plan. "I'll work on the Merilee case until I get answers or you say it's time to give up. I have to be careful flashing my badge around, but I have ex-cop friends who help each other out. Some are private investigators, and lots of us on the force, me included, help them out when they need a little confidential info."

Landry called it unfair to let Harry work gratis, but Cate disagreed. "We can't afford an investigator at the moment, and Harry needs something to fill his time. Why can't he work on Merilee while we're doing the network stuff? If he's careful, of course."

Landry said, "Okay, but the network will reimburse expenses. Gas and whatever. There's something you can work on right now."

Earlier, they had gotten good information from the mailbox-to-go place in Baton Rouge, but Landry thought getting a license wasn't all this was about. He believed that mailbox wasn't really for James's use. He hadn't even opened a bank account or applied for a credit card after changing identities. His name was on the box, but Landry thought someone else—likely Stuart Pinelli—controlled it.

He asked Harry to find out who collected the mail from that box, adding, "The property tax bill goes there every year, and somebody pays it. Other mail may show up too—we don't know what else it might be used for—so let's find out. That guy who owns the mailbox store helped you out before. Think he'll do it again?"

"With my charm and persuasive personality, who could resist helping me? This calls for a face-to-face meeting. I'll head on back to Baton Rouge after lunch and stop by there before I go home."

Although it might take time, Harry was certain he could pull this off. He wasn't kidding about being persuasive; a police officer seeking answers intimidated most private citizens. People weren't necessarily afraid, but most were cautious and respectful.

The mailbox store was busy. Some people were retrieving mail from their boxes while a dozen customers waited in line to ship packages. Three employees—two females and a much older man Harry bet was the owner—rushed here and there handling the crowd. He took his place in line and at last moved to the front, hoping to get the man but ending up with a young lady.

"I'd like to speak to the owner for a moment," he said in a voice loud enough the man could hear.

He was taping up a large box with an Amazon logo on the side, and he spoke without stopping or looking up. "Little busy right now. What can I help you with?"

Harry stepped out of line and moved closer. "I'm Lieutenant Harry Kanter. State police. I spoke with you the other day about a mailbox."

"Sure. Sorry I can't talk now, but we're swamped. Come back at ten 'til six. I'll talk to you then."

Harry left, pleased that the owner seemed willing to cooperate. When he returned, there were no customers in line, and a UPS driver was hauling packages on a dolly out to his truck.

Once the driver left, the man lowered a mesh gate and turned off a neon "OPEN" sign in the window. His employees continued loading parcels and mail into large postal service bins.

"What can I do for you, Lieutenant Kanter?"

"That mailbox I asked about. Number 3703. Can you show me where it is?"

The man pointed it out on a wall filled with identical ones. Through a tiny window in it, Harry could see something inside. "Looks like they have mail," he said. Before he could ask, the owner said postal regulations prohibited anyone but the box holder from seeing it.

"No problem. Any idea how often someone picks it up?"

"We all sort the mail every morning when the postman brings it, but only I stuff the boxes. When it's busy like today, I might not see someone come to get mail, but I can say this box is empty every Tuesday morning when I stuff it."

"So the person comes on Mondays? Do you know what he or she looks like?"

"I do. Let me check the card." He opened a file cabinet, pulled the one marked 3703, and said, "Clifford Latour. It's in his name. My word. He's had it for twenty-five years. Way before my time. I bought this place in 2013, and for a while, a man picked it up. Recently it's been a girl. Hard to forget, actually. If you saw her, you'd understand why I say that." He gave Harry a wink.

Harry nodded. "Today's Friday. Would you allow me to come in on Monday and watch the boxes until she comes?"

"Not without a warrant if you're planning to confront her or arrest her. I don't want any trouble in my store…"

"No, no. Nothing like that. I just want to see who she is. I won't talk to her at all."

The man paused before replying, "If I can help in an investigation, I don't see why not, but I'm holding you to your promise not to cause a scene in here. We open at eight. I don't recall what time she comes, so you might have a long wait. Look at that row of desks over by the wall." He pointed to five computer tables, each with a monitor, keyboard, and mouse. "The fourth one doesn't work. You can sit there as long as you need, and you won't be in anybody's way."

Harry arrived on time and waited three hours and eighteen minutes. The moment she walked in, he knew that his quarry had arrived at last. She was young—maybe twenty-five—with long blond hair, and she wore a black pantsuit, a white shirt, and high-heeled shoes. Black-framed eyeglasses gave her an academic look. Whoever she was, she worked somewhere that required its people to look sharp.

The woman walked over to box 3703, turned the dial a few times, and opened the door. She took out three white envelopes, closed the door, spun the dial, and left with Harry close behind. The proprietor breathed a sigh of relief. That cop had kept his word.

She got in a late-model Ford Escape and backed out of her parking spot. Harry's car was in the end space facing out, and he easily slipped into traffic behind her. He knew how to tail someone, and he maintained a safe distance even though she never gave him a glance. She drove the speed limit, used her signal to change lanes, and after three miles, she pulled into the multistory parking garage of a downtown building.

Harry followed her up a ramp to the second level and passed by as she found a spot. He pulled into a handicapped slot, walked behind her through the garage to the elevator entrance. When the doors opened, he stepped into the car behind her. She pressed the button for the third floor, and the doors closed.

"Morning," she said with a bright smile. Noticing he didn't press a button, she asked if he was also going to the third floor. He said he was, hoping she didn't ask anything more. And she didn't. When the doors opened and they stepped out, she turned to the right, used a card to open an unmarked door, and let it close behind her.

He looked to the left where a tastefully decorated

reception area stood behind double glass doors. There was only one office on this floor, and on the wall of the waiting room hung a large round sign. A seal, actually.

The seal of the United States Senate.

This was the field office for Louisiana's senior senator, Patton Fortier.

CHAPTER FIFTY-THREE

Landry and his gang took a break, joined Harry in the conference room, and listened to what he'd learned. Although they wouldn't have been that surprised to hear Stuart Pinelli owned the place, they were surprised to learn the mystery went all the way into Senator Fortier's office.

This might point to the senator's personal involvement, although it was possible the goings-on at Merilee had been a side project of Pinelli's alone. Perhaps some clerk in Fortier's office had been Stuart's gofer, picking up the mail every week and bringing it back to…someone. But who? Stuart Pinelli was dead, but the project continued. Who received the mail these days?

"Wonder if there's a funeral planned for Stu?" Landry said, and a few minutes later Harry looked up from his laptop and said, "Yep. It's tomorrow afternoon at two. Notre Dame Catholic Church in St. Martinville. Burial to follow in the cemetery on Bridge Street. Why do you care?"

"Because I'm going."

"To pay your respects," Cate quipped. "The man planned on killing you, remember?"

"I won't forget that. No, I'm going because it may be the my only chance to get close to Senator Fortier. I want to ask him about the mailbox."

"At the funeral? Isn't that a little gauche?"

Landry laughed. "Gauche is my middle name."

Harry went along to keep Landry company, and they got two breaks. The first came when the senator showed up. There was no assurance he'd return to Louisiana for the funeral of an aide, albeit a senior one, but he did. Outside the church after the funeral mass, they got their second break. Despite having a security detail, Fortier paused to greet people, as he always did. He shook hands, hugged and cheek-pecked the ladies, and shook his head at the tragedy of losing a man in the prime of life.

Landry joined a small queue of people who waited to greet the politician. When it came his turn, Senator Fortier said, "Howdy, friend. Sad day, isn't it?"

There was no time for small talk. He had a few seconds at best, so he gave it his only shot. "What's your involvement with Merilee Plantation?" he blurted.

Taken aback, Fortier snapped, "What are you talking about? What are you doing here?"

"I'm Landry Drake, sir. I'm with—"

"I know who the hell you are. You're at a man's funeral, for God's sake. Have you no tact?"

He took a chance. "With all due respect, I watched Stuart Pinelli die. Tact isn't a word I'd associate with a person like him. Someone from your Baton Rouge office checks a mailbox every Monday. Stuart set up that box twenty-five years ago. Who handles Merilee for you now that Pinelli's dead?"

In a fluid motion, Fortier turned to one of his goons and snapped, "Get this asshole out of here!" and turned to the next person in line. By the time Fortier's bodyguard jerked Landry aside, the senator was commiserating with some woman.

"Hold it right there!" Harry ran toward them. "State police. Get your hands off that man."

Unfazed, the heavyset man said, "State police? Let's see some ID. Show me your weapon, old-timer."

Harry reached for his shield, but Landry stopped him, saying, "Let it go." The security man laughed, released

Landry with a shove, and sneered, "Get out of here, both of you. I'll call the real cops if you get near Senator Fortier again."

They said nothing until they were in the car driving away from the church. "That was fun," Harry muttered. "I felt like a total asshole. I understand why you stopped me. Somebody could have called Baton Rouge, and I'd be off the force. But still…"

"You didn't have to intervene. I could have taken my berating and walked away."

"Hey, I was only trying to help…"

"I get it, Harry, and I appreciate it, but things aren't the same for you. They never will be, and that's okay. To answer your question, I rattled the good senator. I didn't expect answers, but he knows someone's digging in places they shouldn't be. Now we wait and see what happens."

CHAPTER FIFTY-FOUR

SENATOR FORTIER TO RETIRE IN THREE YEARS;
ANNOUNCES HUGE TOURISM PROJECT
FOR ST. MARTIN, IBERIA PARISHES

The news that Patton Fortier would call it quits at the end of the term surprised no one. He'd made that promise when he ran three years ago. Patton had been in politics his entire adult life, serving in state government for ten years before running for the Senate. After thirty-nine years in Washington, Fortier had become one of America's most powerful politicians. When a 2005 op-ed piece had dubbed him "the Cajun King," he liked it so much that he used it as his nickname.

The senior senator from Louisiana was a master at pork-barrel politics, and every omnibus spending bill pushed through the House and Senate included millions of dollars for one project after another in Louisiana. He planned to retire as the most-loved man his state ever sent to Washington, and his last project would bring jobs and tourists ready to spend money. That meant prosperity for the parishes along Bayou Teche.

Fortier's grand finale, a lavish and expensive project

near the border between Iberia and St. Martin Parishes, had would be called Teche-Merilee Park and Visitor Center. WVLA-TV, the NBC affiliate in Baton Rouge, carried an exclusive interview with Fortier, excerpts from which were aired by every station in the state. Landry, Henri, Cate, and Harry listened as Fortier made his announcement.

"The federal government has acquired a prime twenty-five-acre tract along Bayou Teche called Merilee Plantation," the senator crowed. "Every parish and town along the river already has its own tourism center, but this will be the granddaddy of them all!" He showed an architect's rendering of the house and grounds. The decaying mansion would be renovated, furnished with period pieces, and opened for tours. A new thirty-thousand-square-foot visitor center next door to Merilee would house a museum, IMAX theatre, and children's play area, and there would be an exciting addition to the culinary scene—a Cajun-themed restaurant operated by the late Wick Ambrose's Atomic Restaurant Group.

"Everyone who met Wick loved him," Fortier gushed, "and his ancestors built Merilee. He grew up there, and I'm proud that the new visitor center will include a restaurant operated by the fine company Wick built from scratch. I predict people from all around—locals and tourists alike— will flock to Merilee to enjoy fine dining. Imagine sitting on a broad patio overlooking Bayou Teche at sunset with a mint julep in your hand and good friends by your side. Tell you one thing, you'll find me on that patio after I leave Washington!"

Landry paused the newscast and asked if anyone's bullshit meter was off the charts by now. Cate nodded, and Henri—who snorted that the word did not belong in a civilized person's vocabulary—called the words those of a pompous man full of himself but lacking veracity.

Harry laughed. "I'm with Landry. Bullshit's the word for what this guy's putting out. I wondered when we'd hear what the Cajun King had in mind for Merilee. What's in this deal for Fortier? Where does he make money out of it?"

They tossed out possibilities. There could be kickbacks

from firms awarded the lucrative contracts for site preparation and construction, but Fortier would be retired before the visitor center opened to the public. Three years wasn't long in the life of a major project, but one thing had to happen first. The federal government had to acquire the twenty-five acres that made up Merilee Plantation. And given Fortier's effusive announcement today, that step might have already happened.

They were certain that whoever was behind the corporation that owned Merilee got a chunk of money for the property, and Harry searched online for a project breakdown to show just how much. That took more time than he imagined, since the visitor center's millions of dollars were a pittance in the trillion-dollar package it was a part of. At last he called the DC office of the state's junior senator, got passed off to a young, helpful aide, and got an email containing the relevant pages. That afternoon they gathered again to discuss it.

He passed out copies of the information and began. "We can't see every line item in the budget, but there's plenty to show us what's going to happen there. The total is fifty million, to be spent over five years. That includes eleven million for infrastructure, including roads, sewer lines, utilities, and a dock and gas station down on the bayou so people can arrive by boat. They'll spend three million to renovate and furnish Merilee and open it for tours. There's twenty-seven million to build the visitor center, the restaurant, and a slew of maintenance buildings. And then there's the number we've all been waiting for. Eight million nine hundred forty-five thousand dollars for land acquisition."

"Wow," Cate said. "Don't they have to get an appraisal before the government can buy land?"

Landry did a quick calculation. "Roughly three hundred fifty thousand an acre if you value the house at zero. It's in such poor condition I can't imagine an appraiser assigning much value at all to it. Even with bayou frontage, the land cost per acre is insane. I'll bet rural land along the Teche goes for under ten grand an acre."

"Perhaps the appraiser assigned a high value to the house because it's a historical structure," Henri offered. "But again, southwestern Louisiana has quite a few decaying antebellum mansions. Even if he put a million dollars on the house, we're looking at far too much cost per acre."

Landry asked Harry to find that appraisal. If it was public information, he wanted to see it.

"And if it isn't, maybe we can see it anyway." Harry laughed. "For the moment, I'm still a cop, after all."

The next morning Cate got a call from Firestone-McCauley, the network's new ad agency in Houston. Three more national companies—one each in the automotive, beer, and retail sectors—had signed up to advertise on TPN. They'd committed fewer dollars than the first one had, opting to start off light and assess viewership after six months. Regardless, it meant more than a million more dollars in the till for the new venture, and they were euphoric. The money would purchase more sophisticated audio-video equipment and provide additional capital to pay the bills and launch the network.

"Where's Harry been all day?" Landry asked as they locked up for the evening. "I just realized we haven't seen him."

Cate said, "You asked him to find that appraisal. I'll bet he's working on getting it for you."

At the end of the workday, they left together, and Henri walked in one direction down Toulouse Street while they headed in the other. Unless the weather was lousy, they always walked the few blocks to their apartment, and tonight it was great —temperature in the mid-seventies with a light breeze coming off the Mississippi. Pink clouds caught the last rays of sunlight; it would be dark soon.

As they neared the cathedral, Landry said, "I'm pumped about our new advertisers. Let's celebrate!" He guided her into Muriel's front door. An unfamiliar face manned the front desk, and Cate commented it was Tuesday, their friend's day off.

The maître d' seated them at the quiet corner table in the bar Landry preferred. He caught the bartender's eye, raised two fingers in the air, and moments later a double vodka tonic with lime and a glass of Malbec arrived. As they clinked glasses, his phone rang, and he scowled until he saw Harry's name. They spoke, and Landry invited him to stop over for a cocktail.

Cate asked if he was coming by, and Landry said no. He was up north in Ruston, four hours away.

"What's he doing there?"

"Working on the appraisal. He's driven over five hundred miles today. I told him earlier we'd reimburse his travel, and once he retires, it might be good to think about hiring him."

Cate cautioned, "Don't mention that to him yet. I'm finalizing a budget to give the bank for our new line of credit. We're burning lots of cash getting ready to launch, so be patient. Harry's not asking for a salary, and let's leave it at that until we see how things go."

Landry told her how fortunate he felt that she took care of the business side of their new venture. His passion lay in the mysteries, not the financial end of things, one reason why Cate was such an important part of the new network team.

They finished their drinks, ordered red snapper dinners to go, walked three blocks, and ate by candlelight on their third-floor apartment's little balcony. At the end of a satisfying day, they kissed goodnight and went to sleep.

CHAPTER FIFTY-FIVE

Harry showed up around noon the next day and found Landry up in the studio, helping Phil Vandegriff unpack equipment UPS had delivered. "Any luck with the appraisal?" Landry asked as they kept at it, removing preformed Styrofoam from boxes and unwrapping the gear.

Harry said instead of answers, now he had more questions. He'd gotten the appraiser's name and address from the same senatorial aide who'd slipped him a copy of the new visitor center budget. The choice of appraisers surprised him.

"Given this is a fifty-million-dollar project, I figured some high-powered real estate firm in Baton Rouge or New Orleans or Houston would prepare it. It surprised the hell out of me that the appraiser was a one-man shop in a town with a population of twenty thousand."

Harry showed him pictures of a shabby structure and said, "His office is an eight-hundred-square-foot storefront in this downtown Ruston building. A sign on the front door says *Andrew Fiske, Real Estate and Appraisals*. It's one big room with a few Army surplus tables and chairs, old metal file cabinets and map drawers. Two people were inside, and the office looked like they hadn't had a walk-in customer in years. I asked a woman at the front for Fiske, and she turned and yelled to the back. The guy came to the front and introduced himself. I flashed my badge and asked to see the appraisal for Merilee Plantation.

"He's an older guy, and his body language showed how nervous he was. He wanted to know why I was after the appraisal, and I said did I have to give a reason for a simple request? That shook him up more, so I pushed harder. I asked him what he got paid for that appraisal, and he started fidgeting around. He couldn't remember exactly. It's also confidential, he said, and I replied that I'm a taxpayer. It was my money that paid him. That got me nowhere, but that had to be one hell of a fee, and I guarantee he knows to the penny how much he got."

Harry pushed harder for a copy of the appraisal, and Fiske said he'd have to call and get permission. "That's when I pulled the old badge out. State business, I told him, and he got really nervous. I asked him who he was going to call and why he needed permission to release it, and he asked me why the police were involved.

"I said it was confidential, same as he told me. I demanded the document now. People in Baton Rouge were waiting for it, I told him. The poor guy began trembling a little. He was starting to lose it."

The man rummaged through a file cabinet, took out some papers, copied them, and told Harry it would be three dollars. He asked him to write his name and badge number on a piece of paper.

Landry said, "Does that worry you? What if he calls headquarters?"

"Can't spend the rest of my life worrying about things. I'm an investigator—it's in my blood, and I'll be damned if some asshole colonel is going to stop me from doing it. Besides, I might not have given the guy my right name. I'm getting a little senile these days. Can't remember how to spell sometimes." He grinned, and so did Landry, but he hoped this didn't come back to haunt Harry.

The document was just three pages, which Landry called surprisingly brief for such a large transaction. Appraisals usually contained comparables—sale prices of similar properties to justify a value—but a single paragraph explained away comps by calling this property unique. Twenty-five acres of bayou frontage and a house constructed in 1843—nothing compared to it. Landry questioned the logic; surely the appraiser could have found sales of other antebellum mansions on other rivers in Acadiana. Yet for some reason, he didn't.

The last page listed the appraiser's background, education, and credentials. Everything there revealed what a lightweight this man was. He specialized in northeast Louisiana real estate, which meant he had little or no experience appraising pre-Civil War plantation homes in the bayou parishes. He held a real estate broker's license, had completed appraisal classes at the local university, and held a Louisiana appraiser's license. The Merilee job had to be the largest appraisal he had ever performed.

Most of the appraisal dealt with property value—slightly under nine million dollars, as they had learned earlier. To Landry, the most interesting valuation was that of the house itself—an astounding two million dollars for the dilapidated seven-thousand-square-foot mansion. Why would a rational person—supposedly an expert—assign that value to Merilee? A new home of that size with every high-tech amenity and a bayou view might be worth millions, but Merilee was in poor condition. Except for its historic value, it would be a teardown. The valuation was laughable, and not a word in the appraisal explained how Fiske had arrived at the number.

Next he listed the twenty-five acres of land at a value of seven million, or two hundred and eighty thousand dollars per acre. A windfall for the seller, Landry thought, but outrageous if you're the buyer...even the federal government, whose penchant for throwing money at projects was legendary.

Who chose this particular appraiser, and why pick him over a large firm with experience in this type of property and the area? Who accepted this outrageous appraisal value, and most importantly, who benefitted from it? The question remained, who really owned Merilee Plantation?

As they wrapped up, Harry's cellphone rang. "Blocked," he muttered. "This may be where the shit hits the fan." He put the phone on speaker and answered.

Harry's guess was on target. When his boss asked Harry's whereabouts, he replied, "On vacation, sir. I'm in Civilian Land, where nobody has the right to ask where I am."

That went over as expected. Talbot snapped, "You've made a serious error, Harry. Why did you go to Ruston?"

"Boy, word travels fast. I had to pick up something for a friend. Is it a crime to be in Ruston these days?"

"You bullied a small-town appraiser into giving you something confidential. And you gave him a fictitious name and badge number."

"I did? If that's right, what makes you think it was me?"

"Because the guy took down your license plate number. He said you intimidated him."

Harry paused and took a deep breath. He was about to make this a whole lot worse if he didn't control himself. "Poor little fella. Hope he's all right now."

"You think this is funny? Here's a laugh for you. Poor little fella's *dead*, Harry. You go to Ruston to see him, and next thing that happens, he's hanged himself."

That news caught everyone by surprise. Harry said, "The appraiser hanged himself? What are you talking about?"

"I have a lot of questions myself. Be in my office in two hours."

Seething, Harry snapped, "What I do on my own time is none of your business, and I say that with all the respect I can muster, sir. You want me, you either arrest me or subpoena me. Otherwise I'll see you when I come back in for my last week before retirement." He rang off the call, took the phone off speaker, and called Sheriff Angelli in St. Martinville.

"Rick, it's Harry. Word is that some appraiser hanged himself. By chance, did that happen at Merilee?"

He listened far too long for a simple yes or no answer. Twice he started to interrupt but hesitated. Angelli was doing all the talking, and at last Harry said, "I understand. Sorry if

I put you in an awkward position. Let me know…no, never mind. Sorry I said that."

Landry asked what happened.

"Talbot's put the hex on me. I guess he's calling around, putting out the word I'm persona non grata at headquarters. Angelli says Talbot made veiled threats about how cooperation went both ways. If Angelli wanted to pass confidential information to over-the-hill cops who should have already retired, he shouldn't expect much help from the state the next time he needed it."

He smiled. "There's one good thing. Angelli cut me a little slack. He answered the question I asked him. That appraiser I met in Ruston—Andrew Fiske? A deputy found his abandoned car last night in a ditch by the Merilee turnoff from Highway 31. When the deputy called in the report, the sheriff sent him on down to the house to check things out. They found the guy hanging from the chandelier, same as the others."

No one knew what to make of that surprising revelation. The others who died there—Wick, Charlotte and their mother, Maria—had ties to the house and its dark history. Andrew Fiske seemingly didn't, and so what had happened?

Landry apologized for sending Harry to Ruston and getting him in trouble. "We'll handle things from here on," he added, but Harry stopped him.

"Now wait a damned minute. I'm your investigator. Not officially, but no damn Colonel Talbot's going to tell me what I can and cannot do as a civilian. Sheriff Angelli may capitulate to that bastard, but unless you fire me, I'm sticking with this case."

Things got tense for a moment. Cate and Henri looked at Landry, who appeared to be considering his options. He said, "You drive a hard bargain, Harry. You're a veteran cop with years of investigative experience, and you're helping us without compensation. It will help us a lot if you continue the investigation, because we're up to our asses in alligators. Be careful and don't push Talbot too hard. He has the advantage—he could ruin the pension you worked a lifetime for, the reputation you earned, and maybe your future as a PI or a small-town cop someday. You may be hopping mad at him, but be careful. He could ruin your plans for a nice retirement."

Kanter snapped off a salute. "Yes, sir! Count me in, sir!"

At six thirty that evening Kanter received an email from Samuel Talbot, Colonel, Louisiana State Police. It was succinct. Harry was terminated immediately, and his pension was suspended pending a hearing by the internal affairs board. Talbot accused him of insubordination, failure to obey a direct order, obtaining information under false pretense, violation of departmental policy, and misuse of confidential information. He must surrender his service weapon and shield to an officer who would shortly arrive at Harry's home and deliver a box containing personal items from his office.

Son of a bitch cleaned out my desk. Bet he had a blast doing that.

Harry knew the cop who came for Harry's pistol and badge, and the cop hated the assignment, apologizing and calling it unfair. Harry gave a dismissive wave and told the man it wasn't his fault. Afterwards, he poured a glass of Jack Daniel's and sat in the darkness.

The longest chapter in my life's story has closed. Thirty-five years with the force that ended with a three-paragraph email. Talbot and I never got along, but I didn't really think it would come down to this. I figured he'd let me retire, but obviously I pushed too many buttons.

He took a long pull of his drink. *Somebody wise said when one door closes, another opens. Or something like that. I refuse to waste time crying about what might have been. I've relied on my cop friends for years, but ex-cops—especially ones who go out like I am—aren't welcome anymore. They're outcasts, as if the bad news might rub off, or the boss might take his vengeance out on them too. And maybe Talbot would. Who knows? Who the hell cares?*

I have other friends now. Landry, Cate, Henri, and Jack. They're doing stuff I enjoy. I'll work with them. For free if I need to, because by damn, I'll keep that pension. The union takes care of its own, and Sam Talbot's too smart to bet his own career on a flimsy case like mine.

He finished his drink and went to bed. Tomorrow would be a new day. A good day.

CHAPTER FIFTY-SIX

Andrew Fiske was terrified. The moment that state policeman left, he told Mrs. Spencer he'd be out for a while. He left his cellphone on the desk; if she needed him—which was unlikely—she knew where to find him.

Boudreaux's beer joint was conveniently located just two doors down the block. Faded, hand-lettered signs on the wall cautioned NO CUSSING and DON'T SPIT ON THE FLOOR. Noisy teenagers crowded around two pool tables, and Andy winced at the crap that passed for music these days coming from the jukebox. Boudreaux could have programmed the damn machine with real music, but when Andy complained, he said the kids' money was as good as anybody else's, and they deserved to listen to what they liked. He added, "Don't worry. I still have 'Moon River' and 'Old Cape Cod' in there just for you. Once they're gone, play to your heart's content."

Dodging empty tables as he made his way to the back, Andy glanced at his watch—one forty-three p.m. No wonder nobody was here—it was a little early in the day. Taking in the familiar odors of cigarettes and beer, he walked up to a long wooden bar. Two other customers—both acquaintances of Fiske's—sat at the far end with beers in their hands, and when Andy picked a stool some distance away, they respected his desire for solitude.

"Afternoon, Sparky. The usual?" Boudreaux asked, and Andy snapped, "I've told you not to call me that." The man backed away, hands in the air. "Sorry, Andy. My bad. Rough day?"

Fiske had known James Boudreaux since first grade. Boudreaux always called him Sparky, but after what had happened at Merilee Plantation, hearing that nickname gave him goosebumps.

"Sorry about that. Yeah, rough day. And yeah, I'll have the usual." He needed a stiff one, and today wasn't the first time he'd knocked back a double rye whisky neat—or two— before two o'clock.

Boudreaux knew his regulars. He'd talk when they wanted conversation, and he'd maintain distance when they didn't. At the moment, Sparky Fiske belonged in the latter category. Shoulders slumped, he stared at the tumbler of whisky, cupping it with his hands. He took a long drink, savoring the fire as it hit his belly.

That damned Stu Pinelli had assured him nothing would go wrong. All he had to do was appraise an old house in St. Martin Parish for a government project, and the appraisal was confidential. Nobody would ever see it; the paperwork was just a formality, Stu assured him. Stu even gave him pictures so he wouldn't have to drive down to St. Martinville, but Andy wouldn't do it that way. Appraising the property without ever setting foot on it might cost him his license. Hell, it might land his ass in prison since the federal government was the buyer.

He knew the size of the acreage and the house, and he had been given the value to use in the appraisal. He considered the number outlandish, but Stu said everyone understood how the government worked. They overpaid for toilet seats and screws. Why not reward some lucky Louisiana landowner with a windfall?

He'd done other work for Pinelli. Small stuff—inflated

appraisals, real estate transactions where he shared commissions with some corporation—shady stuff that might lose him his license, but not enough to spell real trouble. This time he stood to make a hundred grand by signing an appraisal someone else had written. All he had to do was put his John Henry on it, but he refused to sign without visiting Merilee Plantation. He was a licensed professional, after all.

Although Stu didn't like it, he'd agreed because he needed the appraisal fast. When Andy asked for a house key, Pinelli had laughed. "The gate's not locked; if there's debris in the road, just move it out of the way. As far as Merilee itself, you can kick the front door in."

Ever since Stu mentioned the name Merilee, it had sounded familiar. Andy came to the turnoff and saw the historical marker. He snapped a photo for his appraisal—historically significant houses commanded more value—and he glanced at the words on it without giving them a thought.

Kick in the front door, Stu had suggested. That caused Andy to wonder in what kind of shape he'd find the old house. Right now, as he stood on the porch, he got nervous. They weren't just inflating the value of this place—they were sticking it to the government big time. Two million bucks for this dump? No way. Andy would talk to Stu Pinelli. The valuation had to be reduced—perhaps by as much as ninety percent. Andy presumed Stu had seen Merilee, and if so, he'd understand.

Get inside and get this over with. He pushed open the door, crossed the entry hall, and had gotten halfway up the stairs when the words echoed down the ancient mansion's hallways.

Mommy. Daddy. Is that you? Please help me. I'm scared.

Holy crap, there's someone here! A kid, by the sound of the voice. Unable to tell where the sounds came from, he tiptoed the rest of the way to the hallway at the top. He listened in silence, his hand gripping the railing to stop himself from shaking. Nothing. The house was quiet, and Andy decided he hadn't heard a voice after all. It was just a spooky old house making him nervous.

Andy walked on rotting carpet, avoiding holes in the

floor and observing the terrible condition this place was in. It could be remodeled—these old mansions usually were constructed well and remained structurally sound, even if the interior was in shambles. He shot some pictures with his phone and peeked into the bedrooms.

Mommy. Daddy. It's dark. Help me.

Now the voice came from somewhere very close by. Something was wrong about the sound of it. Andy couldn't describe it—the tone, maybe, or the inflection or something. It was like it wasn't human. Not computer-generated either, like those robot voices when you get spam dialed. This voice once belonged to a person—a child—but not anymore. Now came an odd raspy, scary whisper of words, long and drawn-out and plaintive, that made chills go down your spine. Right here, at this minute, Andrew Fiske was more afraid than at any time in his life. He broke out in a cold sweat and his hands trembled as he grasped the railing to keep from falling.

I'm not hearing this. It's the house. It's causing me to hallucinate or something. All I have to do is get out of here. Dear God, help me get out!

Even in daytime, shadows created eerie shapes on the walls. He ran toward the staircase and saw something drifting in the shadows above him. Swaying back and forth, although no air moved in the dank hallway to cause it.

A noose. He saw a rope up there, tied into a noose. A ladder stood nearby, propped up and ready for someone to use.

As Andy ran for his life down the stairs, tripping and catching himself several times, he remembered how he knew the name of this house. Merilee.

This was Wick Ambrose's house. The place where he'd hanged himself. Or someone else did it for him.

Where the same thing had happened to his twin sister.

The house is haunted, for God's sake. I'm in an honest-to-God haunted house.

At the front door he paused and looked around to be sure he hadn't come under some kind of spell. There was a chandelier at the top of the stairs, but no noose hung down. And no ladder stood nearby.

I didn't see all that. My mind played tricks on me. I'm nervous, that's all.

Then the words came, hovering in the air and echoing through the entryway.

Sparky. Sparky, come back!

What? Who said that? As terrified as he was, Andy stopped to listen. How could he—it—know his childhood nickname?

Sparky, please help me.

Gulping breaths of air, Andy ran to his car, jumped in, and locked the doors. He started the engine and put the gearshift in reverse, looking up at the old house as he backed to turn around. Up in a second-floor window he saw a figure. A boy, from the looks of it, wearing a baseball cap. His hands were on the windowpanes, and he was mouthing words. Words Andy couldn't hear…didn't want to hear. But somehow he knew what the boy was saying, and the words echoed in his head.

Sparky, come back. It's your turn. Tag, you're it!

He gunned the engine and drove too fast, hitting every pothole in the rutted road. Tires screaming, Andy veered onto the highway toward St. Martinville. Away from Merilee at last, he forced himself to slow down and take a deep breath.

He'd sign the appraisal, take his money, and be done with this project. Two million for the house was bullshit. In his professional opinion, the decaying old mansion ought to be torn down. And, for the first time in his career, he believed in haunted houses, because Merilee was seriously haunted.

That thing—the ghost—called me Sparky. Nobody knows that name except Boudreaux. And it was playing games with me. Tag. It wanted to play tag.

As he drove back to Ruston, Andy decided to sign Stu's appraisal. This would be his last job for them; from now on, Patton Fortier's flunky could find someone else to do his dirty work. Money couldn't erase the memory Andy would carry about Merilee Plantation. He'd never been that scared in his life.

A familiar voice snapped Andy out of his reverie.

"Sparky…oh, sorry. Andy. Hey, man, you all right? We kind of lost you there for a minute." Boudreaux was leaning over the bar close to his face, and the guys at the far end had paused their conversation to look.

"Yeah, yeah, I'm fine. I just…I've got a lot on my mind, that's all. How about another drink?"

Boudreaux hadn't seen his old friend like this before. Andy had been zoned out for a while. Wondering what the hell a real estate guy had to worry about, he served Andy's drink and went back to visit with the other guys. A few minutes later, Sparky got up, threw a twenty on the bar, and walked out.

"Hey, see you soon, buddy!" Boudreaux called after him, but Andy didn't even wave in response. Sparky simply walked out of his favorite watering hole for the last time.

CHAPTER FIFTY-SEVEN

Last Night
St. Martin Parish

When his car careened off the highway and slammed hard against something, Andy Fiske's liquor-induced fog instantly dissipated.

What the hell just happened? Where am I?

The safety belt dug hard into his chest and arm, suspending him in midair and hurting like hell. The car lay on its passenger side in a ditch in the darkness. Andy moved his legs and arms, decided nothing was broken, and tried to release the belt. As he gripped the steering wheel with his left hand, he hoped he wouldn't slam into the passenger door below when the belt released, and almost dislocated his shoulder when the latch opened. He tumbled across the console and landed upside down. His head lay against the door in a pool of water. A half-full liquor bottle—*his* bottle—lay beside his head. He'd missed hitting it by half an inch.

That would have hurt.

He struggled to right himself in the cramped passenger seat, but after several tries it worked. He didn't hear the car's engine, but the dash lights glowed, which meant he could lower the driver's window without having to figure out how to break it. He climbed out and got his bearings.

The car lay on its side in a drainage ditch alongside a paved two-lane road, but where? He tried to recall what happened earlier. When he left Boudreaux's, he decided not to go back to the office. Instead, he got in his car, stopped by the liquor store for a fifth of rye, and started home.

Then what happened? Andy glanced at his watch. Eight fifty-seven p.m. Hours had passed since the last things he remembered. He took in his surroundings—trees on both sides of what looked like a rural highway. Cicadas whirring, a light breeze moving the grass, but no headlights from either direction. One thing was certain—he wasn't in Ruston.

A dark shape loomed in the mist around fifty feet away. Could be a sign on a post. He took a tentative step and winced at the soreness in his arms and legs. Perhaps he'd been hanging there for a long time before he woke up, because every muscle in his body ached when he tried to move.

It took him several minutes to stagger over to the post, and now he could see a large black sign on it. There were no lights out here, and in the deepening darkness, he came close to see the words. He realized it was a historical marker, one of those you see…

One of those like he'd seen two days ago.

The same one, in fact.

Merilee Plantation.

As a wave of nausea swept over him, he collapsed alongside the dirt road that led to Merilee.

He opened his eyes and gave his brain a moment to reset. The car crash. The sign. Falling to the ground and passing out. But he didn't see the sign anymore. This was someplace different.

Where am I?

He ran his fingers around and felt wooden floorboards. Slivers of moonlight peeked through some dirty windowpanes, allowing Andy to see just a little. He looked to his left. Double front doors. On his right, a sweeping circular staircase.

Bile rose in his throat, and the hair on his arms tingled.

How did I get back to Merilee? I passed out on a road. By the sign. Why am I here?

He remembered the other visit and shuddered.

Don't look upstairs! Don't look up there where the chandelier is! No, he told himself over and over, don't look. He thought he saw something, closed his eyes, and opened them again.

Is a noose hanging from the fixture, or did I imagine that? As scared as he was, he wanted to know.

He pushed himself into a sitting position and looked over at the stairway. He started at the bottom and examined every step, prolonging the suspense and the agony of finding out what might lie at the top. At last his eyes came to the upstairs hallway.

In the half-light downstairs, Andy had seen shapes and doorways and furniture, but the darkness up there—the black hole at the top of the stairs—was eerily intense, like a thick black curtain. Whatever was up there, Andy didn't want to know about it anymore.

Groaning and grimacing from pain and the effort, he stood. He had to get the hell out of this evil place. Something had brought him back here—something that lured him here because he'd dared to interject himself into Merilee's business.

What a crazy thought! Where the hell did I come up with that? Gotta get out of here fast.

He limped toward the double doors. A sound. What was it?

He glanced back and saw nothing, but when he turned to leave, a figure two feet away blocked the door. It was a boy wearing a ball cap and a T-shirt. The boy who knew his nickname and watched him leave the last time he came.

Paralyzed with fear, Andy stammered, "Hey, son. I didn't mean to intrude. I don't even know how I got here."

I brought you here. I want someone to play with.

The boy took a step toward Andy, and he instinctively took two backwards. This awkward ballet continued across the foyer until his foot struck the first riser of the stairway.

You know what you have to do.

Andy looked up. A ladder stood just under the chandelier, and a rope noose hung down from it.

Andrew Fiske's only sin—his only connection with Merilee—had been to sign an appraisal that would help transform the house into a museum. Thanks in part to him, tour groups would walk these halls, poking their heads into bedrooms and closets, and that made Cody Beecham's ghost angry. Atonement would be exacted from anyone who wanted to create a shrine to Wick Ambrose or to give Merilee fame and recognition. This would never be a showplace. Merilee was a place of horror, where a sadistic boy had locked another in a closet and left him to die. It was Andy's hour for atonement. Now. At the top of the stairs.

Tears rolled down Andy's cheeks as he realized his life was over. He looked back at the freckle-faced boy and watched in shock as the phantom transformed into a horrifying specter. Its boyish face became a grinning maggot-covered skull. He could see movement in the eye sockets. Worms.

It glided close enough that when it extended its arm, a bony, fleshless finger touched Andy's shoulder.

Your turn, Sparky. Tag. You're it!

CHAPTER FIFTY-EIGHT

Next Morning

A coffee shop occupied the first floor of Henri's Toulouse Street headquarters. When Landry and Cate arrived at work, they found Harry sitting at a wrought-iron table in the courtyard, coffee in hand.

Cate said, "Good morning. We didn't expect you here bright and early. Do you have news for us?"

"I do. I'm no longer a state police officer."

Landry said, "You retired early. I thought you'd wait a few more weeks."

"So did I, and I didn't retire early, I got canned. I guess yesterday's phone call pissed off the boss. Imagine that. Perhaps I was a little harsh…"

Cate gave a rueful smile. "Perhaps you were, but you endured his abuse a lot longer than most people would have. Your boss is a jerk, to put it mildly."

"Yeah, especially since he accused me of everything but stealing from old ladies. He thinks he can stop my pension by firing me for cause, but I paid my union dues for thirty-five years, and they'll take care of me. When everything shakes out, I'll be on top, pension in hand. I've never been one to hold a grudge, but I'd love to give that slimy bastard a taste of his own medicine. Maybe I'll get my chance someday. Meanwhile, here I am, unemployed and looking for a handout. Got any work for a former cop?"

Landry laughed. "As long as you don't expect a salary, we'll work you to the bone!"

"Bring it on. I need something to keep my mind occupied. And look at this handy little thing I found in the back of a drawer." He pulled a case from his pocket, opened its flap, and displayed a gleaming silver badge with the words *Louisiana State Police* encircling a shield, and a number at the bottom.

Cate said, "They let you keep your badge," but Harry shook his head. This was the shield he'd carried before his promotion to lieutenant. For years it had been a memento in a drawer, but now it might prove useful. He wouldn't call himself an officer anymore. He wouldn't have to—when he needed information, he'd just flash the shield and let it do the talking. It wasn't kosher, but after the treatment he received, Harry didn't care much for protocol anymore.

Landry said, "If you want to help, I've got something for you. The appraiser from Ruston doesn't have to justify his outlandish valuation now, because he's dead. That's convenient, and I wonder if someone planned it. I doubt Sheriff Angelli will tell you anything more, but it's more important than ever to learn who owns the plantation."

"My bet is on Senator Fortier. He's retiring, and Merilee is his last huge federal pork-barrel project. Fifty million dollars isn't enough to raise eyebrows in DC, but it's a big deal in St. Martin Parish. If I know Patton Fortier, he wants to go out on top with a few extra million in his offshore bank account."

Landry considered talking to Fortier too risky. He was the most powerful man in Louisiana, and he could do a lot more to hurt Harry than take away his pension.

"What's a little conversation going to hurt? I'm not going to accuse him of anything. I'm just going to nose around until he gets wind of it and asks me what I'm doing."

Cate said, "Please be careful. Where do you plan to start?"

"They say Lake Pontchartrain's beautiful in the mornings. I think I'll run out to Leon C. Simon Boulevard and check it out."

Landry and Cate didn't understand what he meant.

"Some friends of mine have an office out there in a building by the lake—people who might be interested in finding the person who's using an inflated appraisal to cheat the federal government."

Landry wasn't following him. "Who are you talking about?"

"The FBI. The New Orleans field office for the feds is out by the lake. Think I'll drop in. See you all later." Buoyed by a sense of purpose, they heard Harry whistling as he walked down the carriageway and out to the street. Landry and Cate realized they'd never heard him whistle before.

Later that morning, Sheriff Angelli called to say Rodney and Myrna Beecham wanted to go back to Merilee. When they'd visited earlier, their spirit child had embraced them, and even though Angelli understood how malevolent and vindictive Cody could be, he had said nothing that might dampen their joyful reunion.

The couple was unaware that the ghost that was their son almost assuredly drove several people to their deaths, including two—James Ambrose and Andrew Fiske—after the Beechams saw Cody. Sheriff Angelli had hoped that one visit would allow the parents to finish their lives with good memories of their child. Instead, they wanted to go again, and things could be much different this time.

He thought of ways to dissuade them. He said, "The house isn't safe; plus Cody doesn't always appear when someone's there." But they insisted. If Sheriff Angelli wouldn't take them, they'd go to Merilee without him.

He asked Landry to come along since he understood all this spirit stuff, but Landry corrected him. "I've had more encounters with spirits than you, but to say I understand all this is a gross misstatement. Every ghost sighting has unique characteristics. Spirits inhabit old houses for a variety of reasons and motives. You can exorcise some, but others will never leave. Some go when their house is torn down, while others remain to haunt the land where it once stood."

Landry had been thinking of going back to Merilee with a film crew to see if he could create a *Bayou Hauntings* episode for the new network. After his harrowing experience there when Stuart Pinelli died, the house qualified as a bona fide haunted mansion, and he hoped he could entice Cody to show himself.

He wondered what the sheriff thought about inviting the Beechams to watch the filming. They might even play a part in the show if they saw their son again. Angelli said they had nothing to lose by asking and suggested Landry be the one to do it. They would get back in touch once either had more information.

While Landry and the sheriff planned the visit, out near Lake Pontchartrain Harry sat in the office of an FBI agent he'd known for twenty years. They were such good friends that the man had joined Harry a few times at Bud's, the cop bar in Baton Rouge. Harry disclosed he was no longer with the state police force, saying this time he was investigating on his own.

The agent, whose name was Jim Parsons, took notes as Harry explained what he knew about the involvement of Senator Fortier's aide Stuart Pinelli with Merilee Plantation. Someone had forged a deed long ago, and Harry wanted to know who and why. He enumerated the people who'd died from hanging at Merilee, and he said some people thought the place was haunted. He avoided giving his own opinions about ghosts; Harry needed this guy to help him, not think he should be locked away in an asylum.

When he finished, Agent Parsons asked what Harry wanted from him. "You realize how slowly things move around here," he said. "If the SAC decided today to investigate, it might be months before we interviewed anyone and far longer before bringing charges. And who is there to arrest? Sounds like everyone involved is dead."

"Patton Fortier isn't."

"The senator? You're suggesting we go after a sitting United States senator? If that's what you're thinking, we're talking about years to develop a case, not months. And it would be nipped in the bud before we could get started. There's lots of politics, even here in the FBI. If someone very high up the chain demanded we leave Fortier alone, then that might be the end of it."

Harry said he understood how much time things took, and that wasn't the approach he was asking for. He spent the next few minutes explaining what he wanted, and by the time he left, the agent had agreed to help. Just a little nudge—he wouldn't push hard enough to create an issue for either of them.

Or at least that was the plan.

CHAPTER FIFTY-NINE

Landry and his crew arrived at Merilee in a rented van midafternoon of the next day. Sheriff Angelli and Harry were already there, and the Beechams would come at dusk. Ghost sightings and eerie phenomena seemed to occur more frequently during the night, and that was what Landry elected to do this time.

Phil Vandegriff and two cameramen began unloading equipment as Landry, Cate, Henri, and their director went inside the house to choose where to shoot video.

Despite the kind manner in which Cody had treated his parents earlier, they couldn't be sure that would be the case today, and everyone would be on alert in case of a disaster. Landry knew a disaster might happen, but none of those present today had any past involvement with Merilee. The atonement had been exacted from those Cody held responsible, including the unfortunate appraiser from Ruston, whose involvement was at most peripheral.

For hours, noise filled Merilee's halls and rooms as the crew went about their work. Despite the intrusion, the ghost remained quiet. Even as Landry and the crew shot footage in Wick's bedroom and the fateful closet, nothing happened. It seemed as though Cody had abandoned the house. Landry hoped it hadn't happened, although he worried that the

Beechams might be frightened or angered by the film crew's treatment of their son should he appear.

The Beechams arrived neatly dressed in what Landry's mother would have called Sunday go-to-meetin' clothes. They claimed to be nervous but interested to watch a TV episode being taped. Landry asked them to remain outdoors until everything was ready. If Cody appeared the moment they entered the foyer, he wanted it recorded.

Outside, Landry asked the couple to call for Cody, and when they walked into the entry hall, Myrna cried, "Son, we're back. Are you here?"

The director sat behind an audio-video board in a corner of the hall, viewing nine cameras on the setup before him. Each was positioned in a different part of the house, and any motion would activate them. When Cody's mother spoke, he gave a thumbs-up to Landry, raised three fingers, and pointed upstairs. A camera on the second floor—number three in Wick's bedroom—had activated, picking up movement in there.

Between front and rear cameras, Landry climbed the stairs and stood under the chandelier. "Cody, we'd like to talk to you. Do you remember me? I came another time."

A rustling noise came from Wick's bedroom. Through his earbud, Landry's director said, "Camera three still rolling. Keep talking."

"Cody, I don't want tourists walking through this house and seeing the place where your…sadness and grief took place. The place where you died. If you will talk to us, it might help me convince other people to leave Merilee as it is. Will you show yourself?"

Landry's earbud crackled. "Four rolling." Camera four was in the kitchen at the top of the cellar stairs. Landry wondered about movement there, and in seconds he learned more.

"Six rolling." A wispy form glided from the kitchen into the entry foyer, pulsating and swirling as it took shape and rose, up to the second floor. It came to rest so close to Landry he could have touched it. The whirling stopped, and Cody stood before him. His parents gasped with delight and ran up the stairs.

This encounter was nothing like before. Myrna moved to embrace him, but the spirit flitted to a corner. Every move they made resulted in a countermove. He evaded their approaches and then said, "Don't come here again. This is a place of sorrow, and it is my place, not yours. You must remember me as what I was but am no more. Go now." Cody vanished.

Weeping, the couple held each other a moment before walking arm in arm down the circular staircase. The cameras rolled as they reached the front doors, paused, turned, and Rodney said, "Goodbye, son. We will always love you." A cold gust of wind swept through the house, rattling the windows for a few seconds. The moment the Beechams walked out the door, the breeze disappeared.

The crew shot hours of more footage that night, but Cody Beecham made no further appearances. Landry had experienced such things before. Sometimes spirits would leave the premises after a significant event, but just as often, they remained. Cody could have simply chosen silence.

Later at the studio, Phil and the director would view the footage and decided they had enough footage for an hourlong show. After adding the background of Merilee and the Ambrose family, enumerating the people who died there and asking questions about who owned the property, it would all wrap neatly into the next *Bayou Hauntings* episode.

CHAPTER SIXTY

"Senator Fortier, this is Agent Jim Parsons with the FBI. Thank you for taking my call, sir. I know how busy you are, and I'll keep this brief."

"You mentioned you had a question about the Teche-Merilee Park project. What can I do for you, Agent Parsons?" He listened without interruption until Parsons finished, considered the implications his questions carried, and told the agent he'd call back when he had time.

"With all due respect, Senator, we're trying to tie up a few loose ends, and I'm sure your answers will be helpful. May we talk now, and then I won't have to bother you again?" Parsons couldn't push any harder than this. If Fortier wanted to talk, then Harry Kanter might get what he wanted. If not, no harm done.

Fortier paused and got folksy, using his down-home, Foghorn Leghorn voice that made people think of him as one of them—a good old Sothern boy. "You know, son, you're like that dog tryin' to catch the school bus. You can run and run, thinkin' your goal is just up ahead, but suddenly you realize that thing you wanted—the school bus, I'm talkin' about—is so big and so scary it makes you glad you never caught it. I say all that to say this. I spent years putting together the Teche-Merilee deal. It's the biggest federal project in St. Martin Parish ever, and it's a boon to the people who live there. At last it's a done deal. Passed both houses, got the president's signature, and you come along wantin' to stir up trouble."

Parsons said, "Sir, it's not my intention to stir up anything…"

"I'm doin' the talkin' now, son. You're gonna do the listenin'." Fortier flipped through a Rolodex on his desk until he found the right card. "Is old Wade Hunicutt still runnin' the field office down there in New Orleans? Tell Wade I said hello, and I hope Martha and the boys are doin' fine."

"I will, sir. I just have one last question. Stuart Pinelli claimed you forced him to sign over his half of the corporation that owns Merilee to you when you fired him. Does that make you the sole owner now?"

The senator hesitated. When he spoke next, the Southern drawl disappeared, and he spat angry words. "I hope you have a long, successful career in the FBI, Agent Parsons. I've written your name down in my ledger so I can keep up with you. Leave my project at Merilee alone. If that dog ever caught that school bus, it would run right over him and leave him lying in the dust. This conversation is over."

The agent played the recording for Harry. "I struck out, but there's something to all this. He was seething there at the end. He didn't have to cloak his threats in metaphors. I got the message. It won't be good for me or my career if I tangle with him again."

"I think you did just fine," Harry replied. "That venomous response shows how concerned he is. I'll keep the heat turned up on our friend. And I say don't worry about his threats. He's a lame duck, and I don't see him opening a big can of worms right at the end of his political career."

For Patton Fortier, the remainder of the day after his phone call unfolded like any other. He voted on a bill, attended committee meetings, glad-handed a group of businessmen from Lake Charles on an economic development visit to Washington, and called a constituent to wish her a happy hundredth birthday.

While he conducted business, his mind strayed far, far

away from the mundane tasks at hand. For the first time in his long career, he faced a problem that might not have a good solution. That damned FBI agent found out about the corporation. Perhaps he was fishing, but he'd hit the target square-on.

Damn that Stuart Pinelli. If he hadn't died, I'd kill him myself! The guy got too big for his britches, and after I fired him, he told somebody about the corporation. Guess he figured he had nothing to lose by taking me down with him.

If the corporation's ownership was as protected as Stuart promised, Patton could brush off any accusations about Merilee. Stu had set up the arrangement years ago, and Patton never doubted his assurances that the layers of ownership created a maze no one would penetrate. Louisiana company owned by Cayman Islands company owned by Isle of Man company owned by who knew what else. Bank account in Alabama funded by bank account in the Bahamas funded by some other bank account.

It was complicated as hell, and after looking at the structure just once, he'd locked the file away in his safe. Over many years the taxes and bills got paid on time, and nobody questioned who owned the property. Now, as Stu Pinelli crashed, it seemed he had decided to take Patton along for the ride.

Who gave Agent Parsons the tip about Merilee? After Stuart's death there, Patton had called the sheriff in St. Martinville to get the inside scoop on what had happened. He'd learned that before James Ambrose shot him, something had mangled Stu's face and body. It had to be some kind of animal, but so far nobody said what. Sheriff Angelli had told him Landry Drake was there. So was James and some reporter from a New Orleans TV station. James had held them captive before Stu showed up.

Dear Lord, how that bastard messed things up. Springing Ambrose from jail, the lawyer letting him get away, and getting involved with the ghost hunter were all crazy moves. Patton bet that Stuart did a deathbed confession, spilling his guts about everything right before he died. But if he had, how come the TV reporter didn't call him to ask questions about Stu's sensational revelations?

What if James had confessed in front of the reporter? Maybe the brass at Channel Nine had nixed the story, even though their man heard it firsthand. It was nothing but a rumor about a powerful politician. Patton bet that was why no one contacted him before.

But what about Landry Drake? He'd confronted Patton at Stu's funeral and asked about the mailbox in Baton Rouge. If he found out about that, how much more had he learned?

As much as he wanted to hear how Agent Parsons got his information, Patton didn't call the special agent-in-charge in New Orleans. That would have aroused suspicion and alerted him about Fortier's concern. He had to let this one go. He'd dodged a bullet and told the agent in no uncertain terms to back off. Things would be fine. They always turned out fine for Patton Fortier. With his money and power, why wouldn't they?

He would be back in Louisiana over the weekend, and Patton decided he'd make a visit over to Merilee Plantation. Pay a visit to the place and see how nice it would be once the house got a makeover and opened to the public. Although he'd arranged fifty million dollars for the visitor center, he'd never set foot on the grounds. It was time to go there.

And the senator intended to visit the property alone. He rarely traveled without a driver, but with Stuart gone, he didn't trust anyone else to take him. He'd visit just this once and bask in the glory of accomplishment. He wanted to stand inside Merilee's walls and shout that he, Patton Fortier, United States senator, could accomplish anything. He had unlimited power and knew how to use it.

He drove his car over to St. Martin Parish. The sad state of the mansion shocked him, but it would be a showplace once the federal government's millions started flowing.

He stepped around rotten boards and holes, made his way across the porch and stepped into the house. It was dark and dingy, and he looked all the way up to the cupola, thinking how grand it would be with the sunlight shining through its tiny windows.

"Welcome," someone behind him said, startling the

senator for a moment. He turned and saw a boy maybe ten or eleven years old.

"Hello there, son. What are you doing in this old house? You might get hurt in here."

"Yes, sir, it would be easy to get hurt in here. I come here a lot. Want me to show you something special upstairs? It'll surprise you."

"Sure, boy." As they walked toward the stairs, Patton asked what his name was.

"Cody, sir. Cody Beecham. And you're the senator. You're going to change everything here and let people start walking through the house all the time."

Patton nodded and smiled. Everybody knows me. Even little kids. That's the price you pay for being a famous politician. Can't even go to the boondocks without being recognized.

The little boy stood on the upstairs landing now, beckoning Patton to join him. He didn't notice the ladder and the noose until he got to the top of the stairs.

CHAPTER SIXTY-ONE

FORTIER HANGED!
LOUISIANA LEGEND PATTON FORTIER
DIES AT 75;
SENATOR'S BODY FOUND INSIDE GHOST HOUSE

The words filled the bottom half of the screen, and Patton Fortier's smiling face appeared above as the Baton Rouge newscaster read the story of the senior senator's mysterious and tragic death. Although he always traveled with an aide, this time the senator drove over to Merilee Plantation alone. St. Martinville Parish sheriff Rick Angelli said there were no other footprints outside the house or inside, and they found his fingerprints on the railing where he climbed the stairs to the second floor. At the top, his journey ended. It appeared he climbed the ladder and hanged himself.

Desperate for answers, Sheriff Angelli called Landry first. Instead of an opinion rooted in fact, he got a theory based on years of ghost-hunting experience. The senator had made a grave mistake in underestimating the power of the supernatural, and it cost him his life. He had boasted of his power, but the power of atonement claimed the life of Patton Fortier.

———

BILL THOMPSON

Six months later

Landry, Cate, her father Doc Adams, and Henri raised their glasses in a toast to "The Atonement," the latest *Bayou Hauntings* episode that had aired earlier that evening on the Paranormal Network. Almost a year's work had come down to launch day, and things had gone off without a hitch. A pre-launch media blitz and a targeted advertising campaign on major networks promoted the channel's programs and its host, famous supernatural investigator Landry Drake. Tonight in the French Quarter studio, Landry's director and crew, plus his friend and long-time associate Phil Vandegriff, joined them in popping a bottle of champagne.

Now, two hours later, the four founders sat around a back table at Muriel's, frequently checking the positive feedback flooding social media and basking in the glory that came with a tough job well done. Cate looked up across the dining room and saw Harry and Jack making their way toward their table. When they sat, Landry said, "I couldn't have done it without you two."

Much had changed in the six months since the cops found Senator Fortier's body swinging from a noose at Merilee. Sheriff Rick Angelli knew who killed the politician, but it was impossible to arrest a phantom. Informing the public that Cody Beecham haunted the old mansion would have people thinking their sheriff had lost his mind, and so Fortier's death would forever remain an open, unsolved mystery.

When authorities drilled the senator's private safe, it revealed a treasure trove of information. The feds found a complicated diagram of interlocking companies behind the corporation that owned Merilee, and a list of domestic and offshore banks, complete with user IDs, passwords, and codes to withdraw funds. They also found a piece of paper signed by Stuart Pinelli. It gave Fortier Stu's half of a Bahamas corporation, which ultimately meant the senator owned Merilee lock, stock, and barrel. But for his untimely death, all the profits would have been his alone.

THE ATONEMENT

Millions of dollars had flowed through the accounts over the years. Payoffs from individuals and companies, profits from illegal gains on stocks, bonds, and real estate, and much more. The Merilee money would have ended up there too, but once the illegal activity became known, the US Treasury Department froze the assets.

A corporation owned Merilee, but everyone connected with it had died. Likewise the house itself; no Ambrose family members remained to assert ownership. The Teche-Merilee Visitor Center project was already underway, and a judge ruled that the nine million dollars to buy Merilee Plantation's house and acreage should be awarded to St. Martin Parish, to be used only for further development of the visitors' center project. The money would allow even more experiences for tourists on the property, creating more economic development for the parish.

One significant change to the big project only happened because Landry Drake adopted it as a personal crusade. As part of the media campaign for their show called "The Atonement," Landry appealed to the public to halt the mansion's renovation. He told viewers about Cody Beecham, the tortured, troubled spirit who inhabited the house where he tragically died, and he implored them to call or write their representatives.

Landry's goal was to leave Merilee in its present condition. Spend enough money every year to maintain it, but don't remodel, renovate, tear out, and build up things to create a tourist attraction. Cody Beecham was right. Merilee wasn't a place of joy; it was a place where unspeakable horrors occurred, where perhaps other little boys besides Cody died playing a game of tag with Wick Ambrose, and it deserved to be preserved in its ruined state. Through a chain-link fence, visitors would get a look at the ancient building and see its decaying furnishings through open doors and broken windows, but no tour group would go into Wick's bedroom to gape at the dark closet where Cody Beecham died.

The campaign worked. There was plenty else on the drawing board to attract tourism, and there were dozens of other antebellum mansions within a few miles that would welcome walk-throughs. When the visitor center opened in a few years, the mansion would remain off limits and protected from prying eyes.

Jack Blair's boss, Ted, told him he had a bright future at Channel Nine. It came with a caveat; there would be more work along with more pay, and that meant no time for side gigs with the station's friend and former employee Landry Drake. Jack would see Cate and Landry frequently, but henceforth, those visits would be personal, not business.

Atomic Restaurant Group was acquired by a publicly-held bar and restaurant group that would expand the concepts developed by Wick Ambrose into other Southern cities. Within a year, there would be sister restaurants in Savannah, Tuscaloosa, and Charleston.

Harry Kanter moved from Baton Rouge to New Orleans, got a private investigator's license, and hung out his shingle on Decatur just around the corner from Landry's headquarters. He had plenty of cash to pay the bills, thanks to the police union's civil action filed on his behalf. A judge ruled Colonel Sam Talbot violated the law by withholding Kanter's pension and ordered it reinstated.

Talbot resigned under pressure from the governor, and Harry hired a lawyer to sue the state for the mishandling of his termination. Harry accepted the settlement they offered and executed a nondisclosure agreement. Never one to brag anyway, the document prohibited him from revealing the amount. And he told no one, even Landry and Cate, but it was obvious from that point on that Harry never lacked for money. Over the ensuing months, he would work on several cases with Landry, and Muriel's became his favorite go-to place, where he often shared a drink with his good friends Landry and Cate.

Landry, Cate and Henri spent most of their time working on *Mysterious America,* the new series that would air soon on the Paranormal Network. It would be Landry's first foray into the supernatural outside his home state, but he found a plethora of legends to kick things off.

Landry would visit Merilee only one more time. He went

alone one afternoon to walk down those halls, look in the bedrooms, and experience the place before a barrier and a padlock separated it from the public.

He wondered if he'd see Cody. If so, he'd ensure the little boy knew no visitors would traipse through the house to disturb him. But the house was quiet. There were no plaintive cries and no phantom seeking retribution against those who wronged him.

For Cody Beecham, the atonement was complete.

Thank you!

Thanks for reading *The Atonement.*

If you enjoyed it, I'd appreciate a review on Amazon. Reviews are what allow other readers to find books they enjoy, so thanks in advance for your help.

Please join me on:
Facebook
http://on.fb.me/187NRRP
Twitter
@BThompsonBooks

This is book 8 of The Bayou Hauntings Series. The others are available as paperbacks or ebooks.

MAY WE OFFER YOU A FREE BOOK?
**Bill Thompson's award-winning first novel,
The Bethlehem Scroll, can be yours free.
Just go to
billthompsonbooks.com
and click
"Subscribe."
Once you're on the list, you'll receive advance notice of future book releases and our newsletter.**

www.ingramcontent.com/pod-product-compliance
Lightning Source LLC
Chambersburg PA
CBHW060243100726
47907CB00003B/753